"Tomorrow, Callie. I'll take you riding tomorrow. I think we both could benefit from a few hours away from Becket Hall."

"Thank you, Court." She stepped up on tiptoe and daringly placed a quick kiss on his mouth. But when she went to step away from him his arms closed more tightly around her and he lowered his face to hers, sealing their mouths together.

Cassandra closed her eyes as the strangest feeling rippled through her body, and then raised her arms to hold them around his neck as he showed her that the kiss she'd given him had been far from what a real kiss should be. She felt the tip of his tongue against her lips as he seemed to want her mouth open, and she complied, because saying no to anything Court had ever wanted from her was beyond her power.

"Callie," he whispered against her lips, withdrawing slightly, and then taking her mouth so completely that she could only sigh, and hold on to him for dear life. This was where she wanted to be. In his arms.

This was where she was destined to be. In his life.

Praise for
Kasey Michaels

A Reckless Beauty

"*A Reckless Beauty* [is] a cannon shot. Drama by the boatload, danger around every corner, and heart-wrenching emotion await readers."

—*A Romance Review*

A Most Unsuitable Groom

"From the first page to the last this continuation of the Beckets of Romney Marsh saga is a well-crafted novel. Emotional intensity, simmering sexual tension, characters you care about and political intrigue – plus touches of humour and a poignant love story – all come together in this hugely entertaining keeper."

—*Romantic Times BOOKreviews*

The Dangerous Debutante

"Her characters shine as she brings in fascinating details of the era, engaging plot twists and plenty of sensuality."

—*Romantic Times BOOKreviews*

Shall We Dance?

"Brimming with historical details and characters ranging from royalty to spies, greedy servants to a jealous woman, this tale is told with panache and wit."

—*Romantic Times BOOKreviews*

The Butler Did It

"Michaels' ingenious sense of humour reaches new heights as she brings marvellous characters and a too-funny-for-words story to life. (…) What fun, what pleasure, what a read!"

—*Romantic Times BOOKreviews*

BECKET'S LAST STAND

Kasey Michaels

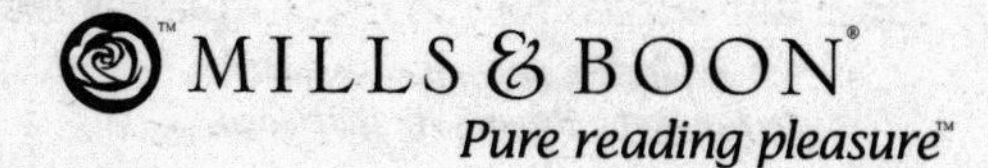

All the characters in this book have no existence outside the imagination of the author, and have no relation whatsoever to anyone bearing the same name or names. They are not even distantly inspired by any individual known or unknown to the author, and all the incidents are pure invention.

First published in Great Britain 2009
by Harlequin Mills & Boon Limited,
Eton House, 18-24 Paradise Road, Richmond, Surrey TW9 1SR

ISBN: 978 0 263 87402-0

037-0309

Harlequin Mills & Boon policy is to use papers that are natural, renewable and recyclable products and made from wood grown in sustainable forests. The logging and manufacturing processes conform to the legal environmental regulations of the country of origin.

Printed and bound in Spain
by Litografia Rosés S.A., Barcelona

USA TODAY bestselling author **Kasey Michaels** is the author of more than ninety books. She has earned three starred reviews from *Publishers Weekly*, and has been awarded the RITA® Award from Romance Writers of America, the *Romantic Times* Career Achievement Award, the Waldenbooks and BookRak awards, and several other commendations for her writing excellence in both contemporary and historical novels. There are more than eight million copies of her books in print around the world. Kasey resides in Pennsylvania with her family, where she is always at work on her next book.

Available from Kasey Michaels
and Mills & Boon

THE BUTLER DID IT
IN HIS LORDSHIP'S BED
(short story in *The Wedding Chase*)
SHALL WE DANCE?
IMPETUOUS MISSES
MARRIAGEABLE MISSES
A RECKLESS BEAUTY

and in the **Beckets of Romney Marsh** series

A GENTLEMAN BY ANY OTHER NAME
THE DANGEROUS DEBUTANTE
BEWARE OF VIRTUOUS WOMEN
A MOST UNSUITABLE GROOM
THE RETURN OF THE PRODIGAL

To my editor, Melissa Jeglinski,
for all her invaluable input, hard work,
friendship and support during two frantic
years of living almost daily with *The Beckets of Romney Marsh*. Couldn't have done it
without you, babe!

BECKET'S LAST STAND

PROLOGUE

1798
An unnamed island near Haiti

IT WAS THE HEIGHT of summer, hot, crushingly hot, difficult-to-breathe hot. But behind the thick walls of the two-story house set among the towering shrubs, nestled among the swaying palms, the air was relatively cool in the large bedchamber. And that air was sweet with the smell of Isabella's perfume.

Courtland sat cross-legged on the wide-planked floor, holding the young Cassandra in front of him, encouraging her to stand on her chubby little legs. But the child wasn't cooperating. She was much too enthralled with the idea of pulling off Courtland's nose, giggling as she reached for him.

"She's too young to stand," Odette the Voodoo woman warned him as she brushed Isabella's long, dark curls. "Her legs will bow like Billy's and she'll roll when she walks, with you to blame for it all."

Isabella laughed, a sound like the sweetest music, as she leaned closer to the large mirror, slipping sapphire bobs into her ears. "Oh, stop teasing our poor Court, Odette," she said, "that's not true. My sweet baby would never roll when she walks. She will glide, like an angel, and she will float in the dance in this London Geoff promises us, the belle of every ball. We will all be so grand, won't we?"

And then she swiveled on the small padded chair and smiled at Courtland, blew both him and the infant Cassandra a kiss.

Courtland felt his heart skip a beat and knew hot color was creeping up into his cheeks, for he loved the beautiful Isabella with every fiber of his thirteen-year-old being. He didn't know that, of course, because love had never been a part of his life before coming to the island. He only knew he lived for her, would die for her. He lived for Cassandra, and would gladly die for her, too, because she was a part of Isabella, a part of his savior, Geoffrey Baskin.

Cassandra went to her hands and knees, her favored form of locomotion, and crawled onto Courtland's lap, stuck her thumb in her mouth, and within moments was asleep in the afternoon heat. He could pick her up, take her to her cot in the dressing room, but it felt so good to hold the small, trusting body that he leaned his back against the wall and contented himself watching Odette brush Isabella's hair…and thinking of the past, of the day he'd first arrived on the island.

The day had begun as usual, with his seven-year-old self being roughly kicked awake by the boot of the man who insisted Courtland call him Papa. But would a father kick a son, make him sleep with the huge, bad-tempered dogs that were allowed to roam free in the shop at night, fight them for the food that was always too little and often too spoiled to eat? Courtland couldn't be sure, but he didn't think a father should treat his son that way.

The other thing that was usual about the morning was that his papa was drunk. Mean drunk, nasty drunk. And Courtland was sick, having eaten some of the meat that the dogs had left for him, and the vile-smelling vomit on the floor beside him was his own. He didn't want to wake up, he didn't want to clean up his mess. He just wanted to sleep. Sleep forever.

But his papa kicked him again, hard, and began yelling about the dogs, something about the dogs. Something about the damn miserable dogs being dead and they'd been worth twice what the boy was, the useless little bastard.

That's when Courtland had heard the worst sound, that of his father's whip being untied from his belt, the braided leather with its several small ends, each tipped with a small lead ball, snapping hard against the floor an inch from his head. He would have cried out, but he'd learned not to do that. He'd learned not to talk at all, not to ever make a sound. It was safer that way. He could almost be invisible, if he didn't talk. Sometimes. Not this morning.

He tried to scramble to his feet, but he was too slow, had moved too late. The whip snaked out again, this time catching him hard across the back, cutting deep into his young skin in at least a half-dozen places. Again. And again. Over and over, until Courtland thought he might die, like the dogs.

But then the blows stopped, and his father cursed, and Courtland heard another man speaking. Quietly, firmly. He dared to lift his head, and saw a tall, dark-haired man dressed in fine black clothes, holding tight to his father's wrist, looking down into his face.

"Billy, take the boy outside. Mind his back as you carry him," the man said as he squeezed harder, and the whip slipped to the floor. "And Jacko, my friend, man the door, if you would, please. This lump of offal and I have something to discuss, and need our privacy."

Courtland had felt himself being picked up, oh so gently, and carried out of the shop, into the morning sun. The man holding him crooned to him, told him he was all right, that the Cap'n would take care of him, that nobody would hurt him, not ever again. That he'd be "just like the other one, most like, God help us all."

But Courtland hadn't really been listening, because the whip had cracked again, only this time not against his back. He heard his father yell, curse. Again, the crack of the whip. His father yelled again, but this time he didn't curse. He had begun to plead, to beg. "Stop! Stop! You can have him—but I'll be paid!"

The whip cracked again, three times in quick succession, and Courtland listened for his father's voice, but it never came. He looked to the door, to the huge, smiling man who stood there, blocking it, and waited for his father to walk out, holding the whip, coming for him once again.

When the door opened, however, it was the tall man who emerged, hesitating only to throw the whip back into the dimness of the shop. He walked over to the man named Billy and held out his arms, so that Courtland felt himself being transferred.

"Hello, son," the man said quietly. "I'm Geoffrey Baskin, and you'll come live with me, if you want. No one will beat you ever again, I promise. What's your name?"

Courtland remained silent, which is how he came to be Courtland, named for a sailor on one of Geoffrey Baskin's ships who had perished of a fever a few months earlier, and he remained silent for nearly six years, until Geoffrey had brought home an angel named Isabella, whose smile and sweet ways had eventually coaxed him into speaking once more.

His very first word spoken on the island had been *Callie,* a gruff, rasping mispronunciation of Isabella's and Geoff's newborn daughter, Cassandra, who would never be called Cassie again, at Isabella's order.

There were other children now, all of them brought

to the island by Geoffrey Baskin. Chance, who had already been in residence when Courtland arrived. A newborn infant, Morgan, was brought back from another trip to Haiti. Three years later a half dozen more children, survivors of an attack on a church on another island. Finally, a wild young hothead named Spencer.

Courtland didn't mix with the other children very often. He didn't speak, and they seemed to think that was funny. He stayed by himself, watching, always watching, always waiting for the first sick singing of the whip before it bit into his back. But it never came.

Isabella. She had arrived instead. An angel as beautiful as his rescuer, Geoffrey Baskin, was handsome. And after years of cautious watching, the young Courtland was ready to give his trust, his heart.

"Dreaming again, Missy Isabella," Odette said, pointing now at Courtland with the hairbrush. "Boy's like a puppy."

Courtland flushed once more and got to his feet, careful to hold Cassandra close as he turned his back, walked over to the open doors that led out onto the veranda that faced the sea.

"Court? Do you see him yet?" Isabella asked, getting to her feet, shaking out the full skirts of her grass-green gown. "I'm so anxious, aren't I? He promised they'd be back before dinner tonight. And then no more grand adventures for my Geoff, not without me by his side as we all sail to our new home. Imagine it, Court. Nearly three hundred of us, all sailing off together, leaving this island behind, a whole new world opening up ahead of us. But still no sign of Geoff?"

Courtland squinted, concentrating on the horizon, the place where brilliant blue-green water met a cloudless blue sky. "No, ma'am, I don't see them. Not yet."

She came to stand beside him, not all that much taller than he, and kissed the soft brown curls on her sleeping daughter's head. "Are you anxious to sail to England, Courtland? Will you miss our small paradise?"

"Papa Geoff says it's time to go. Time to be respectable and safe."

"Being a privateer is respectable, Court," Isabella told him. "Just not respectable enough for my silly husband. He teases that he prefers cold and damp England to our warmth and sun here, and that we will, too. We shall soon see if he's right, won't we?"

Courtland nodded, then looked at the expanse of vibrant greenery and chalk-white sand that led to the water, the horseshoe of land surrounding the natural harbor filled with small houses belonging to the crews of the two ships owned by Geoffrey Baskin. Everywhere was bustling activity as the women added to the small mountains of belongings soon to be loaded on the ships. Transporting three hundred people across the wide ocean was no minor undertaking, but they would be ready to sail within the week.

His gaze singled out Spencer wrestling with Isaac and Rian, two of the boys their Papa Geoff had rescued from the destroyed church. And there was young Fanny, wearing the striped dress cut from extra material from Isabella's new gown; her hair so blond it was nearly white, daring the small wavelets in her bare feet; charging, retreating. He couldn't hear her laughter, not up here, but he knew she was laughing, for Fanny was a happy child, her memory of her mother's death in that same church fading as she grew.

He watched as Fanny began to jump up and down, pointing out to sea, and he followed her direction with his eyes, caught sight of sails flashing in the sunlight as they came around the northernmost part of the island, into the natural harbor. He sighed in relief, knowing Papa Geoff's last adventure as a privateer was now over, that he would be safe. Yes, Courtland supposed he was happy to be leaving here, no longer being forced to worry for his Papa Geoff, his savior, each time the two ships sailed out of the harbor.

"They're back," he said, his breath catching in his throat. "Just as they said they would be."

Isabella kept her hand on his shoulder, also peering out to sea. But then her fingers dug deeper into Courtland's shoulder. "No, that's not Geoff. Three ships, Courtland, see? Three ships, not our two."

Courtland looked at Isabella, saw the worry in her beautiful eyes, and then looked toward the ships once more. What was wrong? No, they weren't their ships, the *Black Ghost* and the *Silver Ghost.* But he did recognize them now; they were the ships of Papa Geoff's privateering partner, Edmund Beales.

"It's all right," he told Isabella. "It's only Beales."

But wasn't he supposed to be with Geoffrey and Chance and Jacko and Billy and the others? Where were the Black Ghost *and the* Silver Ghost? *Why only Beales's three ships? Something was wrong, wasn't it?*

Rian, leaving Issac sprawled on the ground, seemed to already know that, for he was running toward Fanny, scooping her up into his arms, and heading for the main house with Spencer, the two of them shouting, although Courtland could not make out what they were saying. Isaac watched them go, laughing, and then turned to wave to the approaching long boats, already lowered into the clear, calm waters.

It was then that Courtland realized something, knew what Rian and Spencer had seen. It was the ship that lay parallel to the beach. Its gun ports were open, the small cannon being run out. "Ma'am!"

Isabella must have seen it, too. She raced across the veranda, pressed her body against the railing. "Run! Into the trees! Hide! Run, everyone! *Run!*"

Odette was with them now, her black face nearly gray as she wrung her hands together, as they all watched the longboats being pulled, one by one, up onto the beach. "Betrayal. Beales wants more than his share. I did not see this. Why did I not see this?

Sweet Virgin, Missy Isabella, you have to go. You have to go now!"

But Isabella was still shouting, waving her arms in the air, pleading with everyone who had raced out of their small houses and into the sandy clearing to run, run into the trees, to hide themselves.

Courtland stood very still, holding the sleeping Cassandra, refusing to believe what was happening. He flinched at the first gunshot, squeezing Cassandra's small body so tightly that she woke, began to cry. Odette took the child from him and hurried back into the bedchamber.

He joined Isabella on the veranda as more gunshots rang out, to see Edmund Beales standing on the beach now, legs spread, hands on hips, looking across the expanse of sand, up at the veranda.

Another man in black. But although tall, although handsome, he was not Geoffrey Baskin, could never be more than he was, a pale-skinned man with a too-thin face and a mass of black curls, a man who wore leather close against his skin even in this heat, like an animal, Courtland had always thought. Beales was smiling now, and Courtland realized that, for all that he'd seen in his short span of years, he'd never before seen true evil. Not until this moment.

Then one of the ships opened fire from the harbor, and a cannonball hit high in the palm trees to the left of the house, severing one so that its top crashed to the ground.

Children cried, called for their mothers. But the mothers, the old men, the young boys, most all of them were running toward the attackers now, armed with pistols of their own, with metal-tipped pikes, with swords whose deadly blades caught the sunlight.

"*Isabella!*"

"Oh, sweet Jesus protect us," Isabella said at Beales's shout.

"*Isabella!* You're mine now! Isabella! Geoff is dead! You're mine. *Everything* is mine!"

Isabella swayed where she stood and Odette roughly pushed Cassandra, now wrapped tightly in a blanket, into Courtland's arms as she caught her mistress close against her. "He lies. I did not see this, but I would have seen the Cap'n's death. I would have known that in my heart. She kept me from seeing the treachery, my own wicked twin. I am so sorry! Come with me now. Into the trees, to the cave. Now, Missy Isabella! For your husband, your child—*now!*"

Isabella held tightly to the wooden railing for a few moments longer, even as the wives of her husband's crews were put upon by Beales's men, and the older crew, crippled and maimed and gray of hair, fell or were subdued, one by one.

At last she turned away, grabbing Courtland's arm and pulling him back from the open windows. "Take Cassandra, Courtland. Take her and follow Odette. Go with the others, to the cave, just as Papa Geoff has always talked about if we were attacked, remember? Take her now!"

"And you," Courtland said, pleaded. "You'll come, too."

She shook her head. "He doesn't want you, he wants me. If I go with you, he won't stop until he finds us all. I'll be fine, I promise. I'll talk to him, reason with him until Geoff comes to save us. But take Cassandra for me, keep her safe for us. Never leave her, Courtland, not for a moment, not until Geoff returns."

"No! I won't leave you! You can't make me leave you!"

She slapped him. Isabella, the gentle one, the always smiling, laughing one. The one he loved above all others. Slapped him.

"Do what I say! You have to live, Courtland. For your Callie, you have to live. You are her protector! Never leave her, not ever! Promise me!"

Courtland nodded, unable to speak, and Isabella put her arms around him, pulling him and her child close, kissing both their foreheads.

She looked at Odette, who only nodded, and then turned away, stepped back onto the veranda, to stand there, her hands on the railing, daring Edmund Beales to do his worst. "I am here, Edmund. Stop this, and we'll talk! I'll give you what you want—just stop your men, now!"

Odette tugged on Courtland's arm, pulling him out

of the bedchamber, through one of the bedrooms across the wide hallway, onto the veranda there, the wooden stairs that led down the rear of the house. Once on the ground, they ran into the trees, meeting up with one of the other women, Edythe, who carried young Morgan, and they all pressed on together into previously forbidden territory for the children, the sounds of cannon fire, of gunshot, of unholy screams, chasing at their heels.

"They didn't stop," Courtland said, looking to Odette. "He didn't listen to her. I've got to go back, help her."

"You are a child, and you've got to do what she said for you to do," Odette told him, her large brown eyes filled with tears. "If you love her, you'll do as she said. It is all we can do. You know the way? Guide us."

Reluctantly, Courtland led the others deeper into the trees, avoiding the deadfalls Geoffrey Baskin had shown him, the deceptively normal-looking ground that hid deep pits lined with dozens of pointed wooden spikes. On and on they ran, twisting and turning through a path known only to those who had been trained to recognize the signs, until at last they reached the cave.

Some were already there. Spencer, Rian, Fanny, three dozen or more women and even more children sitting wide-eyed and silent in the damp and dark. No more came, not as the screams continued to reach them, as night fell, as some of the young ones began to cry for their mothers, for their empty bellies.

The hours stretched out into an eternity.

At last Courtland could take no more. He reluctantly relinquished Cassandra, whom he'd been holding still for hours and hours, and gave her over to Odette.

He walked slowly, not to avoid the deadfalls, but because he didn't want to see what he felt sure he would see.

The sun was just rising as he stepped out of the trees, skirting the side of the big house, walking onto the beginnings of the wide beach. The wide, red beach. Buzzing with flies; littered with broken, gutted bodies. Women, children, babies. Animals. They all lay on the sand. They hung from trees. Bodies, pieces of bodies.

The three ships were gone.

Young Isaac was among the dead. Isaac, and so many others who had survived the raid on the church, just to die here. Geoffrey Baskin had saved them, taken them in as his own—for this? Why? *Why?*

Courtland went to his knees beside Isaac, pressed a hand to the boy's chest, hoping for a heartbeat, but only came away with blood on his hands. Everywhere he went, every body he knelt beside, he touched, said a prayer for before moving on to the next, and then the next…

The silence rang in his ears like the sound of the whip whistling above his head, ready to sting, to cut. Even the exotic birds in the trees were silent.

At last he turned toward the huge house, his shoulders squaring as he prepared himself for whatever he might face inside those white walls. It was then that he saw the words, written high and wide on the wood. Written in blood.

You lose. No mercy, no quarter. Until it's mine.

He began to run, not knowing if he should be praying to find Isabella, or to hope that Edmund Beales had taken her with him, because then she'd still be alive.

The most fervent of his prayers weren't to be answered, for the first thing he saw when entering the high foyer ringed by the main staircase was the body of Isabella Baskin lying on the stone floor. She looked to be asleep, except that her eyes were open, staring sightlessly at the chandelier hanging twenty feet above her head.

Courtland went to his knees beside her, still hoping she was alive, sliding his hands beneath her, trying to lift her up. But her head fell back, her neck broken, and he looked up at the second floor balcony. Had she fallen? Had she been picked up, thrown over the railing? And why? *Why?*

He left her then, knowing he had to return to the cave, to Cassandra, to Odette and the others. What if Beales hadn't been lying? What if Geoffrey Baskin was dead, what if both the *Black Ghost* and the *Silver Ghost* were at the bottom of the sea? What then?

He couldn't cry, had no time to mourn. This was not the time for tears.

He was, he knew, the oldest male left alive on the island, possibly the only man left alive at all. He had a responsibility.

They all looked to him when he entered the cave, questions in their eyes.

He gathered up the sleeping Callie once more, the blood on his hands smearing the infant's white lawn gown. "I saw her. No one and nothing lives. No one and nothing."

Odette sank to her knees and began keening like a wild animal in pain. All around the cave, women and children screamed, cried, their voices careening, echoing, off the high dark walls.

"I will be the one who tells him," Courtland said, making what was probably the longest speech of his young life. But then, he wasn't a child, never had been probably, and never would be, not after this day. "He needs to see his daughter. The rest of you stay here, wait for someone to come for you."

With the sleeping Cassandra in his arms, once more he made his way to the large white house, to the beach. Flies buzzed everywhere now, but still no birds sang.

He'd have to get Spencer and Rian and the other young boys before the sun grew too hot, form a burial party. So many bodies…

He looked to the horizon, and his heart lurched in his chest when he saw two ships, Geoffrey Baskin's ships, limping toward the harbor, masts without their topmost bits, sail ripped and shredded, flapping loose in the stiff breeze.

Slowly, he made his way across the beach, around the bodies of the dead, Cassandra now awake and laughing in his arms, and walked down the last few yards of the hard-packed sand nearest the shore, into the gently lapping clear blue-green water until it reached his knees.

The small wavelets caressed his shins, and each one spoke to him in Isabella's voice. Over and over and over again:

You are her protector. Never leave her, not ever. Promise me.

Courtland listened carefully to Isabella's plea, to Cassandra's happy gurgles, as he waited. Stoic. Refusing to feel.

He remained there, not moving, not reacting, as the boats were hastily lowered. As men jumped from the ships, frantically swimming toward the shore. As they waded through the shallow surf, and then began to run. As they shouted out the names of those they loved, their wives, their children, and no one answered.

He only began to shiver, to cry, as his Papa Geoff splashed toward him through the surf, slowly shaking his head, wordlessly begging Courtland not to tell him of the destruction Edmund Beales had wrought in their small paradise, the death he'd brought with him…

Romney Marsh
1815

CHAPTER ONE

"WHAT ARE YOU DOING?"

Courtland Becket said something unlovely under his breath as the hammer came down hard on the side of his thumb rather than the small brad he was tapping into place.

"Cassandra, how many times have I asked you not to sneak into my workshop without knocking?"

"Dozens, I suppose," she said, hopping up onto the workbench, her slipper-clad feet crossed at the ankle and swinging back and forth tantalizingly close to Courtland's face as he sat on his work stool. "You know I don't listen when you bluster."

"I do *not* bluster," he said, tapping the brad home and then inspecting the finished project that had occupied him for most of the morning. "There. Done. What do you think?"

Cassandra leaned forward and took the thing from him, held it up in front of her. "Very fine workmanship, Mr. Becket, as always. You do exemplary work. What is it?"

He took the thing back, prepared to show her. "It's for Rian, to help him on with his boots. Look—these two hooks go into the loops at the top of either side of his boot. The hooks are connected to this handle. Rian positions his foot in the boot as best he can, and then attaches the hooks, then pulls. He'll still probably have to stamp his feet entirely into the boots, but this should help him a lot."

"Amazing. Let me try it. To see if it really works, I mean," Cassandra said, hopping down from the workbench.

"You aren't wearing boots," Courtland pointed out, as he'd been doing his best to keep his gaze averted from her slim, shapely ankles as she had deliberately goaded him by dangling them in his face.

"Yes, but there's a boot over here. Rian's? Of course it is, so you could test your brilliance." She slipped out of her right shoe and grabbed the boot. "So, pretending I only have the one arm and hand, I simply step into the boot as far as I can, and then—oh, pooh, it went on by itself. I didn't realize Rian had such large feet. And the top comes up past my knees. How on earth do you men walk in these things?"

Courtland sat back on the stool, smiling as Cassandra comically clomped around his workshop in the boot, her skirts pulled up, her tawny curls bobbing as she stepped, limped, stepped again.

She knew what she was doing, of course. She was

bedeviling him again. On purpose. With full deliberation and malice aforethought.

And he was watching her, entranced, again. Unable to help himself. Wondering how long it would be before he had to leave Becket Hall forever, or else break her heart.

"Enough, Cassandra. Why did you come down here?"

She boosted herself back up onto the workbench and lifted her right leg toward him, wordlessly telling him to remove the boot for her. Which would expose her bare leg all the way to her knee.

He'd rather chew the last of the metal brads in the pocket of his leather apron.

"Papa wants to see you in his study," she told him, lowering her leg, at which time Rian's boot simply slid off her foot and onto the floor. "Hand me up my slipper, if you please, you big spoilsport."

Courtland bent down, retrieved her slipper, and raised himself up in time to see her bare foot extended, her leg uncovered to her knee as she held up her hem once more. "Cassandra, for the love of God…"

She smiled down at him as he took hold of her bare ankle and pushed the slipper onto her foot. "There, that wasn't so painful, was it? Honestly, Court, anyone would think you've never seen a female ankle before."

"And if I say I have, that would mean you'd then quiz me about whose ankle it was that I've seen, so

I'm not going to say it," Courtland said, getting to his feet as he untied his apron and laid it on the workbench. "Who else will be there?"

"Where?" she asked him, grinning like the minx she was. Her mission in life, for today, forever, seemed to be to do her best to drive him mad, send him screaming into the Channel to drown himself, just to be away from her. The temptation of her.

"Never mind, I was a fool to ask. I'll find out soon enough."

Cassandra hopped down from the workbench again, chasing after him as his long strides took him out of the basement workshop and toward the stairs leading up to the first floor of Becket Hall. "Spencer, and Rian, and Jack. Jacko, of course. Oh, and Chance."

Courtland turned around, causing Cassandra to bump into him. She looked up at him, smiling, and he could smell the sweet jasmine in her hair. "Chance? When did he get back?"

"I didn't mention that? Honestly, Courtland, if you didn't spend half your time moldering down here in the cellars, you'd know more. Chance and Julia and the children arrived at least an hour ago. He may have news on Edmund Beales."

"I do not molder."

"I suppose moldering is in the eye of the beholder, then," Cassandra said, dancing past him and up the steps, leaving Courtland to follow after her. He always seemed to be following after her, even while trying to tell himself that she'd become too old for him to consider her his personal responsibility…and old enough to know that her grown-up self caused him problems he refused to face.

As a child, she had tagged behind him everywhere, and he'd been flattered, delighted. She'd taken her first real steps to him. She'd run to him when she fell, scraped her knee. As her papa, now known to the small world of Romney Marsh as Ainsley Becket, hid in his study, turned away from the world in his grief, it had been Courtland who had sat Cassandra on his knee, taught her sums and her letters, read her stories, held her hand when the storms raged in off the Channel.

He'd tied her sashes when they came undone, taught her how to fly a kite, sat her on her first pony, held her above the waves when, as all Beckets had to do, she learned to swim.

He'd instructed her to stay away from the shifting sands that ran along the shore to the east of Becket Hall. He'd shielded her from the teasing of her older siblings, explained to her that her papa did indeed love her, very much, even if sometimes he was too sad to look at the child who, day by day, more closely resembled her dead mother.

And that had all been fine.

When Cassandra was two. When she was five, ten. But at fourteen? Yes, that's when it had all begun to change, slowly at first, without him really noticing what was happening.

She still followed after him everywhere he went. But now it was to tease him, to goad him, to dare him. Look at me, Courtland. Look, I'm growing up. What will you do with me now?

She was his sister, damn it!

No. Not his sister. Never his sister.

He knew who he was. He knew who she was. She was the daughter of the house, Ainsley's child. He was the mongrel, the boy who had slept and eaten with the dogs, the boy who had been an object of pity, brought home because what else was to be done with him?

He owed Geoffrey Baskin—Ainsley Becket—his life. His loyalty.

Ainsley Becket owed him nothing, least of all Isabella's daughter.

Courtland shook his head, disgusted with that part of himself that refused to accept what had to be, and bounded up the stone steps to the main floor of the large house, turned and headed for Ainsley's study. He needed to concentrate on Edmund Beales, the monster so long thought dead, but the same man Rian had gone head-to-head with only a little more than a month ago, in France.

Beales had come out of that encounter wounded, but not defeated, not dead. And now he knew that Ainsley, his old partner Geoffrey Baskin, also still lived.

A reckoning was coming, and coming soon, and the tension inside Becket Hall was fast becoming unbearable.

All of the Beckets had gathered in Romney Marsh a month ago, to talk, to plan, to prepare for that final reckoning, discuss the many ways Edmund Beales might come at them. When, and where. Would he chose sudden violence, or stealth?

It had been a large gathering, all eight Beckets and their wives and husbands, a menagerie of children.

Morgan, now the Countess of Aylesford, and her husband Ethan, their young twins, Geoffrey and Isabella.

Chance and his wife Julia, bringing with them their three children.

Fanny—good God help them all, now the Countess of Brede—and Valentine, the most long-suffering and piteously besotted fellow in creation.

They'd joined Eleanor and her husband, Jack Eastwood, who resided at Becket Hall along with Spencer and his wife Mariah, and their two children.

And Rian. Rian and his new bride, Lisette. Edmund Beales's daughter.

God. Lisette's introduction to the family had caused some tense moments, and still did, unfortunately, especially with Jacko, Ainsley's second-in-command during the years in the islands.

But they were all together again, all of Ainsley's eight "acquired" children who had survived the attack on the island; his seven hostages to fortune, and the child of his beloved Isabella.

Almost eighteen years after that last day, that

terrible, unforgettable day, they had rebuilt, grown, possibly even healed.

The ships, the *Black Ghost* and the *Silver Ghost* had been dismantled once they'd reached what would be called Becket Hall, the boards used to construct Becket Village, housing the survivors of the attack on land, the betrayal at sea.

Life, often painful, had moved on…only to have Edmund Beales resurface, bringing danger to all of them.

Courtland had never asked Ainsley about the warning Beales had written in the blood of his victims: *You lose. No mercy, no quarter. Until it's mine.* He didn't think it was his place, especially when Ainsley had been so cruelly hurt, outwardly strong for his crew, for the survivors, but dead inside for too many long years.

No one had asked when they'd all first come together again last month. But perhaps it was time. Time to know what it was that Edmund Beales had wanted and could not find, the reason behind the tortured bodies, the eventual massacre.

Until it's mine.

They had all thought Beales wanted Isabella, but it would seem that the man had coveted more than his friend's wife. What? What had the man wanted? What might he still want?

Courtland stood outside the closed door to the

study, certain it would be he who would finally be the one to ask that question.

CASSANDRA ENTERED THE drawing room to see Julia sitting with Mariah, the two with their heads together, speaking quietly.

"Secrets?" she asked, sitting down beside Julia. "Don't tell me one of you is breeding again. I'm too young to be an aunt so many times over."

Mariah colored beneath her flame-red hair, and dipped her head. "You weren't supposed to guess. We all have enough on our plates with Elly at the moment, with…with everything else that's going on. The men need to feel free to concentrate on finding Beales, putting an end to this long nightmare."

Cassandra hid her surprise at having guessed correctly, for she'd just been, she thought, speaking nonsense. "Elly's fine, Mariah, isn't she? And the baby won't be arriving for another month or more. I don't know how she stands it, being confined to her bed this way."

"Elly *can't* stand it," Mariah said, smiling. "But Odette is, by and large, a powerful force, more powerful than any one of us. And she seems to have gotten Elly and the baby this far, so it's impossible not to listen to her."

"I'll agree with that," Julia said, smoothing down her skirts. She wasn't a beautiful woman, but she had presence, Cassandra had always thought. Presence, and a keen, sharp-eyed intelligence. Chance adored her. "I still hang this ridiculous *gad* around my neck when we travel, much as I know it's all superstitious nonsense. An alligator's tooth, if that's truly what it is? Nonsense, I keep telling myself. But I wouldn't be without it."

"She gave one to Lisette, you know," Cassandra told them quietly. "To protect her from her papa's evil, the evil of Odette's twin, this horrible Loringa Rian saw in France. I think she should have given her a second one, to protect her from Jacko."

"He's still being so nasty?" Julia asked, frowning. "Chance and I noticed it when we were here last month, but we'd hoped Ainsley convinced Jacko to come to his senses. After all, Lisette isn't responsible for her father's…actions."

"Jacko's not the only one," Cassandra said, grabbing the dish of sugared treats from the table between the couches and placing it in her lap. She'd lost what Odette called her baby fat last year, but it wasn't because she had given up her love of sweet things. "Lisette won't walk over to Becket Village without Rian or Jasper going with her. Jasper is so huge, nobody will even look at him, even though he's really the kindest creature in nature, according to Lisette. I think…I think Rian and Lisette are going to have to leave Becket Hall when this is all over. Lisette, just by being here, opens old wounds for some people, even though none of it, what happened, what might happen next, is her fault. After all, she saved Rian's life. That should mean something to our own people, shouldn't it?"

Mariah and Julia exchanged glances Cassandra couldn't interpret. "What does Ainsley say?" Mariah asked.

Cassandra shrugged, popped another piece of the chewy candy into her mouth. "He doesn't say anything. You know Papa. He just sort of *looks* at people, and they know he doesn't approve. So no one will do anything terrible. But Lisette feels the dislike, she has to, poor thing. And you'll be leaving, too, won't you, Mariah? Once this is over?"

Mariah smiled. "Lining us all up like ducks, Callie? Why?"

Cassandra didn't realize she was being so obvious. "No reason. I know Elly would never leave Becket Hall, not of her own volition, and Jack seems happy with that. But Papa?" She shook her head. "He had another letter from Mrs. Warren last week, you know."

Once again Mariah and Julia exchanged glances, this time smiling at each other. "Marianna Warren? Really?" Mariah commented. "They only met the one time, and that was years ago. So they keep up a correspondence? I didn't know."

Cassandra rolled her eyes. "Oh, of course you do. Spence writes to her ship captain—Abraham, is it? And that's where you and Spence will be going, I already know that, I guess. This place known as Hampton

Roads. Papa has several maps of the area. They've been arriving from America for years. And…and he's purchased land there, a huge parcel along the water. For his ships, you know? He doesn't think I know that part, but I do."

She waited for her sisters-in-law to react, which didn't take long.

"Ainsley's thinking of leaving Becket Hall? Leaving Romney Marsh?" Julia shook her head, looking astonished. "He won't even travel to London. He goes nowhere."

"Fearing arrest for piracy so long ago in the islands, no thanks to Edmund Beales," Mariah said, and then sighed. "Ah, but once Beales is gone? Any real chance of trouble from that quarter would be gone with it, and Ainsley would be free to go anywhere without fear of exposing all of us to the same charge. But he'd go to America? Not London? I never imagined, and I doubt Spence has, either. My goodness. Delightful to think we'd be living close by, but still shocking."

"How do you feel about that, Callie?" Julia asked her. "Chance and I would never leave England. I know, because we've discussed it. We want our children to grow up here. Are you asking to come live with us rather than relocating to America? Because you're most definitely welcome, unless you want to live with Fanny and Valentine, or stay here with Elly and Jack and—oh." She sat back on the couch, grinned at

Mariah. "It's Court, isn't it? You're lining up all your ducks, but you don't know where Court fits in that line, do you? And you think *we* know?"

Cassandra put down the candy dish and twined her fingers together in her lap. "I don't think he'll stay here, that's all. Becket Hall doesn't need so many masters, or it won't once we're free to travel anywhere. Jack and Elly love this house, love Romney Marsh, and Papa would want someone to live here in any case. Fanny's settled, Chance and Morgan are settled. Rian and Lisette will go somewhere else, they really have no choice, do they? You and Spence are already planning your own move to Hampton Roads."

"Which, counting to eight on my fingers, leaves Court, and you," Mariah said, nodding her head. "Oh where or where will you go? I imagine Ainsley assumes you'll go where he goes. But will Court be equally happy to go there, as well? Especially when offered the opportunity to at last rid himself of his shadow?"

"I'm not his shadow!" Cassandra said, knowing that wasn't true.

"Ah, Callie," Julia said, leaning over to kiss Cassandra's cheek. "You've been nowhere but here. You know so little of life, of men. And you're young, too young to be thinking of marriage to anyone."

Cassandra looked above the fireplace, at the portrait of her mother. "Mama wasn't any older than me when she married Papa. He was at least a dozen years her senior. I know, because Court told me."

"And now we'll tell you something you already know," Julia added quietly. "Court sees you as his sister. Perhaps, some day, he'll change his mind, see what the rest of us see. But not now. There's too much going on now, with Beales out there somewhere. This isn't…this isn't a happy time. Truly the wrong time."

"But it *has* to be now, Julia, don't you see?" Cassandra explained tightly. "Edmund Beales will be gone soon, out of our lives, and everyone will scatter to the four winds, I just know it. We won't all be held here anymore, in this limbo Odette calls our lives all these years. If Papa leaves—if Court and I end up on opposite sides of the ocean before he admits to himself that he can't live without me? What will I do? Whatever will I do?"

Morgan's voice came at them from the doorway. "Oh, alas. Alas and alack! What will I do? Whatever will I do? Poor Court, poor *me!*" She crossed the room in her usual graceful, long-legged strides, a raven-haired beauty of lush proportions, and then plopped herself down next to Julia. "Callie, I never thought you were such a dolt. You want him, then you go get him, *that's* what you do."

"That's what *you'd* do, Morgan. Oh, wait, that's what you did, isn't it? Poor Ethan is still trying to figure out what happened," Julia said, laughing.

"I crossed an ocean to get to Spence," Mariah said. "Of course, I mostly wanted to box his ears for him, but that's neither here nor there, is it?"

"The whys don't matter," Morgan said, rubbing her hands together, clearly eager to enter into a conspiracy. "It's the *how* we're concerned with, if Callie really wants to bring Court to heel."

"Yes, *how?* I've tried almost everything, and he still refuses to think of me as anything but a baby," Cassandra asked, leaning forward on the couch.

"True, true. And you're all grown-up now, aren't you? We just need Court to finally accept that delightful change. This might take some serious thinking, although I am already entertaining one possible idea, and it will take our minds off this tense waiting, waiting for Beales to show himself," Morgan said, reaching for the depleted sugar treats in the candy dish. "Ladies? Can we please entertain suggestions from the floor? You start, Julia. I'll leave my idea for last."

"And, knowing you, Morgan, that's probably a good thing," Julia said, looking at Mariah and winking. "It will at least delay, if not spare our blushes."

Cassandra looked to the other women, one by one. "You think I could do that?" she asked, her heart pounding.

"Do what?" Morgan asked innocently, popping a sugar treat into her mouth.

"Seduce him, of course. That is what you're suggesting, isn't it?" Cassandra asked, and then waited while Mariah slapped Morgan's back, to help dislodge the candy stuck in her throat.

"Ah," Julia said, sighing theatrically. "Our little girl is all grown-up now, isn't she? This should help divert our minds from worries over Edmund Beales."

CHAPTER TWO

"YOUR PARDON, SIR? Sir Horatio Lewis and Mr. Francis Roberts to see you, sir."

Edmund Beales did not look up from the papers on his desk, aware that the men were standing just inside the door, but perversely refusing to acknowledge that fact. "Thank you, Walters. Please keep them waiting. A half hour should be sufficient to depress their any remaining pretensions."

"Uh…um…sir? That is, they're…here."

Beales smiled, swiveling on his chair to look at the two men who, although they were not standing there, hats in hand like supplicants, were in fact only minus the hats. Their joint demeanor was that of inferiors come begging…most probably for their miserable, pathetic small lives.

"How utterly tactless of me. Gentlemen, do come in." Beales did not rise from behind his desk. Nor did he offer his hand other than to wave rather languidly in the direction of the two deliberately placed uncomfortable chairs facing the massive desk that had once graced one of Bonaparte's many residences. Not that the man had much need of such a glorious piece of furniture now, freezing his skinny shanks on the rocks of Saint Helena.

He'd had the desk shipped to his new mansion in Portland Square, along with other treasures he'd collected over the past two decades, leaving behind in Paris the few pieces "collected" during his privateering days he had deemed impressive enough to keep. He hadn't been much interested in collecting chairs, or rugs, or other furnishings all those years ago, the way Geoff had been. An oversight, one he regretted now, but there was nothing that couldn't be corrected with ample infusions of money, of which he had more than a sufficient amount.

Still, the Emperor Napoleon's desk? That was rather a coup. Perhaps he should have a brass plaque attached to it, so that all could know of his prize. Ah, but that would be the old Edmund Beales, and spoke too much of flash and dash. Today he was a solid citizen, sober and earnest and… "Oh, for the love of heaven, gentlemen, sit down. I'm not going to bite."

Sir Horatio was the first to speak, but not until he had squirmed uncomfortably in his chair, as if doing his best to avoid a tack someone had placed there to poke at his enormous backside. "We, um, we didn't know you'd be returning, Mr. Beatty. Your departure two years ago—is it two years now?—well, it was rather precipitous, wasn't it? And…and so soon after poor Rowley disappeared. His house burning down like that, his dear wife fleeing to the country, seemingly to bury herself there, as yet to return to society."

"This cheers you?"

"Rowley disappearing?" Mr. Roberts asked rather incredulously, and then winced, as if sorry he had spoken, drawn attention to himself. "Not that we don't know where he went to, not with Horatio here working at the Admiralty. Died just a few weeks ago, you know. Hanged himself in his cell, poor bastard."

"Hell of an end for a man with so much ambition," Sir Horatio said, touching his hand to his neck cloth.

Beales nodded, assuming a woebegone expression. "Yes, yes, shall we all drink a toast to the memory of the dear Earl of Chelfham, who destroyed a most profitable enterprise for us all with his stupidity and greed. Who is to say if the ending of the war wouldn't have been different if the Red Men Gang had been able to keep up its guinea runs these past years. Not being able to pay his soldiers was not the greatest of our friend Bonaparte's problems, but it certainly had an impact. Although we've all learned a valuable lesson, haven't we, gentlemen?"

"Not to back the wrong horse," Mr. Roberts said, and then once again bit his lips together, as if regretting his words.

"Yes, that, as well," Beales agreed, smiling

thinly. "But I was referring to Lord Chelfham's belief that he could hoodwink me, try to steal from *me.* From me, gentlemen—can you imagine? I only regret being unable to get to him sooner, ease the pain of his incarceration and his guilt over his betrayal of the rest of us. But when at last the opportunity presented itself, I made certain it was a stout rope. Do you think he was grateful for the time, effort, and considerable expense I incurred having someone insinuated into his lordship's plush prison? I've wondered about that, or if he still thought his pitiful life worth living. And yet, I feel I owe the man something for the services he did render me in the past, which is why you are here. Gentlemen? Some wine?"

"I'll get us some," Mr. Roberts volunteered, jumping up from his chair to play at servant. "Over there, yes?" he asked, pointing to the lavish drinks table set up in one corner of the large study.

"Ah, Francis," Beales purred, placing a few small dark green leaves between his teeth and cheek. "Still the master of the obvious, I see. None for me, thank you. I long ago found my own way to paradise."

Beales chewed on the coca leaves, releasing their invigorating, mind-expanding juices as he watched Francis Roberts pull the lead crystal stopper from the decanter and then fill two glasses, spilling only a few drops in his nervousness. Once the gentlemen had been served and Roberts was back in his chair, a careful, two-handed grip on the fragile glass, he said, "And so, delighted as I am to see you both again, I'm afraid this meeting of ours is not purely social. There is—"

"Mr. Beatty?" Sir Horatio cut in, raising his hand like some slow-witted student unable to understand the simplicity of two plus two. "You don't mean to take up where, well, where we left off when our smuggling enterprise was so sadly compromised? With Bonaparte gone for good now, there really is no reason, unless you wish to begin trading in brandy and silks and such, rather than gold guineas."

"No, no, never return to the same well once it has gone dry, Sir Horatio," Beales agreed, inwardly wishing to wring the idiot's fat neck for daring to interrupt him. Ah, well, he wouldn't need the man much longer. "I am sufficiently well situated, for the moment, monetarily, and can only hope the same for you both. I do, as I've already alluded to, have this one small, niggling problem standing between me and a happy existence here in London."

Francis Roberts must have seen this as his cue, for he sat forward on his chair, his hands gripping the wooden arm rails. "Whatever you need, Mr. Beatty, sir, consider it already done."

Fools rush in, Beales thought, blessing the gods for peopling the earth with so very many of them ripe for the picking.

"Why, thank you, Francis. That's so kind in you. I'm quite touched, truly. Almost as if I don't hold both the rather large mortgages on your estate. And you, Horatio? Are you likewise amenable?"

"Oh, yes, yes indeed. Anything I can do to be of service, as always."

Beales watched as the man flushed uncomfortably. No need to mention the sword of Damocles he held over Sir Horatio's head. After all, whose business was it if a man wished to keep his lover in a picturesque cottage near Bath? Even if that lover of such long-standing is one's own nephew—a young man also in the employ of the so-discreet Edmund Beales?

Knowledge. Power. Knowledge was power. And Edmund Beales did so appreciate both.

"Very well," Beales said after the silence in the room had grown, at least for his two visitors, decidedly tense. "First, for reasons my own, I am, for the nonce, no longer Nathanial Beatty. Erase, if you please, that name from your memories. In fact, erase me from your memories. Both for only a small space of time, but until I give you permission, you do not know me, have never met me. Understood?"

Francis Roberts actually began to smile, as if just given a gift from above, but quickly covered his mouth and coughed into his fist. Obviously not quite as stupid as he looked, Beales thought. He might keep him.

"Then what will we call you?"

Beales looked at Sir Horatio from beneath heavy eyelids. *Him* he most definitely would not keep. The man was a stepping stone into the rarefied society of

Mayfair, as were all the others, but his usefulness would end soon.

"You will not call me anything, Horatio, for you will not know me," Beales explained as he would to a child. "You will see me on the street and nod your head in passing as you would to any gentleman you encounter, but that is all. Are we understanding each other now, or shall I write it down for you, have you memorize it and then recite to me tomorrow, so I can be certain you have taken such complex information into your brainbox, hmm?"

"No, sir," Sir Horatio said, looking into his empty wineglass as if wishing it full again.

"Very well. Now, if we may proceed with my crisis of conscience?" Beales picked up a piece of paper from his desk, turned it about and slid it across the surface toward Roberts, the smarter of the two men, if it was possible to differentiate between Dumb and Obtuse.

Roberts picked up the paper, read aloud, "'Geoffrey Baskin, captain, the *Black Ghost,* now known by the name Becket and residing somewhere in Romney Marsh, most probably near the Channel. Jacko, no surname known, captain, the *Silver Ghost,* probably also somewhere in Romney Marsh—'"

"Yes, yes, I know what's written on the page, thank you, Francis," Beales said, waving away the man's words. "Now, let me tell you their crimes, shall I? Because these men must be located, gentlemen, and brought to justice for the crimes of piracy and murder against the Crown. Found, tried, convicted and hanged…within the month, if possible. Can you do this?"

"Piracy? Where?" Sir Horatio asked, frowning. "Smuggling, God knows, and even some ship wreckers still operating in Cornwall. But piracy? Not in these waters."

"Indeed, no. Francis holds the paper containing all of the pertinent information. We're speaking of a time before the turn of the century, gentlemen, in the waters somewhere off Haiti, and a convoy of several ships from three nations, joined together to protect each other in dangerous waters. The French and Spanish ships are of no account to us, of course, but the English ship that was, sadly, sent to the bottom carried not only property of the Crown and its captain and crew, but also the Sixth Earl of Chelfham—yes, gentlemen, the older brother of our dear departed friend Rowley—along with his lady wife and young daughter. Monstrous, just monstrous, wouldn't you agree?"

"Rowley's older brother?" Sir Horatio looked to Francis Roberts. "That's how Rowley came into his title, remember? His brother was lost at sea? Damn and blast, murdered by pirates? Did you know that?"

Roberts shook his head, his gaze still concentrated on the paper in his shaking hand. "This was all so long ago. There's…there's proof?"

"All you might ever need," Beales said, steepling his fingers in front of his chin. "A letter, dictated on his deathbed by one of Baskin's outraged crew and witnessed by none other than our mutual friend Rowley himself. In fact, we may also have living evidence, much to my own astonishment, as Rowley tearfully informed my, um, my agent before his untimely suicide, that his brother's child—the young daughter?—may still survive. My only possible conclusion is that she was either roughly abused by these horrible men at the time of the attack and then murdered, or that she remains a captive of Baskin's all these years later, possibly living the life of a servant, poor thing. Name of Eleanor, I believe Rowley told my agent. I had dismissed the information at the time, thinking Rowley needlessly sentimental as he looked death in the face, but have since come to believe him most wholeheartedly. If you can locate her, this would help to prove our case against Baskin, yes?"

"A crime against humanity!" Sir Horatio exclaimed, his eyes gone wide. "I assure you, Mr. Beatty—that is, I assure you, *sir,* that I will bring the full concentration of my post to bear, to locate and prosecute these two monsters, and to rescue the wronged Lady Eleanor, if she survives."

"Romney Marsh," Francis Roberts said quietly. "Brings them to Dover Castle once we find them, and into my jurisdiction. That's why you summoned—

that is, happy to be of service, sir, as always. It will be a quick trial, with this Baskin and his cohort and anyone else we might find hanged in chains. You have my word on that, sir. The horror, sir. That poor child!"

"Yes, yes, a horrific tragedy, truly. And, for all of his treachery, which had to be punished, you can see why I feel I cannot be happy until these men who committed crimes against Rowley's family—and the Crown, gentlemen, lest we forget that—are brought to the bar of justice. Before Christmas, if you please, gentlemen. You will keep me apprised of any and all developments, most especially Baskin's location once you ascertain that, of course. Only then will I believe dear Rowley rests in peace." Beales stood up, signaling that the meeting was over.

Once the two men were gone, Beales sat back in his chair, smiling for the first time in weeks. Ah, to see Geoff and whoever else was left alive from the old days brought to *justice.* What a wonderful thought. And it would be the Crown, and his hired apes, that would do the deed, all without Beales being forced to dirty his own hands. After all, why keep a dog and then bark yourself? Let his minions scuttle about, locate Geoff and the others. For his part, he would be content to visit Geoff in his cell, and make a bargain. The Empress for the lives of his now totally unprotected women.

Not that he was prepared to keep any such bargain. Why should he, once he had the Empress? The old days wouldn't be entirely gone until every last person who could place him in the islands was also gone—breed, seed, and generation.

Beales took a small key from his pocket and used it to open a box he'd taken from a bottom drawer of Bonaparte's desk.

He sorted through the dozens of dossiers he'd been collecting for many years, at last deciding on one in particular. Yes, the dear Reverend, and a man so generously opening his house to young orphan girls, leading them to God via nightly lessons on their knees in his bedchamber. Highly placed in the church. A fairly impressive if long-winded speaker able to rouse his audience to do his bidding. Located on the fringe of Romney Marsh, he was close enough to summon at a moment's notice to raise the rabble against Geoff, demand a rash of executions.

After all, what was life without a little entertaining *theater?*

Beales continued to sort through the papers, smiling over several sheets blank save for the shaky (forgivable, as the man had been under considerable duress at the time) signature of Rowley Maddox, Earl of Chelfham, scrawled at the bottom. If necessary, Rowley might need to *witness* a few more deathbed confessions before Geoff was measured for the chains he'd hang in at Dover Castle.

So many dossiers, he'd soon need a larger box to keep them in. And perhaps he should organize them, as well. Alphabetically? he thought, reaching into his pocket for a few more coca leaves. By name? Or by vice?

By vice, definitely.

"To know a man's virtues has its uses," Beales ruminated, closing and locking the box once more. "But to know his vices is to provide the key to every door…"

He rubbed at his chest, his wound healed but still plaguing him from time to time, as Lisette had managed to nick his lung with the point of the scissors she'd used to attack him. Her own *papa.* He looked forward to seeing her again.

Ah, but mostly he longed to see Geoff, his old friend and partner. He longed to see him defeated, despondent, his family dead, his crew to be hanged alongside him in chains.

And the Empress, once thought lost to him? His, his alone at last, as she was meant to be.

Revenge truly was a dish best served cold….

CHAPTER THREE

CASSANDRA SAT BUNDLED up in her heavy blue cloak on the bottom step of the stone stairs leading from the west side of the terrace, watching the large group practicing their maneuvers on the brown shingle beach. It would rain soon, as it always did in November, but they would keep on marching, their rifles on their shoulders, unheeding of the weather.

Sergeant-Major Hart's shouts could be heard above the cries of interested gulls and the waves crashing with more than usual vigor against the beach, proof of a storm somewhere in the Channel.

Clovis Meecham marched alongside the ranks of men and women, also barking orders and, as always, a few skipping children who could not resist the fun tagging along behind him, all of them looking what they were; old men from the days on the island, young boys, mothers and even grandmothers, men more used to striding a deck at sea than parading on dry land.

But her papa had told her that the villagers wanted to keep busy, preparing themselves for possible attack.

In the harbor, the sloops, the *Respite* and Chance's own *Spectre,* as well as the new frigate her papa had ordered were all fitted out to sail at any moment; casks of fresh water replaced weekly, extra sail stowed away, food and munitions crowding every compartment.

Becket Hall was prepared for attack, for a siege. The ships were ready in case an assault came by sea. Everyone had a single bag packed and lined up in the secret storeroom just behind her, the one accessible via several concealed inner passages her papa had designed into Becket Hall, and that led directly out onto the beach.

Plans. Plans, and more plans, all because Edmund Beales still lived. The man who had murdered her mother and so many others still walked the earth.

Nearly eighteen years of hiding, of watching over their backs, of never feeling quite safe.

It was enough to challenge one's faith in a merciful God.

"Don't gnaw on your thumb like that, Cassandra."

She looked up to see Courtland walking toward her, appearing as if from nowhere, because he'd been checking the storeroom again, and had exited Becket Hall via the door that, when closed, blended completely with the dark stones.

"I'm not gnawing, Court," she said, wishing he hadn't caught her out indulging in the nervous habit that even she had thought she'd left behind years ago. "I was…I was thinking. I was thinking how unfair life is, to keep knocking some people down, again and again, while others sail through all of their years, unknowing, unscathed."

"Oh, my. That is profound. But life is life, Cassandra, and each of us gets rained on a time or two, one way or another. Which, speaking of rain, is going to happen to you soon, if you don't go inside before the storm makes land."

"I know, but I want to stay here a while longer. I like the feel of the wind before the rain. And the sea smells so…wild."

"Then I'll sit with you a moment, if you don't mind. All that awaits me inside are more lists to be checked, and rechecked, to be sure we haven't forgotten anything." He sat down beside her, folding the edges of his dark brown woolen cloak over his knees, and Cassandra looked at him, sitting so close beside her, yet with his gaze heading out to sea, his thoughts probably there, as well.

Jack Eastwood was handsome. Her papa and her brothers Chance and Spencer were handsome; Rian could actually be called pretty, even with his left arm mostly gone.

But Courtland was different.

He wasn't as tall as the others, his build more solid. He wore his light brown, loosely waving hair long, almost to his shoulders, and he'd taken to covering the bottom half of his face with a neatly trimmed beard and mustache. To annoy her, or at least that's what he said.

Spence called him a plodder, Chance laughed and said Courtland did things slowly because he carried the weight of the world on his shoulders. Rian teased that Courtland had been born an old man, with no adventure in him.

And her papa said he could think of no one he would trust more to keep a cool head in a crisis.

Cassandra supposed Courtland was all of those things. Solid. Solemn. Careful. Dependable.

Did no one else notice the sparkle in his blue eyes? Did no one else see the passion in the man, tightly held in check at all times, and yet begging to be set free, to soar?

She remembered how it was to be held safe in his arms. Her protector, her knight in shining armor.

Besides, he was adorable.

"I hate the way it feels, being here, constantly on guard, waiting for the second shoe to drop," Cassandra told him, to break the silence. "This is my home, Court. Why does it feel like an armed camp?"

He pulled his gaze away from the horizon and smiled at her, and her heart did that familiar small flip in her breast. "We've always been an armed camp, Cassandra. We've just never been so obvious about it before, that's all. Are you afraid?"

She shook her head. "Not as long as you're here, no. You'd never let anything bad happen to me."

His smile faded. "Cassandra, you sound like some vacant-headed miss in a fairy tale. We all protect each other, that's our way. But I need you to be afraid, just a little bit. I need you to depend on yourself, in case I'm not here."

She placed a hand on his forearm. "But where would you be, if not here? Are you going to London? I know Chance is going there again, Julia told me, to search for Beales, but you won't go, will you?"

He shook his head. "No, I'll stay here. But there are times when I'm assigned to the ships, and if an attack were to come while I'm at sea on the *Respite,* I need to know that you will obey Ainsley, do exactly what is expected of you, even if that means boarding the frigate and heading to America. No hesitation, Cassandra, no arguing. I need to know that."

Cassandra pushed her tongue forward, to moisten her suddenly dry lips. "But you'd come for me in America. Just as soon as you could?"

He looked away from her. "I don't know if that's a good idea. Once this is over, once Beales is out of our lives, I might decide to travel the Continent for a while, or possibly look for an estate of my own. I've been reading quite a bit about farming. A useless enterprise here on the Marsh, but there are some interesting things being done in crop rotation elsewhere in Kent."

"Is that so?" Cassandra said, then bit her lip.

"I know, I'm boring you to flinders, aren't I? Which means I don't suppose you'd like to hear about an American inventor I've read about for some time now. There's talk of a submersible boat he might consider testing somewhere here in England, and—Cassandra, stop looking at me like that."

"How am I looking at you, Court?" she asked him blinking furiously, as tears were daring to sting at the backs of her eyes. "Am I perhaps looking at you like a woman who realizes that the man she loves would rather sink to the bottom of the sea in a submersible boat than be with her?"

"Cassandra, please don't say things you can't possibly mean, not—what in bloody blazes did you do to your hair!"

She'd been so angry with him that she hadn't realized that her hood had fallen back in her agitation, and she quickly raised her hands to her head, attempting to hide the surprise she'd planned to spring on him at the dinner table, when there'd be others there to deflect his anger. "Nothing. I did nothing to my hair."

"You *cut* it," he said accusingly as she tried, without success, to pull the hood back over her hair. "How could you have—why did you do that?"

"We didn't cut it, Court. For pity's sake, all we did was put it up, see?" She turned her back to him and began pulling out pins, letting them fall to the ground as she pulled and tugged at her annoying curls until they tangled around her fingers, tumbled down past her shoulders, all her childish ringlets blowing crazily in the breeze from the Channel.

"Thank God," he said, reaching out to touch a thick ringlet that had fallen directly between her eyes.

"Yes, yes, thank God," Cassandra said, pushing the lock of hair behind her ear, not that it did much good, for her hair was so fine, even though she had masses of it, that it just fell into her face once more, it and several others. "You say that because you don't have to brush it, Court. There are days I wish I could be sheared, like one of the sheep. I hate my hair. I *loathe* it. It…it makes me look like a baby."

He looked at her for a long moment, and then shook his head. "Someday you'll change your mind about that, Cassandra. Probably the first day you step into Society and the gentlemen trip over themselves, rushing to your side."

"I don't *want* gentlemen tripping over themselves, Court. Why do people think I should want that? Morgan says she'll give me a Season, and then amuse herself by turning away the undeserving, vetting all those who propose marriage to me, and even have Ethan place bets at his club as to who first will compose an ode to my stupid, upturned nose."

Courtland smiled. "Your nose isn't stupid, Cassandra. It's delightful, and fits your face very nicely. Although I believe I'd rather Julia introduces you to Society. Morgan would probably help you fall into scrapes every second day."

"It doesn't matter, because I'm not going into Society, joining a gaggle of simpering little girls on the lookout for an advantageous marriage. Papa will go to America, I'm daily more certain of that, and I will have no choice but to go with him, the unmarried daughter, the spinster. And all because you, Courtland Becket, are the biggest fool in nature."

"Because you love me," he said, pulling the hood up over her hair, tucking her curls away from her face. "Cassandra, you have no idea what that word even means. You're too young."

It was an old argument, and she had no new answers.

"My mama knew she loved Papa when she was no older than I am now. A year from now, she was a mother. I'm not a child anymore, Court, except to you."

"You're a child as long as you act like a child, Cassandra," he told her, putting his hands on his thighs, as if preparing to stand, walk away from her.

But not this time. This time she wouldn't let him dismiss her so easily. As Morgan had told her just the other night, it was time she took the initiative.

"Is this the action of a child?" she asked, grabbing on to the edges of his cloak and pulling herself toward him.

Before he could react, push her away, she aimed her mouth at his, sealing herself against him with more enthusiasm than finesse, for it was her first kiss.

She felt a shock, a shiver, run through them both. Hers delicious. His, probably more one of surprise, hopefully not disgust.

She let go of his cloak and flung her arms around his neck, holding him close, grinding her lips against his, goading him into reacting, daring him to remain his stoic, quiet, immovable self.

For a moment, she felt his mouth soften.

For a moment, she felt his arms raising up, as if longing to clasp her close, hold her against him.

For a moment.

And then he pushed her away and stood up, looking down at her in that stern, solemn way he had, that fruitless display of being So Grown-Up when she was Such A Child.

"Cassandra…" he began, and then sighed. "You shouldn't have done that."

"But I did do it," she told him, getting to her feet. "And you liked it, I know you did."

"No, sweetheart, I didn't. I know we're not brother and sister, we're not bound by blood. But that still doesn't make it right. You're Ainsley's daughter, a man I owe my respect, my admiration, and definitely my life. It would not be fair to him, or to you, to deny you the world that's out there because of some wrongheaded idea you've got that you and I are destined to be together. And I'm too old for you, in any case. Years too old."

"Papa was nearly as old as you are now when he married my mother. We have a life to live, Court, and you're wasting it, being so stubborn."

He smiled, seemed to relax somewhat in his skin.

"Is that supposed to be in the way of a proposal, Cassandra? If so, I think the wrong person is speaking here. And this person is *not* speaking of proposals."

"Only because *that* person is thick as a plank!" Cassandra said, losing her temper. "Just you wait, Courtland Becket. One day you will go down on both knees, begging for me to love you, and I will snap my fingers—like this!—and laugh in your aged face."

She turned on her heel and lifted her skirts as she ran up the steps, chased by his voice. "And don't put up your hair again!"

Tears were stinging at Cassandra's eyes by the time she threw open the French doors to the drawing room and burst inside, intent on crossing the room and heading up to her bedchamber, to have herself a good cry, probably, or to curse Courtland in private.

"Callie? Where are rushing in from, sweetheart?"

Cassandra stopped, wiped at her eyes. "Nowhere, Papa," she said. "It's…it's coming on to rain."

He folded the newspaper he'd been holding in front of him and motioned for her to join him on the couch. "It's difficult to find a moment not crowded by so many other people, isn't it? Let's take advantage of this one, shall we?"

She nodded, untying her cloak and folding it over the back of a chair, pretending not to notice when her father looked at her hair, that was as wild as the wind could make it. "Is there something you wanted to discuss with me, Papa?"

"Must there be something in particular to discuss?" he asked her as she sat down beside him, kissed her cheek.

Cassandra believed her father to be the most handsome man in creation, and had no doubt her mother had taken one look at him and fallen desperately, totally in love. Even now, with silver working its way into his coal-black hair, he had the look of a prince, perhaps even a king. Tall, slim, straight.

She looked at the portrait of her mother, life size, hanging above the large fireplace, and wished, not for the first time, that her father had posed with her, so that she could just once see them together as they were on the island, young, wonderfully in love, and so very, very happy.

"Mama was so beautiful," she said, sighing. "Do you still miss her?"

"Every day," he said, also looking at the portrait. "You're so very like her, you know."

Cassandra shook her head, having heard this before, but never believing it to be true. Posed in a gorgeous, full-skirted striped dress of vibrant hues, her ebony hair hanging in ringlets past her shoulders, eyes such a vibrant green, her mother had been glorious, so alive, Cassandra had often, as a child, felt certain she would jump down from the painting at any moment to give her daughter a hug. "I'm small, like she was, but she was so colorful and I'm so…so bland."

Ainsley Becket laughed, rubbing at her curls. "I can think of many ways to describe you, pet, but bland would never be one of them. You've got your mother's features and curls, but my mother's more honeyed coloring. And she was also a beautiful woman. I look at you, Cassandra, and see the women I love. I thank God every day for you."

Cassandra blinked furiously, fighting back tears once more as she leaned her cheek against Ainsley's shoulder and he put his arm around her. "You never told me that, before, Papa. About your mother. Was it sad, leaving her to go to sea?"

Ainsley was quiet for some moments, and Cassandra believed he was thinking about what he would say to her next, how he would say it.

"Cassandra, I'm not proud of my past, and offer no excuses for what I've done, for there are none. But I know you're old enough to hear this story now," he said at last. "My family made its living smuggling from the shores near Deal, until my father was caught and hanged at Dover Castle and my older brother and I escaped on the first ship leaving port, a ship heading for Haiti, although we had no idea where we were going. Haiti? We'd never even heard the word. We could have been sailing to the moon, but we had no choice. It was either the ship or the hangman, or at the very least, transportation. I was thirteen, my brother four years older. We didn't even have time to say goodbye to my mother, and by the time I was in a position to write to her—once I'd learned to write—it was to discover that she'd died mere weeks after we'd sailed."

Cassandra sat up straight, amazed at one part of the story. "You have a brother? You never told me that, Papa."

"Will and I sailed with some fairly unlovely men for several years, learning our craft, until he was killed during an assault on a Spanish ship. The captain gave me my share and Will's, and I combined that with everything we'd saved over the years, bought my own small sloop, a true wreck of a ship," he said, smiling at some private memory.

"How old were you then, Papa?"

"All of twenty. And rather full of myself, I suppose. I managed to hire a crew, and had some small successes as a pirate. Very small successes. A year later Jacko and I met over exchanged fists in a wharf-side pub, he explained Letters of Marque to me, and we became licensed privateers. I was, hopefully, on my way to respectability and, eventually, a return home, to England. From the very beginning, my objective was to return home."

"Until Edmund Beales betrayed you, tricked you into attacking Eleanor's ship and becoming a pirate again," Cassandra said, sighing. "There isn't a conversation that doesn't lead back to Edmund Beales, is there? Not for so many years." She looked up at the portrait once more, tears spilling onto her cheeks. "He took so much from you, Papa, from all of us. I hate him!"

Ainsley took a handkerchief from his pocket and wiped at her cheeks. "Don't hate him, Cassandra. Be aware of him, be alert to danger, prepare yourself as we are all doing, but don't waste your time hating the man."

"Lisette says he's a monster."

"As his daughter, that's quite a damning indictment of the man. But, yes, Edmund Beales is a monster. One of his own making. But he's also brilliant, as I learned to my great sorrow when he engineered his betrayal of us so many years ago. We can't underestimate him. Which brings me to something I've been considering for some weeks now. Until this is over, until Edmund strikes at us and is defeated, I want to send you, all of the women, to Chance's Coventry estate."

Cassandra shook her head, sending her curls falling into her face. "No! No, Papa, don't do that. Please don't do that. Lisette should go, probably, as she should never have to see her father again. But I can't leave you, and I know Morgan would never agree, or Mariah or Fanny. Oh, and Elly! Papa, she can't leave. Not with the baby coming in another month."

"I agree. Odette and Eleanor will have to remain here."

"But, Papa, if Elly stays, why should the rest of us go? Elly will want us here with her, I'm sure. And how could any of us be so far away, not knowing what's happening here at Becket Hall? No. I won't go. I won't, Papa."

"I lost your mother…"

"I'm not my mother, Papa. I'm me, Cassandra. And we know he's going to strike at us this time. We're prepared, we're ready."

"Are we?" Ainsley asked, as if posing the question to himself. "Edmund excels at treachery, and we're preparing for a frontal assault. A battle, a war. I've agreed to all that we're doing, but I'm not certain any of it means anything."

"Then we can stay?" Cassandra asked, pushing her question as her father looked up at the portrait of her mother. "If you really don't believe he's going to attack us, there's no reason for us to go, is there?"

"Oh, he's going to attack, Cassandra," Ainsley told her, looking at her, his usually bright eyes unaccustomedly dull. "Soon. I only wish I knew how."

"It doesn't matter how," Cassandra said bracingly, leaning against his shoulder once more, praying her father had now given up the idea of sending her away from Becket Hall, away from Courtland. "You'll defeat him. There can be no possible other ending."

CHAPTER FOUR

COURTLAND WALKED ALONG the shore with his head down, the brim of his hat shielding him from the wind, his unquiet thoughts occupying all of his attention.

She'd kissed him.

Christ Almighty, she'd kissed him!

He hadn't seen it coming, hadn't suspected she'd ever do anything like that.

And the hair? She'd looked so grown-up. Not prim, definitely, but not the child he was used to seeing, doing his best to dismiss as a perennial pest, God bless her, believing herself in love, when she was too young to know love. Wasn't she?

Eighteen. Cassandra was eighteen.

He was, he thought but couldn't know for certain, thirty-one.

Ridiculous! Unacceptable!

God. She'd kissed him.

Worse, he had almost kissed her back, almost put his arms around her, drawn her closer against his body.

Taught her how to kiss.

Which, he knew, would be disastrous, if her inexperienced, almost clumsy attempt had been enough to send him reeling like some raw youth.

He stopped, bent to pick up a few stones, held them in one hand as he began tossing them, one by one, into the sea. He threw hard, launching the stones as if they were his thoughts, his damning, betraying thoughts.

And then he hesitated, his arm drawn back, as something Cassandra had said to him danced lightly in his brain. *We thought.* That's what she'd said, wasn't it? The idea to put up her hair hadn't been hers alone. *We.*

"Damn it!" he said, throwing the stone past the third line of waves making their way toward the beach. His shoulder hurt, he'd thrown so hard, and he dropped the rest of the stones, began walking parallel to the water once more.

This is what happened when all the Becket women gathered in one place. Trouble. Mischief. Deviltry.

And he knew who the ringleader had to be. Morgan. The woman was a mother now, a countess. You'd think she would have curbed her deviltry at least a little bit, become more sober, circumspect. Then again, look at whom she'd married. Ethan was almost as bad as she was. If their twins grew up to be half as troublesome as the two of them, it would be only simple justice.

Courtland turned to his left, making his way across the beach and into the main street of Becket Village, home to the crews of the *Black Ghost* and the *Silver Ghost,* those who had survived the massacre, and paused, as he always did, to look at the mermaid masthead carved so many years ago by Pike, the ship's carpenter, and set deep into the sand, looking out at the sea they'd all forsaken.

Pike had been dead these past five or more years, a victim of the Red Men Gang, and the reason Courtland had first donned the black mask and cloak of the Black Ghost and ridden out to protect the local smugglers, little knowing that the Red Men Gang had been headed by Edmund Beales.

Life was so odd, and it seemed to travel in circles, as Ainsley was prone to say, each one drawn smaller than the last, until the past and present collided.

Courtland mounted the wooden flagway, heading for The Last Voyage, the one place Cassandra could not follow, and the pint or two of ale he felt necessary at the moment, hesitating only when he heard hoofbeats coming toward him through the misty dusk.

"Chance," he said, waiting until his brother dismounted from his large stallion, Jacamel, and stepped up on the flagway. "You're alone?"

"Rian and Ethan are somewhere behind me," Chance said, lifting his hat and pushing back his nearly shoulder-length blond hair that had escaped the ribbon he used to secure it at his nape. "Our brother handles the new mare well, but Ethan insists the two still have to get to know each other better, especially since Rian's learning how to direct Miranda only with his knees."

"Leaving his hand free to hold a sword or pistol," Courtland said, nodding his head. "If anyone can do it, Rian can. Although I question his choice of name for the mare. Miranda?"

"Lisette chose it. If she'd told him to call the damned horse Mud Fence, he would have done it. She holds quite a bit of power over our youngest brother," Chance said as they entered the tavern. "I don't know that I like that."

"Because she's Beales's daughter? She proved her loyalty, Chance. Hell, she tried to kill the man."

"Granted. But she also helped keep Rian in France for months after he could have returned to us, with us believing him dead all that time. She only had her epiphany about her father when he killed that servant who tried to help her, or so she says. We have no proof the man is dead."

Courtland lifted the two mugs Ivan poured for them and carried them to a table in the corner. "I believe her," he said before taking a long drink from the mug. "And so do you. What else bothers you about Lisette?"

Chance smiled, toasted Courtland with his own mug. "I'm that transparent? Rian told me that, once this mess is over, he and Lisette will go to New Orleans, to claim land and money left to her by her grandfather. That makes two now, you know, with Spence and Mariah heading for Hampton Roads. I've never considered myself particularly sentimental, but

I find I dislike the idea of having two of my brothers on the other side of the ocean."

"Not just Rian and Spence," Courtland said, looking into his mug. "Ainsley has purchased property in Hampton Roads. A boat-building company he acquired at no small price. He'll be leaving us, too, taking Cassandra with him."

"Ha, that is a piece of news I already knew, thanks to Julia, although I won't believe he'll leave here until he actually sails away," Chance said, and then smiled. "But if he does, you'll go, as well. According to my wife, Callie wouldn't have it any other way."

"Cassandra has nothing to say about where I go, what I do."

Now Chance grinned. "Oh, brother mine, you're as thick as you ever were. Maybe I should have knocked you down more often. But I suppose, as your brother, I should warn you—the ladies are plotting your demise. Julia says it is to keep their minds away from thoughts of Beales, but I think they're using our old enemy as an excuse to cause mischief."

Courtland lifted his hand, and Ivan brought him a fresh mug. "I already figured that out, earlier. Cassandra put her hair up today. She looked ridiculous."

"Did she now? You know, I've always thought she'd grow up to be a pale imitation of Isabella, but she hasn't. She's her own person, and even though she's my sister, I can say with a clear conscience that she is a very lovely young woman. If we were to take her to London for a Season, she'd have half the eligible gentlemen clogging up my drawing room every day. Maybe all of them."

"And that's where she belongs," Courtland declared hotly, wishing he didn't sound so angry. "Not here, not with me. Fanny was the same way with Rian, believing herself in love with him, until she met Valentine. Proximity. That's all it is, but Cassandra refuses to believe me when I tell her so."

"Which you do, daily," Chance pointed out, accepting a second mug from Ivan. "You know, our Alice is only ten now, but females, I believe, are females. And do you know what I've learned from my daughter? The more I tell her she shouldn't have something, the more she wants it."

"Meaning?"

Chance shrugged. "Meaning, brother mine, that maybe it's time you stopped protesting so much. Give Callie a small taste of your attention—and not the doting uncle, brother, father, whatever you think you are, but the *man*. Once you stop treating her like a child, perhaps she'll stop acting like one, and leave you alone."

"Do you hear yourself? What you're suggesting? I can't do that. My God, man, she's Ainsley's daughter."

"I'm aware of who she is. I can remember Isabella. God, she was beautiful. Inside and out. I was mad for her at seventeen, and so were you, following her like a puppy hoping for a treat. That's probably how Callie sees you. I don't know why, you're such a stodgy old nag, but she truly believes herself in love with you."

"Who's in love with whom?" Rian Becket said, pulling out a chair and sitting himself down even as Ivan brought him a mug of ale. Even mussed, coated with road dust, he had the look of a young Greek god. "Tell me everything, and don't leave out any of the juicy bits. Quick, before Ethan comes in to tell you how I fell off Miranda and bruised my pride."

"You fell off a horse?" Courtland looked at his brother, visually checking for injuries. "You've never fallen off a horse. Rian, maybe you're pushing too hard."

"And there she goes—Mama Courtland, believing herself in charge of everyone," Chance said, lifting his mug. "Rian lost an arm, not his wits. He'll master the horse, just give him time. And a few falls, if that's what's needed."

"Thank you, Chance," Rian said, grinning at Courtland. "Now, who's in love with whom? And note my use of *whom,* which I think reflects very well on Ainsley's incessant lessons over the years."

"Callie thinks she's in love with Court here," Chance supplied quickly.

"*Pfft!* And here I thought you were going to tell me something that isn't already abundantly clear to everyone, and has been since the little hellion entered her teenage years."

"You know," Courtland said sourly, "I came here to drink alone. I should have known better."

"Never drink alone, Court," Rian warned him. "Not when we're here, more than ready to increase your misery. Did you know the ladies have been giving Callie lessons in how to seduce you? Lisette told me last night. Her contribution, by the way, was to tell Callie to toss any maidenly shyness to the four winds. I blush to think what else she said, and didn't repeat to me. When it comes to love, women hold all the cards, and we men can only pretend to have any say in the matter. Hullo again, Ethan. What kept you?"

"Your Miranda seems to have picked up a stone," the Earl of Aylesford said, seating himself. Having ridden the same roads as Rian and Chance, Ethan looked as if he'd just finished a long session with his valet; nattily dressed, every blond hair sleekly brushed back from his finely-boned face. A man could look at him and see a well-dressed, amiable fool of fashion—and that man would very, very wrong. "I walked her up to Jasper at the smithy. I'd like to say he met me halfway, carried Miranda on his back the rest of the way, but none of you is probably deep enough in your cups yet to believe me."

"Don't think my giant couldn't do it, if pressed," Rian said, grinning. "Have I told you how he carried both Lisette and me out of that burning house, running with us both as if we were no heavier than feathers?"

"Twice," Courtland said.

"Three times, at the least," Chance added. "Although I still chuckle over the cannon, I'll give you that."

"No matter what, he's quite a find," Ethan said. "And I'd trust any of my horseflesh to him. In fact, I've already considered stealing him away from Waylon, who promised to break my head if I so much as tried."

"The day may come when Jasper does take you up on the offer to be part of your horse farm, Ethan," Courtland said, trying to keep the men concentrated on any subject other than him and Cassandra. "Once everyone feels free to leave Romney Marsh, much of this village may cease to exist, having served its purpose."

It was a valiant try, but Chance must have seen through it, for he said, "Court is all a-twitter because Callie might be sailing off to Hampton Roads with Ainsley, leaving him to molder here, dying of a broken heart."

"Oh, for the love of God—" Courtland got to his feet, pushing back his chair with some force. "When did I become an object of amusement to you all? This isn't funny. I think Cassandra may be out to…to seduce me."

"I think so, too," Chance said, and looked to Rian. "You?"

"Oh, yes, definitely," Rian said, smiling up at

Courtland. "Shall we have a drink to the shameless little minx?"

"Spence and I discussed just this subject last night," Ethan told them, wiping his mouth with the back of his hand—an earl in name, but not one who worried overmuch about his manners when out of sight of the society he wished to have believe him a fool. "We're considering placing bets as to the timing of the thing, actually. We've tentatively settled on fifty pounds to the winner. Court? I give you two weeks before you succumb. Spence says a full month, but we all know he's never right about anything. At least I hope so."

"Three weeks, and we each ante up fifty pounds for the winner," Chance said, holding out his hand. "Rian?"

"Chance took my guess," he said, winking at his brother. "Very well, fifteen days. I could say thirteen, but our dear brother is made of sterner stuff. Aren't you, Court?"

Courtland sat down again, with a thump. "Aren't any of you the least bit concerned that Cassandra is, in all but blood, my *sister?*"

They all looked to one another and answered almost as one.

"No, I don't think so."

"Callie doesn't seem to be put off by it—or that ridiculous beard."

"I can't speak for myself, having only married into the family," Ethan said, "but Morgan seems to think you and Callie are fated. And my wife, I warn you, is not averse to helping Dame Fate along, when she thinks it appropriate."

"I know what it is," Chance said when Courtland glowered at them, one after the other. "You think Ainsley wouldn't approve. God, Court, the man thinks the sun rises and sets on you. You really should be embarrassed."

"He thinks the sun rises and sets on all of us," Courtland said, feeling his cheeks growing hot, for Ainsley's approval was all he'd ever wanted out of life, ever since the day the man had saved that life. "We've all been very, very lucky to have him."

"Even when he thinks we should all leave him before Edmund Beales makes his move, get as far from him as possible. Save ourselves." Chance balled his hands into fists. "Sometimes I just want to knock him down."

"He's a father, Chance," Ethan said quietly. "Just as you and I are fathers. What would you do if you believed having your children with you needlessly exposed them to danger?"

"You make a valid point, Ethan, considering that I'm sending Julia and the children back to Coventry once we reach London," Chance said. "But I was seventeen the day I stood on the deck of the *Silver Ghost* as we sailed out of that damn mist and into the middle of a half dozen ships to our two, because Beales and his three ships had slipped away during the night, leaving us to be slaughtered. I was seventeen when I walked onto the beach to see it stained red with the blood of old men, women and small children. I'm going nowhere. My place is right here, and Julia understands that."

Courtland closed his eyes, Chance's words bringing back memories he fought away every day, and Isabella's words to him. *You are her protector. Never leave her, not ever. Promise me.*

"We all belong here," Rian said quietly. "Courtland? You won't leave, we all know that. Callie most especially. You're her rock, you know. Her rock and, God help you, her *target.*"

"You just want to win the bet," he complained, lifting his mug to attract Ivan's attention. "And now, if you don't mind, I think I'd like to sit here and get myself very, very drunk. Does anyone care to join me?"

Chance laughed again. "Are you kidding? We're all married, Court. Falling into a bottle is for the free and unfettered, that don't have to answer to a wife. Enjoy yourself, this may be the last time you'll be able to toss up your accounts in your chamber pot without abjectly apologizing between retches."

"You're all wrong. All of you. If none of you care for Cassandra's happiness, I do. And that happiness doesn't lie with a man like me."

"A man like him. As if he has two heads, or something, and not a brain between them." Ethan chuckled softly as he lifted his mug. "A toast, gentlemen. To Courtland Becket, one poor, deluded bastard."

"Hear! Hear!" they all agreed, clinking their mugs together, and Courtland sank low on his spine in the wooden chair, believing the entire world, save him, gone mad.

CHAPTER FIVE

"DOMINOS?"

Eleanor Eastwood looked levelly at Cassandra, saying nothing, although her dark eyes spoke volumes.

"All right then, not dominos," Cassandra said, knowing that look. "Chess? I'll even magnanimously allow you to beat me."

"I always beat you, Callie," Eleanor reminded her. "And, before you ask, I don't wish to play Hearts, I don't care to read another book, hem another gown for the baby, have another slice of cake, nor will I ask you to plait my hair. What I want to do, Callie, is to scream. Loud and long."

Poor Eleanor, confined to her bed all summer and now into the fall and winter, as well. She looked so small in the huge bed, except for the swell of her belly beneath the covers. Eleanor was, as they all said, their lady. Small-boned, regal, fragilely beautiful, but possessing a will of iron that had no one in confusion as to who was in charge of Becket Hall. That their *grande dame* should be hidden away upstairs, unable to quietly ride herd on all of them had to be endlessly frustrating to her.

Cassandra attempted to stifle her smile, but it was no use. Her sister was the most sensible, calm, collected person in the universe, and seeing her so agitated was almost amusing. "Oh, you sad thing. You won't be locked up in here for much longer, will you?"

Eleanor pleated the covers with one hand as she looked up at the cut velvet canopy over her bed. "One moment more will be too much longer, Callie. Would you like to know how many roses are in this canopy? Six hundred and forty-three. And I loathe and detest every single one of them." She sighed. "Oh, I'm sorry. I'm being such a sad complainer, aren't I?"

"If someone put me to bed for—what is it now, seven months?—I would be much more than a sad complainer. I would be carted off to Bedlam, that madhouse in London."

"Bethlehem Hospital, yes," Eleanor said, smiling at last. "And I shouldn't be anything but happy that this baby is still where he or she belongs, waiting patiently to grow and be born. Odette swears it's a boy, you know. I'm at the point where I don't care what it is, as long as it's healthy, and arrives before Christmas. Now, tell me what's going on downstairs The entire place is a shambles, I just know it is."

Cassandra shook her head. "Jack and Odette would have my head. You're not to do anything save to lie here and think pleasant thoughts, remember?"

"Easier said than done, I'm afraid. And, since I'll worry anyway, why don't you tell me what's going on concerning that terrible man?"

"Courtland?" Cassandra said with a grin.

Eleanor picked up a small pillow and tossed it at her sister. "We'll get to him in a moment. You know who I mean."

"I can't tell you anything about Edmund Beales because nobody knows anything about him other than that he's out there somewhere, looking for us as desperately as we're looking for him. You know that Chance and Julia and the children left this morning for London, don't you?"

"They came to say goodbye, yes. And Alice gave me a drawing she'd made of Odette, Lord love her. It's a good thing Odette can't really turn little girls into toads. Only Chance is staying in London, however, sending Julia and the children on to Coventry with their London servants and some others to watch them until this is over. You, I understand, were supposed to have gone with them."

"Papa relented," Cassandra told her, quietly glorying in her victory. "He realizes I'm a woman now, and capable of making my own decisions."

Eleanor pushed herself up against the raft of pillows behind her. "I imagine that's why you're considering Court a terrible man right now. He wasn't happy for you to remain?"

Cassandra shrugged as she sat down on the edge

of the bed. "He hasn't said. Actually, he's not speaking to me at the moment, which is fine with me, for I'm not speaking to him. He told me to never put up my hair again. Who is he to tell me how to wear my hair?"

"Yes, indeed, who is he? As if his opinion matters a jot to you one way or the other. After all, you don't care a snap for him, correct?"

Cassandra allowed her body to list over to one side until she was lying on the covers, her head on Eleanor's knees. "He drives me insane."

"That seems only fitting, as turnabout is fair play," Eleanor teased, stroking Cassandra's tumbling curls. "Morgan and Mariah were in here earlier, visiting, and looking extremely guilty and altogether too pleased with themselves. What have our conspirators advised you to do now?"

"You *know?*" Cassandra sat up, pushed her hair out of her face. "Morgan said not to tell you because you're so…poor spirited, and would probably ring a peal over all our heads."

"Poor spirited? Is that what she calls being sensible?" Eleanor said, reaching for her cooling cup of tea. "Although, to Morgan, anyone a step below the rank of hellion is too boring to contemplate. Are you all so certain I disapprove?"

"You don't? Really?" Cassandra allowed her shoulders to relax. And then she made a confession she hadn't shared with Morgan or the others, because it was all just too embarrassing. "I kissed him two days ago," she said, watching Eleanor's face closely for her reaction.

"Is that so? My, and Morgan suggested this course of action?"

"Well, no…not directly. She just said—they all said—that Court has to stop seeing me as a child. So I…I just…"

"Ambushed him?" Eleanor suggested, handing Cassandra the empty teacup. "What did you do, jump out from behind a statue and hang yourself around his shoulders like a limpet?"

"It wasn't *that* bad," Cassandra said quietly. "Almost, but not quite. We were sitting on the steps below the terrace and I just…I just turned to him and, well, *launched* myself at him, I suppose you'd say. It was very impulsive, not well thought out at all. But the entire thing seemed perfectly logical at the time."

"Oh, I'm sure it did, after Morgan filled your head with nonsense. Cassandra, that probably wasn't a good idea. You know what a stickler for propriety Courtland can be. You'll have to be less obvious. *Launching* yourself is not being less obvious. Next time, you might want to find a way to make him think the kiss was his idea."

Cassandra's eyes went wide for a moment. "You're giving me advice?"

"Why shouldn't I? It would seem everyone else has, yes? And this is a baby I'm carrying, and we all know how babies are made. You and Fanny may have called me Saint Eleanor a time or two behind my back when I tried to school you in proper deportment, but I am a woman, you know. And, speaking of Fanny, please tell me *she* didn't give you advice."

"Well, Fanny didn't say too much, as she and Valentine were in a hurry to get back to their estate. Something about a small fire in the kitchens, or something. A messenger arrived yesterday evening with the news, and they left this morning soon after Chance and Julia. But you know that, too, don't you? Nobody hid that from you?"

"Yes, I'm allowed that sort of information, since Brede Manor didn't burn to the ground, thank goodness. It's probably better to have Fanny and Valentine gone, in any case, if things become, well, complicated. No one will know Fanny is a Becket, and Valentine shouldn't be involved in anything that could end in violence. He has his place in Society to consider, his Earldom."

"Not to hear him talk about how much he'd like to be the one who personally puts a ball between Beales's eyes," Cassandra said, sighing. "All of them, all the men. It's all they talk about. Like little boys. They really want to see it come to a fight, Beales sailing into the harbor, his cannon run out, ready to deliver a broadside, or riding across the Marsh with one hundred well-armed men behind him, set to attack us. Do men never tire of war?"

"Are you including Court in this group of bloodthirsty avengers, Cassandra? I would have counted on him to be more subdued."

"I suppose he is. He seems more interested in protecting us than in destroying Beales. He and Papa closet themselves together every morning, going over their plans as if something changed during the previous night."

"And what are their plans? To defend Becket Hall, that is?"

Cassandra shook her head. "Oh, no, I'm not going to be tricked into telling you things Jack says you're not to know."

"But I feel so helpless, lying here. I've rolled enough bandages to wrap every other man here from head-to-toe if the occasion arises, and I've been over and over our list of supplies, until I could tell you precisely how many sacks of flour we have stored away, how many dozens of candles. Anyone would think we were Troy, about to come under siege. And all with me stuck here, unable to help. It's so frustrating!"

"How should I be less obvious, Elly?" Cassandra asked, seeing that her sister was becoming agitated. If Odette were to enter the bedchamber now, Cassandra knew she'd be shooed out, probably with a flea in her ear and an admonition that she never return.

"Very well, I'll stop complaining." Eleanor took Cassandra's hand in hers. "I doubt you should listen to me, sweetheart, when it comes to attracting a man. After all, I watched Jack from afar for over two years, hiding my feelings like some silly ninny, before I finally got up the courage to…well, that's neither here nor there. Was Courtland really angry when you kissed him?"

"I'm not sure. I think he was surprised. Oh, I know he was surprised. But then, just for an instant, you know, he seemed to…he seemed to *soften* toward me, as if he didn't really mind all that much. *That's* when he got angry!"

"Angry with himself," Eleanor concluded, nodding her head as if this made perfect sense to her. "Poor, poor Courtland. He loves you so much, and has always loved you. What a surprise it must be to him that this love has been slowly shifting from the avuncular to the…ah…never mind. Do you know what I think? I think you should ignore him, Cassandra, just for a few days. Let him think you're upset at his reaction to your kiss."

"Well, I most certainly am not *happy* about his reaction. But what good will that do?"

"I can't be sure, but I think it might make him begin to reconsider your association. The baby he helped care for hasn't been a baby for a long time. He may need, however, to be introduced to the adult Cassandra. Because they're two different people, aren't they?"

"Sometimes," Cassandra admitted, sighing, for if nothing else, she knew her own faults. "Sometimes I still act like an idiot child. Chasing after him, teasing him, driving him to distraction—all the things he's always told me I do."

"Then don't do them anymore. It's that simple. He is accustomed to reacting to the way you act—behave, that is. But, if you no longer behave as he has come to expect, then he will also have to change his own behavior and conclusions as they concern you. That only makes sense, doesn't it? It could, actually, be rather delicious to watch. While I'm stuck up here, drat it all."

Poor Eleanor. Cassandra decided she'd suffered enough. "Let me comb your hair. It's all tangled in the back, from lying against those pillows."

"Oh, I suppose so," Eleanor said, sitting up. "Jack must think I've got birds nesting in my hair at times. But aren't I keeping you from something?"

"Not a bit of it," Cassandra said, grabbing the brush from the dressing table and climbing back up on the bed, kneeling behind her sister. "I can't think of anything more enjoyable than spending time here with you."

"Which explains why you're pulling my hair out of my head—ouch!"

"Sorry," Cassandra mumbled, trying not to giggle. But she'd talked so long with Eleanor that she'd lost track of time, and Jack would be coming into the bedchamber at any moment, while Mariah kept Odette occupied checking on young William Henry's supposed putrid throat. "Oh, see how pretty you look now? Let me get you that bed jacket over there, and put it around your shoulders. I think I feel a chill."

"Cassandra," Eleanor said sternly as her sister dashed away, running back with the lace-edged bed jacket, "*what* are you doing? And don't tell me you invited everyone in here to my prison to entertain me, because I'm in no mood to be cheered by a gaggle of people who can come and go as they please while I'm stuck here like some—Jack? I thought you were all meeting over at The Last Voyage to decide who next goes out on maneuvers with the *Respite*."

"Yes, I imagine you do think that, since that's what I told you," her husband said, smiling at Cassandra.

He'd changed his clothes since she'd last seen him, and his dark blond hair was still damp from his bath. Jack always had a rather lean yet *rugged* look about him, riding out on the Marsh daily, his skin darkly tanned, making the laugh lines around his mouth and eyes stand out in relief when he smiled. He looked dangerous, while Eleanor looked the Compleat Lady. And they loved each other very much. "Thank you, she looks beautiful. Not that you aren't always beautiful, darling, so don't go pulling a face at me. Now, are you ready to go downstairs?"

"Down— Downstairs?" Eleanor shook her head, looking incredulous. "What did you all do, lock Odette in the cellars? She won't let me leave this bed."

"What Odette doesn't know won't hurt us, or at least not until she finds out," Jack said as Cassandra pulled back the covers and helped Eleanor on with her slippers, not that her sister's feet would ever touch the floor, and then arranged her long nightgown so it covered the scars on her ankle. "At Morgan's suggestion, we're having a musical evening, and as you've been such a brave little soldier for all this time, we thought we'd include you."

He slipped his arms beneath her and she wound her hands around his neck as he lifted her from the bed, high against his chest. "Well, look at me, Cassandra, holding my entire family in my arms. Gives a man pause, I'll tell you."

"Just don't be so nervous that you trip with your family as you go down the stairs."

"My darling wife, always so trusting."

"I was only teasing, Jack, poking fun at my new weight that you couldn't have been expecting. But, to speak of being trusting, and I don't wish to appear ungrateful, not when you've all gone to so much trouble—but will Spence be singing?"

"Not if there's a merciful God," Jack said, carrying his wife toward the door, Cassandra following behind, so happy for her sister, who'd found her Jack, and who would soon, after so much heartache, have her own child to hold.

COURTLAND WALKED DOWN THE hallway toward the music room still holding a sheaf of papers filled with drawings of the first and second lines of passive defenses he and Ainsley had commissioned a few weeks earlier, all of them now in place.

Thankfully, Ainsley had at last been able to convince the women in Becket Village to leave. Except for the stubborn Becket women and some of the household staff, who refused to leave Eleanor, who could not be moved without imperiling her unborn child. They'd taken their children inland with them, out of the way of battle and safe from the defenses that now made the area dangerous even to its inhabitants. They had all gone together, but would break off for predetermined destinations in small villages scattered throughout Romney Marsh, so that no one would raise an eyebrow at an influx of over one hundred new inhabitants descending on the same place.

Becket Hall, Becket Village, were now little more than armed camps…and one musical evening meant to entertain Eleanor.

Mentally, not really needing to consult his lists, Courtland reviewed their defenses.

Deadfalls fitted out with wooden spikes and seamlessly hidden beneath the landscape were now located in the tall reeds to the East, behind the treacherous, shifting sands along the shoreline that were their own deterrent.

Protective trenches had been dug around the Western and Northern sides of Becket Village, in places more than twelve feet deep—good for burying Beales's dead hirelings once the assault was over,

Spence had joked. Again, these defenses were camouflaged with grasses and shrubs, ready to snare the unwary, and too wide for most men to jump across them if they were discovered.

The shingle and sand beach and the first dozen or more feet of shallow sea in front of the village and Becket Hall itself had been studded with sharp sticks of wood tied together to make large structures that, to Courtland, looked like enormous children's playing jacks, preventing small boats from landing easily and then slowing any force trying to make its way across the beach. Only those who lived at Becket Hall knew the paths through these obstacles that wouldn't end with a foot impaled on hidden nine-inch metal spikes Jasper and Waylon had fashioned in the smithy.

Casks of black powder had been placed at strategic spots, but with the near constant November rains, there would be no possibility of keeping the fuses dry, so the explosives had been removed again just that afternoon.

Men had been assigned to the crow's nests of all three ships even as they lay at anchor, as the mostly flat land was not conducive to lookouts onshore, and they worked on twelve-hour shifts, their eyes constantly training on all four corners of the horizon. Ethan would take the *Spectre* out in the morning for three days, to cruise the coastline, on the watch for any ships that appeared too interested in this approximately one-mile-square area of the coastline.

All of which left only the front of Becket Hall apparently vulnerable to any sort of sustained assault. Purposely open to assault, if one were to be deceived by the innocuous appearance of Becket Hall, which looked like any other large, architecturally uninspired, even ugly country house.

If one didn't look too closely, that was. Because Becket Hall was anything but ordinary. The dark stone hid a multitude of gunports, two entire half floors between the ground and first floor, the second floor and the third. In fact, Becket Hall had been built as if it was a ship, complete with cannon salvaged from the *Black Ghost* and the *Silver Ghost,* and what wasn't reminiscent of a ship could be compared to a maze of false walls, passageways, secret staircases and the like.

Ainsley, a student of history and its battles, had longed for peace. But he had, when designing and ordering Becket Hall built long before planning to take his family there, prepared for war by constructing a deviously placid-looking fortress, a remnant of his two dozen or more years spent living in the dangerous islands, where no man could succeed for long without gaining himself a few dangerous enemies. And although there had been several complaints over the years about the length of the staircases that actually rose a full floor-and-a-half, and the drafts in winter caused by the gun ports that fine tapestries and paintings could not possibly fully alleviate, no one was unhappy with the house at this dangerous moment.

Ainsley had described the tactic of driving attackers toward Becket Hall as opening the wide end of a funnel, luring attackers into that wide end, and then forcing them down, down, into the smallest part of the funnel, so that they could feed out in front of Becket Hall only a few at a time. Easy targets…

"And here he is at last, the late Courtland Becket," Morgan said from her seat on one of the striped satin couches.

Courtland looked up, scanning the number of occupants of the music room, as he'd been rather staring at the floor as he walked, his mind still on all their plans, and suddenly felt he had just been forced out of the bottom of a funnel. An easy target.

"Elly? You're downstairs?" he asked, knowing his question more than begged the obvious, as his sister was reclining on another couch, a soft blanket over her legs and the almost perfect roundness of her stomach. He hadn't been to see her in several days, and felt ashamed of that fact. "I…I was going to come up and visit with you tomorrow…"

"And you'd be welcome," Eleanor told him. "But it's delightful to see you tonight, as well. You will sing for us, won't you?"

Morgan got to her feet. "Certainly he will. He and Callie will sing a duet, won't you? I've already picked the music. Right after Spencer gives us a tune, of course."

"Oh, God no," Courtland said, subsiding into a

chair beside Ainsley, whose shoulders were shaking suspiciously. "Where's Cassandra?"

"She and Mariah are still upstairs, placating Odette, who just found out her chick has flown the coop," Ainsley told him. "Doesn't Eleanor look wonderful?"

"She does, yes, as long as she pretends not to notice the way Jack is hovering over her, I suppose. This is all Morgan's idea, isn't it? Although I have to admit, it's a good one. We all need to turn our minds away from Beales for a while."

Ainsley took the papers from Courtland's hand and folded them, tucked them into his jacket. "I agree. To that end, I'd like you to arrange some sort of party for the crew over in the village for Sunday afternoon. Beales has had six weeks or more to find us, and nothing has happened yet. We cannot expect everyone to continue existing with such constant tension without some sort of temporary outlet for that tension. Ollie tells me he's more than willing to sacrifice a supply of good pigskin by donating his largest pig to us to roast on the beach. Plenty of food, Courtland. The only thing we will measure out more carefully will be the ale. We can't afford to let our collective guard down that much."

"A good idea, I suppose, if it ever stops raining," Courtland said, and then his head snapped back involuntarily as Mariah and Cassandra entered the room. "My God, I told her not to—"

He quickly shut his mouth, after all, Ainsley was

sitting directly beside him, but he couldn't take his eyes off Cassandra, who had changed out of the simple dress she'd worn at dinner, exchanged it for a sunny yellow watered-silk gown he felt sure had lately occupied Morgan's closet. Cassandra certainly had nothing quite so revealing in her own wardrobe, he was certain of that.

And what was that hanging around her neck and wrist, in her ears? Rubies?

Courtland shot a look at Ainsley, who only smiled and shrugged. "I always enjoyed when Isabella wore them," he said, as if anticipating the question. "I should have given Cassandra the set on her eighteenth birthday, I suppose, but better late than never. Don't you agree?"

"Er, yes, certainly, sir. The jewels are yours to give where you will. Isabella wears them in the portrait in the drawing room, doesn't she?"

"Yes," Ainsley said, his expression closing for a moment. "But with Cassandra's coloring, they look equally striking with that gown. Excuse me for a moment, son, I…I think I'll take these drawings to my study."

Courtland watched him go, knowing what Ainsley had been thinking when he looked at his daughter, saw the yellow gown. Isabella, only a year older than Cassandra was now, and always so vibrant, so gloriously alive, had worn the rubies with her colorful striped gown. The same one Ainsley had dressed her body in before carrying her deep into the interior of the island, to hold her one last time, to sob and shout at God while a stone-faced Jacko stood guard and a much younger Courtland had watched from his hiding place amid some nearby bushes, devastated by both Isabella's death and Geoffrey Baskin's grief.

He watched Cassandra now as she and Morgan stood at the piano, poring over sheet music together. Morgan was whispering furiously and Cassandra was shaking her head, just as quietly and furiously objecting to those whispers.

And she was wearing her hair up again this evening, pulled back quite severely from her forehead and tied with a pale yellow ribbon, the mass of barely contained curls falling down onto her bare back.

Her profile, uncluttered by the usually errant ringlets was so pure, so wonderfully sculpted, Courtland found it difficult to draw a breath into his lungs. When had she gone from pretty child to beautiful woman? Where had he been, that he hadn't noticed?

And now that he had, what in bloody hell was he supposed to do about it?

"Something wrong, Court?" Spencer asked, sitting down beside him in the chair Ainsley had just vacated. He looked the Spanish *Grandee* this evening, his linen crisply white against his black evening attire. "You're wearing a sort of pole-axed look, in case you were unaware of it."

Courtland blinked himself back into the moment.

"That's because I just heard you plan to sing something. If I promise to fashion another knife-sleeve for you, would that change your mind?"

"I'll have you know my wife enjoys my singing."

"Your wife is delusional," Courtland told him, grinning. "You know all the words. You're loud enough. But when the dogs over in the village start howling, you might want to consider shutting up."

"Very funny. Where's Ainsley taken himself off to, do you know?"

"He needed to check something in his study," Courtland said, still unable to take his gaze off Cassandra who, he just that moment realized, had been avoiding looking at him.

"It's Callie, isn't it? Seeing her this way probably upset him." Spencer looked across the room at his sister. "She looks just like her. Why haven't I ever noticed that before now? The hair? That's probably it. Can't call her the baby anymore, can we? No, our Callie's all grown-up, isn't she? Court?"

Courtland didn't answer him, but just got to his feet and walked over to Eleanor, to bend down, kiss her cheek. "Are you in on this?" he asked her quietly. "Or can I appeal to you for help, for some sanity?"

Eleanor lifted her hand to cup Courtland's cheek. "A plea for sanity? This from a man who wears all this fuzz on his cheeks, just because a certain young woman told you she finds beards unappealing?"

"Then you are in on it," Courtland said, sighing. "What am I going to do, Elly?"

"Follow your heart, Court, not your head. Not in matters that are of concern only to the heart. What other advice could I possibly give you?"

"I was thinking the suggestion of a sharp sword and a long walk into a woods might be appropriate," Courtland said, smiling weakly. "Why did she have to grow up, Elly? And, for the love of God, why now?"

CHAPTER SIX

"DID HE SING YET?" Ainsley Becket asked as he slipped back into his chair beside Courtland as Lisette played an only slightly tentative bit of some French tune on the Bartolomeo Cristofori piano Courtland knew some unhappy matron never saw safely transported from her home in Padua to Jamaica. The harp in the corner, a magnificent piece, had been retrieved from a French ship. Both captures had been under Ainsley's Letter of Marque from the English government, completely legal and acceptable, but sometimes Courtland felt he was living surrounded by other people's belongings, and the thought made him uncomfortable.

"Sorry, but no. You'll have to suffer along with the rest of us," Courtland told him as Lisette finished and everyone applauded politely and Rian banged on his chair seat with his hand and called out *Brava!*

"Rian," Mariah said before Lisette could step away from the piano. "Why don't you and Lisette play something together?"

Rian looked at her owlishly.

"Oh, for pity's sake, don't look as if I just suggested you fly to the moon," Mariah scolded. "Lisette can play the…well, the left-hand notes, and you can play the right-hand notes. Or whatever they're called."

Spencer bent his head, rubbed at his forehead. "Only you would suggest something like that, sweetheart. Rian, you don't have to—"

"No, no, of course he does," Lisette said quickly. "Rian Becket, shame on you, not telling your own wife that you play, all the while I sat here, insulting this beautiful instrument with my infantile plinking. Come over here, come over here right now, and we'll play something together."

Rian got to his feet, smiled at the others in the room. "My bride, the nag. Coming, darling. What shall we play?" He sat down next to his wife, who had turned the page in the songbook to the next song, and after a few fumbling starts, the two of them played together, Rian's strong right hand carrying the melody as Lisette slipped her arm around his waist, leaned close against him, moving her honey-blond head in time to the music.

Courtland looked over at Ainsley, who was blinking rather rapidly, and quickly looked away, gave the man his privacy. It had been so hard on all of them, believing Rian dead after Waterloo, coming to terms with his injury when he did return, bringing Edmund Beales's daughter with him.

“He used to play so beautifully,” Ainsley said after a moment, as if to himself. “Yet I’ve never enjoyed his music more than I do tonight.”

Mariah led the applause when the tune was over, literally jumping to her feet, and Rian stood up from the bench, held out his hand to Lisette, holding tight to her as he bowed, and she dropped into a deep curtsy. Then he lifted her hand to his lips, looking deeply into her eyes as he kissed her fingertips.

“She’s just what he needs, Ainsley,” Courtland said, watching his brother’s amazingly handsome face, the smile that turned it beautiful.

“Yes, she is. She cajoles, she bullies, and she gives without reservation. I would forgive her a thousand sins, for the love she bears my son. I only wish Jacko could see that,” Ainsley said, and then sighed. “And now, as we’ve enjoyed ourselves mightily, it’s time to be punished. Spencer is about to abuse our ears. Are you sure there isn’t some emergency you and I need to attend to for, oh, the next quarter hour?”

“Sorry, sir,” Courtland said, and only hoped the quarter hour could stretch out even longer, if not into infinity—for Spencer was an enthusiastic but far from accomplished singer—so that he could be spared singing a duet with Cassandra.

Cassandra had sat very still on a chair in one corner for the past hour or more, looking excruciatingly proper, as well as heartbreakingly beautiful. She had never once met his eyes (eyes he couldn't seem to stop turning in her direction). Strange. It wasn't like her to hold a grudge. And what had he said? That she shouldn't put up her hair again? It was up tonight, wasn't it, at least partially, so she'd ignored his disapproval, as she always did.

No, this had nothing to do with her hair. It had to do with that kiss. That kiss, that had seemingly come out of nowhere, shocking him, thrilling him…frightening him.

Had that kiss been a turning point, a corner that, now that it was turned, meant they could never again go back to where they'd been all these years?

No more Cassandra following him about, teasing him, bedeviling him, flattering him, bringing turmoil and constant sunshine into his life?

Had he turned her away one too many times, so that now she believed him, even agreed that there could be nothing more than friendly, familial affection between them?

That gown, those rubies…the hair. All outward signs of something he should have seen for himself without the aid of Morgan-engineered props. Cassandra wasn't a child anymore. She was eighteen, of an age to go to London for the Season, be put on the marriage mart. Old enough to have a home, a husband and a child of her own by this time next year.

The thought of Cassandra in London, looking as

she did tonight, put a hard knot in the pit of Courtland's stomach, and he actually moaned, low, under his breath. Or so he thought.

"I heartily agree," Ainsley whispered, leaning close to him. "Moan, groan, plead with the boy to stop—all three have occurred to me. But look at Mariah. She's gazing at him as if he's got the voice of an angel. Love, Courtland. Blind and deaf. Please, for the love you bear this old man, go get Cassandra out of that corner and the two of you sing something that won't have my ears bleeding in a moment."

"Yes, sir," Courtland said, getting to his feet to applaud loudly before Spencer could take a breath and begin the twelfth verse of a song that would have benefited from being not only less lengthy, but by being sung by someone who could at least hold a tune in a bucket. "Wonderful, Spence! But now I think it's our turn, before Jack insists on taking Elly back upstairs. Cassandra?"

She got up from her chair, smoothed down her skirts, and walked over to the piano, shaking her head as Morgan attempted to push a sheaf of sheet music at her. "No, not that one, please," she said quietly, but Courtland heard her.

"But this is the perfect song for the two of you," Morgan insisted.

"Morgan, have you learned nothing of diplomacy since becoming a countess?" her husband, Ethan, asked her, and then smiled. "No, no. Please, consider that a rhetorical question. Push on, darling, you push so well."

"Is something wrong?" Courtland asked, now standing close enough to Cassandra to smell the sweet lavender in her hair. "Don't you want to sing with me, Cassandra?"

"It's not you," she told him. "It's the song. I think we should find something else."

"Nonsense," Morgan said, shoving the sheets at Cassandra again, so that Courtland took them from her. "Since Elly shouldn't do anything but lie here and enjoy herself, and Rian isn't…well, he isn't prepared to accompany you, I thought you should sing something that really needs no accompaniment. Yes?"

"And tact," Ethan added from his chair. "There are some strides still to be wished for there, too, sweet wife."

"Oh, hush, Ethan," Morgan told him, not even turning to look at him. "It's the perfect song for a duet."

Courtland looked down at the sheet music in his hand. A pretty enough tune, but one that was really a battle between a man and a woman, each asking the other to do impossible things to prove their love. A duet, yes, but also a duel. Did he really feel up for a fight tonight, even a musical one? "'Scarborough Fair?'" He shook his head. "No, I think Cassandra's right. Isn't there something else?"

"Oh, no, Court," Eleanor said as she readjusted the

blanket over her rounded belly, and Courtland knew he had lost the last of his allies. "I adore the song. And it's the perfect duet. Please?"

"They hate us," Cassandra whispered from between clenched teeth, and she and Courtland took up their places alongside the piano.

"Worse than that, Cassandra. They're enjoying themselves. You may think twice before you ask their assistance again."

She looked up at him, her eyes shooting blue-green sparks at him. "Just sing your part, and let's be done with this charade," she told him, taking the sheets from him and plunking them down on the piano. "You know the words."

"Very well, yes, I do. If you're ready?"

She nodded, and then turned away from him, to face the middle of the room, beginning on her own, her sweet soprano joined before the second word by his clear baritone:

Are you going to Scarborough Fair?
Parsley, sage, rosemary and thyme,
Remember me to one who lives there,
For she once was a true love of mine.
For he once was a true love of mine.

Courtland was aware of Cassandra with every fiber of his being as he sang the next verses alone, beseeching his listeners to inform the woman they met to sew him a cambric shirt without any seam, wash it in water from a dry well that has never seen rain, dry it on a thorn that has never borne a blossom, "'And then she'll be a true love of mine.'"

Do the impossible, he was singing, and then you'll be my true love.

Cassandra looked at him for only an instant, and then tipped up her chin, and sang out clearly to their audience. He was to find her an acre of land between the salt water and the sea-strand, plough it with a lamb's horn, sow it all over with only one pepper-corn, reap the field with a sickle of leather, gather the crop with a rope made of heather.

She turned back to him as she sang the last verse:

When he has done and finished his work,
Parsley, sage, rosemary and thyme,
Ask him to come for his cambric shirt,
For then he'll be a true love of mine.

Do the impossible, as impossible as the feats you ask from me, she had sung back to him, and then you'll be my true love.

Courtland heard Spencer's chuckle, for he seemed to know that this was no longer a song between Courtland and Cassandra, but a dare, a duel, with neither of them giving ground.

And that's when some small voice inside Courtland's head said, "May as well be hanged for a sheep as a lamb," and he took hold of Cassandra's icy-cold fingers, turning her so that they faced each other completely as they sang the final verses together:

If you say that you can't, then I shall reply,
Parsley, sage, rosemary and thyme,
Oh, let me know that at least you will try,
Or you'll never be a true love of mine.

Love imposes impossible tasks,
Parsley, sage, rosemary and thyme,
But none more than any heart would ask,
I must know you're a true love of mine.

Cassandra never faltered, her voice as strong and pure as his own, her gaze never leaving his until Eleanor said in hushed tones, *"Oh, my stars."*

Only then did Cassandra pull her hands free of Courtland's and run from the room.

He took two steps after her before Ainsley stood up in front of him, shook his head.

"Let her go, son. She's taking large steps, and sometimes strides of that length can put a person off balance. The same, I might say, goes for you."

"But it was wonderful to watch," Morgan trilled from behind him, and Courtland felt his shoulders stiffen as he turned toward the French doors and headed out onto the terrace, into the dark and the wind and the rain.

He strode across the stone terrace to lean his hands on the balustrade, cursing himself under his breath, cursing Morgan for her meddling, cursing the night for being so cold and wet, ruining his new jacket.

And then he raised his head, looked out into the Channel, toward a horizon devoid of stars on such a miserable night…and saw one twinkle, then disappear.

He leaned forward, straining his eyes, holding his breath. Waited.

There! He saw it again.

Not a star. A light. Shown, and then quickly shuttered. Shown again, shuttered, shown.

Then nothing, not for a full minute. Courtland knew that, because he counted off the seconds out loud along with the beat of his heart.

Again, but coming from a different spot, a good half-mile from where he'd first seen the light.

Light, darkness. Light, darkness. Light, darkness.

A signal. The signal returned. A warning: I'm here, in the dark, don't get too close; just close enough to maintain contact.

And a heartbeat later, from the harbor, where their three ships lay at anchor in front of Becket Village, came a voice, carrying clearly over the night air.

"Two sails to starboard!"

"Sonofabitch," Courtland bit out as he pushed away from the balustrade and raced into the music room, dripping rain all over the floor.

"I was wondering how long it would take to cool

you down," Morgan said, laughing. "Seems not long at— Court?"

Courtland strode past her, Ethan, Spence, and Rian already on their feet, following him, while Jack reached over the back of the couch to take Eleanor's hand in his. "Sir, two ships about a mile out, running dark, but signaling each other."

Ainsley slowly got to his feet. "All right then everyone," he said, his voice as calm as if the drenched Courtland had told him it was raining. "This could be nothing more than some smuggling operation that has nothing to do with us, but we can't afford to ignore another possibility. Gentlemen, your attention, please. Rian, find Jacko. Spencer, get yourself to the village to put things into operation there. Jack, carry your wife upstairs, and then meet us, ready to hoist sail on the sloops, as they're more easily maneuverable in the dark. Ladies, your pardon. Please follow Jack, locate Cassandra. It will be your choice who remains with Eleanor and who stays in the nursery with the children."

"With Chance gone, who do you want in charge of the *Spectre,* sir?" Courtland asked as they made their way to the Ainsley's study. "I will gladly—"

"I'm sure you would, Courtland, thank you, but I need you here, as you're most familiar with our land defenses. Jacko will command the *Spectre* in Chance's place. I'll take the helm of the *Respite.*"

Courtland stopped so quickly that Rian barreled into his back. "*You,* sir? But you haven't—"

"All things end eventually, Courtland, even my self-imposed penance, I suppose. Don't fret. It may be nearly twenty years since I've stood a deck, but I think I remember a thing or two."

"Yes, sir!" Courtland said, grinning in spite of himself. "What are your plans, Cap'n, if I may ask?"

"We'll merely watch from some distance away, confront whoever is out there if necessary, board the ships peacefully," Ainsley said as Jacko, still tucking his voluminous shirt into his trousers, slammed into the room. "You hear me, Jacko? We are reconnoitering for the moment, and that's all."

"I hear you, Cap'n. Means I've got to take myself back upstairs to get my jacket, don't it?"

Ainsley smiled as he took a uniform jacket complete with ribbons and gold epaulets from a cabinet in his study. "That it does, Captain. Have the Union Jack raised on both sloops, with the *Respite* taking on the blue, please, as I think I'd enjoy playing a rear admiral for the duration."

"Aye, aye, sir!" Jacko said, executing a perfectly terrible salute before lumbering back out of the study.

"You'll board them as English Naval officers?" Ethan asked, grinning. "I hadn't heard this clever bit of strategy. Splendid, sir."

"Workable, Ethan, although we don't plan to board them unless they turn to fight. We only wish to watch them once we're clear of the harbor and circle about before showing them our lights, as if approaching from the East, a contingent of the Waterguard out on patrol. We let them see the flag, the uniform as I stand at the rail. They sail on, we sail on, as if we've somewhere important to go. They turn toward the harbor, and everything we've planned for will be put into effect. Running without lights? These could be smugglers, or they could be Beales's ships, scouring the Marsh shoreline for us under cover of darkness," Ainsley said, turning back to Courtland once more, a bicorne hat now in his hand. "You know what to do if we're forced to engage."

"Yes, sir. You have nothing to worry about here."

"I have everything to worry about here. I brought this on all of us." Ainsley shrugged into the well-tailored jacket of a Royal Naval officer, strapped on the sword Spencer handed him. "Shall we be off?"

Courtland watched them all leave the study, part of him wishing he could go with them, be in on any action that might take place on the water, but his saner self knew he was needed here, at Becket Hall.

He went in search of Jacob Whiting, who found him in the hallway.

"We're closing all the drapes, Court, just as we're supposed to, and dousing all but the candles in the hallways. Ollie and the others with land duty are on their way from the village to man the gunports."

"Very good, Jacob. And the women?"

"All of them with Mrs. Eleanor or the little ones,

save Callie. Can't find her nowheres, Court, and we been lookin'."

"Damn! All right, thank you, Jacob. This could all be for nothing, but will serve as fine practice for all of us in any case. Who's up on the roof?"

"Sheila."

Courtland stopped short. "Sheila? Your *wife* is our sentry on the roof?"

"Best eyes of all of us, Court. Think she's part cat, I truly do. She'll let us know right off if she sees somethin'. Showed her where the pull rope is for the alarm bell, an' all."

"I suppose that's good then," Courtland said, sighing. "I don't have time for this, but I'll go find Cassandra, and then join you on the second cannon level. Keep the ports facing the marsh closed for now, but open those facing the Channel."

"Already done, Court. We been practicin' this for a while now, you know. Turnin' a pretty house into a fortress, lickity-split, with its own defenses tucked up inside, ready to pop out. No need for great stone walls around *this* man's castle, eh? The Cap'n, his mind works a real treat, so we all say."

Courtland smiled at last. "That it does. I've always likened this house to a ship Ainsley just happened to build on land. And I know you'll do just fine, Jacob. We all know what we're to do, don't we?" Then he shook his head. "Your *wife* is our sentry on the roof? God, we live in a world gone mad, don't we?"

Jacob only grinned before taking himself toward the kitchens and the staircase tucked behind a seemingly solid wall of pantry shelves, and Courtland headed for another set of secret stairs, these leading down to Odette's private quarters, her altar room.

With Odette upstairs, sleeping in the dressing room of Eleanor and Jack's bedchamber these last months, her chambers were the first place Courtland thought of looking for Cassandra, as no one else would think to search those rooms.

He took a candle from a table in the hallway and stepped carefully onto the dark stairs, to see a soft glow ahead of him, at the base of those stairs.

He had guessed correctly.

"Cassandra?" he called out as he entered the room that seemed part sorcerer's cave, part church, complete with altar. But the thick candles burning on that altar illuminated enough of the room to tell him that Cassandra wasn't there.

He was about to turn around, think of somewhere else to search, when he heard Cassandra call his name.

"How did you find me?" she asked, opening the door cleverly cut into a corner of the room, the one that led to the large, secret storeroom, and entering the main chamber. Obviously she'd heard someone coming down the stairs, and gone into the storeroom to hide herself. "Better yet, Courtland—why? Anyone would think the last thing you'd ever want is to look for me if I'm not in sight."

She was still dressed in the pale yellow gown, and the light from the candles set the rubies around her throat and wrist to glowing with red fire. "Why did you come down here, Cassandra? To ask Odette to put a curse on me? Should I expect to have my teeth begin falling out anytime soon?"

Cassandra shrugged her slim shoulders. "Odette keeps some of my mama's things down here. A lock of her hair, one of her silver-backed brushes, a small portrait—over there, on the altar, see it? Sometimes, when I want to feel close to Mama, I come down here, talk to her a little. Someone's always walking in or out of the drawing room, so I can't talk to her portrait over the fireplace without someone overhearing me. Odette doesn't mind."

"So you were down here, talking to your mother?" Courtland knew he should be grabbing her, hauling her up to Eleanor's bedchamber, and then getting himself back to the business at hand, but he was so transfixed by the sight of Cassandra in the candlelight, the words she was saying to him, that he held his tongue.

"You think I'm silly. You knew her, Courtland, I never did. Lisette…Lisette told me she never knew her mama, either, but that she dreams of her, and then she seems real. I've never dreamt of my mama, not even one time. I…I wanted her to seem real. That's all."

"Oh, Jesus," Courtland swore under his breath.

He'd wanted to hear what she had to say, but this was the worst possible time to sit with her, comfort her. "Your mama used to sing to you," he said, taking her hands in his. "She had a beautiful voice, just like yours. She loved you very much, would have done anything for you. She just couldn't live for you, Callie," he said, slipping into his childhood name for her.

"No. She died for me, instead. I know. And you protected me. It was all so long ago, but now it all seems so close. The island, all of it."

"This will be over soon, I promise," he told her, longing to pull her into his arms, protect her. Love her. "We're not going to have to live this way anymore, always wondering if and when the past is going to come back in an attempt to destroy us."

Cassandra took a step forward, leaned her forehead against his chest, and he fought the urge to lift his hand, push his fingers into her warm, living curls. "Everyone else has something to do, everyone but me. I'm still the child, to everyone, most especially Papa. I'm…I'm as useless here as a wart on the end of Prinney's nose."

Courtland laughed aloud. "And where did you hear that saying?"

She lifted her head, smiled at him. "Spencer? Chance? I don't remember. Do you think I'm useless, Courtland? That I'm nothing but a useless child?"

He looked down at her, saw the nervousness behind her smile, and shook his head. "No, sweetings, I don't. Now, just to prove me right, I'm going to tell you that Ainsley's gone out on the *Respite* because we saw sails out in the Channel."

"Papa? He's gone aboard ship? *Papa?*" She stepped away from Courtland, raising her hands, as if to stop Courtland from saying anything else until she'd digested this unbelievable information. "Um… all right. Who else is with him?"

"Jacko's on the *Spectre.* The rest of them—they're somewhere. I'm in charge here."

She nodded her head several times. "All right," she said again, her breathing quick, and shallow. "And the women? They're all with Elly and the children? Yes, of course they are, so I'm not really needed there. Tell me what to do, Courtland, and I'll do it."

He knew she was serious, and that he'd damned well better give her a serious job of work to do. "Sheila Whiting's up on the roof, watching the land approach to Becket Hall. But she's the only one up there, and it's dark, and it's raining."

"Then that's what I'll do. My case is down here in the storeroom with the others, and I've got clothing and shoes in it, so there's no need to take time to go back to my bedchamber if I can just run up the backstairs to the roof," Cassandra said, lifting her hands to the back of her neck, trying to unclasp the ruby necklace. "Here, help me with this, and with the buttons on my gown. I can be changed and up on the roof with Sheila in a few minutes. I'll take a slicker from the hooks in the kitchen-way, so I don't drown up there."

She turned her back to him as she lifted her hair out of the way. "Court? Don't just stand there. Help me."

Well, she hadn't dissolved into a pool of tears, he'd give her that. But now she wanted him to—oh, hell.

"Turn your back toward the candles, Cassandra," he said, and then worked the catch on the necklace, placed it on the altar, sparing only a moment to realize that now something else of Isabella's was there.

Then he got to work on the buttons, at least two dozen small silk-covered buttons that must have been designed by some imp of the devil to confound a man's thick and, at the moment, clumsy fingers. "Hold still, Callie," he ordered, trying to undo the buttons and at the same time not touch her skin.

"It would be better if you worked from the top down, Court," she told him as she stripped off her bracelet and earbobs. "Once you have most of them open I can just slip out of the gown. It's Morgan's, and even with her maid altering it this afternoon, it's a little bit big."

He did as she said, leaving the buttons at her waist and beginning with those at the top of the gown. He would have realized his own error, eventually, he supposed. Or perhaps he'd just been prolonging the inevitable, for each button he set free of its mooring revealed more of Cassandra's white skin, the delicate bones of her spine. Her back was bare now, almost to her waist, golden in the candlelight.

He stopped what he was doing.

"What do you have on beneath this gown?"

She was still holding her hair up off her shoulders, her head bent. "Nothing. You don't wear anything beneath a gown like this, Courtland. Morgan told me there's no way to hide straps and things, so you just put it on and— Court?"

"I…I'm still here," he said, blowing out a breath as he realized exactly what Cassandra meant. "So, you've got a good hold on the front of the gown?"

Cassandra looked at him over her shoulder. "Yes, I'm holding tight, I promise." Then she sort of *wriggled* inside the gown. "Two more buttons should do it, I think."

"It'd damn well better," he grumbled, and undid two buttons, no more, and then quickly turned his back. "Can you get it off now?"

She didn't answer him.

"Callie? I said, can you get it off now?"

Her answer was to toss the gown over his head, and he slowly pulled it down over his face as he heard her laugh, followed by the sound of her slippered feet running toward the storeroom.

He stood there, slowly counting to one hundred, planning to give her no more time before he left her where she was, and considering what the Devil thought Hell might be like, since he was fairly sure he was already living in it.

"Ready," Cassandra said from behind him. "Courtland? Are you just going to stand there, holding on to that gown?"

She stepped in front of him, taking the gown and folding it in half, placing it over a nearby chair. "It'll be fine here. Morgan doesn't want it back in any case."

Courtland nodded, looking at her, dressed now in a plain round gown that, he felt fairly certain, was still her only covering save the soon-to-be ruined white satin slippers. How in bloody hell could he look at her, looking so circumspect to others, knowing what lay, or didn't lay, beneath that modest gray material?

"If you're ready?"

"I am," she said, but didn't move toward the stairs. "Court? Are you afraid? I'm afraid. Is it all right, to be afraid?"

He smiled ruefully. "Afraid? Callie, I'm terrified."

She tipped her head to one side, as if considering his words, and then—looking anything but a child—she smiled at him, lifted her skirts slightly, and ran up the stairs.

CHAPTER SEVEN

CALLIE SAT WITH HER back against a chimney pot, her legs drawn up tight against her chest, shivering.

The night had been long, cold and constantly wet, but otherwise uneventful. She'd divided her time watching the land approach to Becket Hall with Sheila Whiting, and then crossing the roof parapet to strain her eyes looking out over the dark Channel, wondering if she wanted to see lights somewhere, or if that light might be the flare of cannon, signaling possible disaster.

And, she was ashamed to realize, at some point she had given in to the cold and wet and sat herself down out of the worst of the rain and fallen asleep. She'd awakened all at once, relieved to see that Sheila was still patrolling the roof, as indefatigable as ever, and scrambled to her feet.

"How long was I sleeping?" she asked the woman, rubbing at her arms, wishing her teeth would please stop chattering. "I can't believe I fell asleep."

"Ten minutes, no more," Sheila said. "Didn't need

you anyways, you know. Got the men below, all of them watchin', too. I was pretty much up here to ring the alarm bell, 'cause I'd probably see 'em first. I've got real good eyes."

Cassandra tried to suppress a shiver. "You've already said that, Sheila, at least half a dozen times. And I've told you a half a dozen times that Courtland sent me up here."

"Humph! Probably to keep you out of the way."

"You know, Sheila, that's just plain mean," Cassandra told her, stepping closer to the woman. "I'm not a child anymore. I was given a job of work to do, and I did it."

"With your eyes closed," Sheila pointed out, grinning. "Didn't even see the sloops slippin' back into the harbor, did you?"

Cassandra turned her back and walked away, knowing the woman was right. She had fallen asleep. Her intentions had been so good. How could she have allowed herself to fall asleep? They were right, they were all right. She was still a child.

"I'm going back downstairs," she told Sheila. "I'll send someone up here to relieve you."

"No need. My mam's got our little Jacob and our Jane Anne with her, gone all the way to Appledore with some of the others, so I can stay up here anytime anyone wants me to stay up here. My eyes are that good. And I don't get sleepy."

"All right, that's it," Cassandra said, turning

around and heading toward Sheila once more, not stopping until she was less than a foot away from the other woman. "You don't like me, do you, Sheila? Why don't you like me?"

The older woman sneered down at her. "We're all supposed to be the *crew,* that's what Mr. Ainsley says. Everybody just as good as the next one, that's what Mr. Ainsley says. All except for you, Cassandra Becket. The fairy princess, that's who you are. Just doin' what you want, flittin' around, ridin' your horse, takin' long walks on the shore with your nose in the air, Court tellin' us to leave you alone, you're still a *child.* Well, I seen the way you look at him, the way you chase him, tease him. Child, is it? You're nothin' but a—"

"Sheila!"

Cassandra turned around at the sound of Courtland's voice, and saw him striding across the roof, fire all but spitting from his eyes. "Court, no. It's all right. Sheila and I were just—"

"Go downstairs, Cassandra," he ordered without looking at her, because he was looking straight at Sheila Whiting, who was doing her best to disappear inside her hooded rain slicker.

For a moment, Cassandra was going to obey him. But only for a moment.

"No, Court, I'm not going anywhere until I decide to go somewhere. Sheila didn't say anything that's not true. So I…I want to thank her. Yes, that's what

I want to do. Thank you, Sheila," she said sincerely, looking at the woman. "I promise to do better in the future, and not just…just walk on the shore with my nose in the air."

"Oh, for the love of God," Courtland muttered, grabbing her by the arm. "Come on, you're half-drowned, and shaking like a cat in a wet sack. Sheila, someone will relieve you in a few minutes."

"Let go of my arm," Cassandra said once they were back inside the house, poised at the head of the steep stairway. "Even this *child* knows how to make her way down the steps unaided."

"She shouldn't have said that to you," Courtland told her once they'd reached the landing to the second floor and the concealed doorway that led out into the long hallways to the bedchambers. "Ainsley is the head of this household, and you're his daughter."

Cassandra slipped out of the slicker, and immediately shivered again, because the slicker hadn't been enough to keep her from being soaked to the skin, to the bone. "Is that what you tell them, Court? That I shouldn't have to do anything save be Papa's daughter? That's…that's *insulting*. And what's worse, I *allowed* it to happen. Little Cassandra, wandering about here, mooning over Courtland like some… some insipid *child!*"

"Callie, don't do this," Courtland said, reaching for her, but she put out her hands, pushed him away.

"No! No more, Court, no more. Isabella's daughter, the Cap'n's daughter. Poor little orphaned baby, her mama dying, her papa hiding himself away for years, mourning the woman he loved. Be kind to her, be gentle with her…treat her like a child. And, Lord knows, don't give her anything *important* to do. I am *not* a child anymore, Court, and I refuse to be treated like one."

He shook his head. "I don't know, Cassandra. At the moment you're acting as though you belong back in the nursery. Now, listen to me. Go change those wet clothes and get into a warm bed while we—"

Without thought, of either the action or the consequences, Cassandra slapped him, hard, across the face.

"Oh, God, Court, I'm sorry. I—"

He held his hand to his cheek, shook his head slowly. "No, you've no need to be sorry. I've been slapped before in an effort to bring me to my senses, remind me of my duty to the family. Only, the last time, it was your mother who did me that favor. And I shouldn't be giving you orders as if you're still a child. *Please,* go get yourself out of those wet clothes, Cassandra, and only go to bed if you want to go to bed. Your father probably will want to see you, in any case, explain what happened here last night."

"You tell me first," Cassandra said, her palm tingling, for she had slapped him with all her might. Slapped him, yes, but she would not run. She'd apologized, and now she would stand her ground.

That's what a grown-up would do. "Those ships. Whose were they?"

"We can't be certain," Courtland told her, folding her slicker over his arm and then leading the way into the hallway and carefully shutting the concealed door so that the long mirror on it blended with the rest of the hallway. "By the time our ships got out there they were on the run. Your father chased after them all night, but never spotted them again. No moon, no stars—and a very large Channel to hide in. Not smugglers, that's fairly certain, because they'd be heavily laden with goods from either France or here, and not able to maneuver as well as these ships did. Whoever was in charge of those ships knew what he was about."

"So we're going to think they were Beales's ships?"

"We are," Courtland said, "because that's the prudent thing to do. Beales himself, possibly, and with the ships there for only one reason—to reconnoiter this area. If they hadn't already decided they'd found the right place on the Marsh coast, they know it now that we've gone out after them, not that we could have allowed them to come sailing in here without going out to challenge them. This all could be over in a matter of days, Cassandra. Will you promise me that you'll wait that long before you and I..." He sighed. "We have a lot to talk about, you and I."

"I know," she said, hugging herself to keep warm. "And I have a lot to think about. I'm so sorry I slapped you."

"Don't be. I deserved it, for more reasons than you could possibly know," Courtland told her, and then turned on his heel and headed for the front staircase.

Cassandra watched until he'd disappeared around a turn in the hallway and then ran for her room, wondering if she would seem too much the spoiled child if she rang and asked someone to fetch her hot water for a tub.

In the end she decided that everyone else must have had the same sort of sleepless night she'd had, so she made do with cold water from the pitcher and then quickly dressed in her warmest gown, tying back her damp hair at her nape before she went in search of her papa, finding him in his study, leaning over the large table that was always covered with maps.

"Papa, good morning," she said, kissing his cheek. "You were out on the water."

"Yes, I most certainly was," he said, returning her kiss. "Do I still look giddy with the excitement? Jacko informed me that he might have to knock me down, in hopes that might remove the smile from my face. Ah, Cassandra, how I've missed being onboard my own ship. In command. Oh, and now you're frowning?"

Cassandra attempted a smile. "I'm sorry. It's just that…I think you men enjoy this sort of thing. Don't you? The danger?"

"I'd say that's what makes us men, Cassandra. The thrill of the chase, the prospect of a good fight at the end of that chase. But it's not that simple. For so many long years, we've wondered if the past might come back at us in some way. We hid here—I hid here. Waiting for the blade to fall is worse than having it fall, it would seem. Now, at last, there's a chance to put the past where it belongs, and move on with our lives, no longer captives of that past."

"What will happen now?"

Ainsley shook his head, dismissing her question. "There's no reason for you to worry about that, sweetheart."

"Papa," Cassandra said, her eyes pleading that he understand, "look at me. Please. I'm not a child anymore. I'm eighteen, the same age Mama was when you married her, brought her to the island. I know you want to protect me, but please don't try to keep me wrapped in cotton wool. This is my life, too. She was your wife, yes, but she was also my mother."

Ainsley put his arms around her, drew her tight against his chest, and she closed her eyes, fought back tears as he kissed her hair, her forehead. At last, he put her from him, his hands on her shoulders as he looked at her for a long time.

Then he sighed, suddenly looking very tired, and began to speak. "We're isolated here, which is good, in many ways, but also leaves us very much on our own, responsible for our own protection. Everyone seems to think Edmund will attack in force, and I have planned for that eventuality, as you know."

Cassandra nodded, her heart singing. She knew she wasn't going to like what he said, but she rejoiced inwardly that he was at last trusting her with the truth. "The defenses on the beach, in the marshes around the house and village. All the stores we've stockpiled, the plans for escape, if necessary."

"Exactly. It's what we'd expect from Edmund, after sailing with him for so many years. Quick, violent attack." He dropped his hands, sighed. "But time changes people, and his tactics may have changed, as well. We know now that he's been with Talleyrand in France, at the conferences of the Allies. He seems to work behind the scenes now, his actions more covert, not at all the Edmund I knew. The only thing that's certain, Cassandra, is that he is coming at us. Soon. You see, I still have something he wants. Something I believe he wants even more than he wanted the profits from our days as partners, even more than he wanted your mother."

Cassandra cocked her head to one side, unable to understand her father's words. She'd always believed, everyone had always believed, that Edmund Beales had coveted her mother, had decided that her father could leave the island, give up the life of a privateer, but that he, Beales, would retain possession of all they'd earned over the years, take possession of the beautiful Isabella as if both were somehow his by right.

"You're puzzled?" Ainsley said, smiling wanly. "You wish to be treated as an adult, Cassandra. I'm going to tell you something only Odette, Jacko and Billy know. I'm going to tell you about the Empress."

"A woman?"

"This will easier if I simply show you." Ainsley walked over to the map table, pushed the sliding stacks of maps away from the front edge and depressed something up beneath the tabletop. A small drawer opened, and Cassandra approached, fascinated.

"You'll feel the lever easily, once you know where it is. I'll teach you, later. For now, just look at this. Hold out your hand. Be careful, Cassandra, it's heavier than you'd imagine, but still fragile."

He reached inside the drawer and extracted a small leather bag tied at the top with a silken cord. He untied it, dumping the contents into Cassandra's palm.

"Oh, my!"

"Yes, oh, my. The Empress, Cassandra, probably the finest, largest emerald ever to come out of South America. We likened it, Edmund and I, to stories we'd heard about the Mogul Emerald first known about in the late Sixteenth Century. That particular emerald was inscribed on one side in some Islamic language, with a decorative carving on the other. The Empress is still just as it was taken from the ground. Rough, uncut, but probably larger than the Mogul Emerald. I'd been the one to find it, so it was kept on the island. We'd always divided everything equally, Cassandra, Edmund and I, but to cut this stone would be to halve its worth, or even worse. I hadn't told him, but I was going to give it to him the day Isabella and

I sailed to England. As a sort of recompense to him for my being the one to dissolve our partnership."

Cassandra still couldn't take her gaze away from the stone that had to be more than ten centimeters high, and the sweet, beautiful color of spring grass. She shook her head slowly. "It's…it's beautiful. Isn't it?"

"In places, yes. In order to see its full beauty it would have to be carefully extracted from its less beautiful moorings. Edmund, as do many others, believes emeralds hold special powers and impart good luck and success to their owners. I disagree with him on that, considering what happened to all of us."

"Where…where did you find it?"

Ainsley took the stone from her and replaced it in the bag, closed the secret drawer once more. "In the usual way. We took it, as English privateers claiming a prize. We had no idea when we boarded the French ship that we'd find anything half so valuable, but there it was, waiting for us. Harvested in Colombia, on its way to France. By rights, it should have gone to the Crown, but Edmund convinced me to keep it, just for a while. Just…just to be able hold it, look at it. It? Not to Edmund. To Edmund the stone was a woman. The Empress. Looking back through the years, I realized that Edmund began to change then, become more secretive, often sitting quietly as if thinking deeply, making plans. And then I told him I thought the time was right to return to England with my family. That must have surprised him, forced him to act."

"Who would get the emerald? That's what he wondered, didn't he? Because he was already planning a way to have it for his own?"

"I'm certain of that now, yes. I only wish I could have known then, all those years ago."

"She's worth a fortune, isn't she? The Empress."

"In pounds sterling? Yes, a fortune, a very great fortune. But to Edmund? I think Edmund felt it was worth more than mere money. I think he believed—believes—the Empress is his promise of immortality or, failing that bit of ridiculousness, a good luck talisman that will guide his footsteps from one victory to another. Edmund is coming here for me, yes, but what he wants most is the Empress. If I thought I could trade that stone for our lives, I'd do it, find a way to do that. Unfortunately, that won't be enough for him, as he needs us all dead so that he can move in society without the same fears we have of being discovered, being branded pirates. Luck? That stone has been nothing but bad luck. Disaster. I nearly threw it into the sea as we left the island, except that Edmund would never believe I'd done such a thing. If anything happens to me, Cassandra—"

"Papa, please don't say things like that."

"Cassandra, don't interrupt me," Ainsley said almost sharply, and she lifted her chin, kept her silence. He was right. This was no time to do anything but listen. Later, she would cry.

"If…if I'm no longer here, Cassandra, and

Edmund is still a danger to you, give the stone to Courtland. Explain that Edmund wants it, and trust him to do what's right, how to use it if he thinks he can…bargain with it, I suppose."

She nodded once more, unable to speak for the mingled fear and pride tightening her throat. Her papa was speaking to her, really speaking to her as a person and not just his child, for perhaps the first time in her life. And he was saying horrible, frightening things. "Court and I will decide, together. It's my right."

He smiled now, this handsome, solitary man she'd considered a near god for all of her life. "You're your mother's child, aren't you? All right, Cassandra. There is something else that worries me, and I think you'd be the best one to trust in the matter. I'm putting you in charge of Odette."

"Excuse me? Papa, we all know that no one is ever *in charge* of Odette. She's in charge of us. I want to help, not be shuffled off to do nothing."

"She's not well, Cassandra. Frankly, I believe she's only holding on for two reasons. Eleanor's child, and the chance to confront her twin, Loringa. Although I can't understand how Odette believes she can face down her sister, not as sick as she is. She's been ill for a long time now, and only told me to explain why she didn't, as she says it, *see* Rian and his troubles sooner."

Once again, Cassandra refused to think beyond the assignment her father had given her, trusted her to take on. She could not think about Odette as the woman who had raised her, told her stories about her mama, hugged her, scolded her, taught her—had been for so many years the linchpin that held the Beckets together. "What's wrong with her, Papa?"

"She won't say, at least she won't talk to me, only telling me that it is a discussion for women. Nobody else knows, Cassandra, and Odette would probably have my liver and lights if she knew I'd told you, so you'll have to be very careful not to fuss over her too much, let her know that you're aware she's not well."

"Yes, Papa, I'll be careful. But shouldn't Jack know, even if we don't tell Eleanor? With the baby coming, I mean."

Ainsley stepped behind his desk, sat down, looking up at Cassandra. "I don't know. Odette promises me she'll be fine, able to help Eleanor through her lying-in, and I've decided to believe her. I'm asking you to keep a close eye on her, help her where you can, and tell me if you think she's…well, you understand."

"If she's too sick," Cassandra said, and now a tear did escape, run down her cheek. "I can't believe this. Odette's just always…been there. A part of my life. And with her sister out there somewhere with Beales? What does she think she can do about that?"

"Another question I can't answer, sweetheart, and hope I never have to answer. Loringa is not the sort of woman we want to see here at Becket Hall.

Odette's opposite in every way, save the fact that they look as alike as two peas in the same pod."

"The other side of the same coin, good and evil," Cassandra said, wiping at her cheeks. "And Dahomey, so they're both equally powerful in their Voodoo."

"Loringa once killed a woman," Ainsley told her as he picked up a letter opener, balanced it between his fingers. "She *willed* her to death for coveting Edmund. I wouldn't have given such a spell or curse any credence if I hadn't seen it, but when someone believes in the power of the Voodoo, these things can happen. And Odette, quite naturally, believes in the power of the Voodoo, the power of both the good and the bad *loas.* If Loringa comes after her, if she's strong, Odette will not be able to stand against her. Don't let her leave Becket Hall, Cassandra, not even to go to the village, not until this is over."

"And it will be over soon, Papa. Beales will make his move, as Courtland calls it, very soon."

At last, Ainsley smiled. "And if Courtland says it, then it must be true? You looked very beautiful last night, Cassandra. The picture of your mother. I was, and am, quite proud, although I think I'm feeling very old, knowing that my daughter is now of a marriageable age."

Cassandra felt her cheeks growing hot. "He thinks I'm a child, and I sometimes think he's right. But that's going to change, Papa. May I…may I have your blessing?"

"If I could," Ainsley said, "I would send you back to the nursery, never to grow up, never to leave your selfish papa. But that isn't possible. Of course you have my blessing. But more, Cassandra, you have my confidence that you know your own mind, and your own heart."

"I do, Papa," Cassandra said earnestly. "I've always known."

"So has Courtland," Ainsley said quietly. "Unfortunately, sweetheart, he often confuses his heart with what he believes to be his responsibility. Let's get this nightmare of Edmund Beales and the past behind us, and then I think I'd very much enjoy watching you teach him the difference."

CHAPTER EIGHT

A WEEK PASSED, one tense with watching, waiting. Chance had sent two messages to Becket Hall from his townhouse in London, neither one telling them much other than that, if Beales had indeed returned to the city, he was playing least-in-sight, not going into the thin society of the dwindling Little Season.

They'd had a small fright with Eleanor, who began to labor, but Odette gave her something vile to drink—this according to Cassandra, who seemed to be Odette's shadow these past days—and the pains stopped.

What never seemed to stop was the rain and wind coming in off the Channel. Damp days and gray skies and the enforced confinement were all combining to make the Beckets begin to chafe at that confinement, and at being in each other's presence, constantly.

Morgan, always restless, had been the first to grab a cloak and ride out onto the Marsh, Ethan following after her on his splendid white Andalusian stallion, the two of them returning some hours later, suspiciously smiling, the back of Morgan's cloak suspiciously littered with bits of straw. The two of them then disappeared into their bedchamber for the remainder of the day.

Neither Morgan and Ethan nor Rian and Lisette had come down to dinner, prompting Spencer to make a rather ribald joke about idle hands being the devil's workshop, a bit of silliness his dear wife tersely informed him had not been in the least bit amusing.

Then Spencer and Mariah disappeared to their own bedchamber immediately after dinner, leaving Cassandra to look at Courtland, who only shrugged, reddened a bit above his beard, and muttered something about heading over to the village to make certain the assigned patrol had returned without incident.

Cassandra had only nodded, telling him that she was going upstairs to check on Eleanor and Odette, and with that encouraging piece of news Courtland relaxed, said goodnight to Ainsley, then silently berated himself for being glad to be out of Cassandra's company.

Because he wasn't glad. He was confused, off-balance, constantly thinking about her, about the way her back had looked in the candlelight, bared to the waist, open to his touch. Constantly reliving those moments, as well as the moment she'd slapped him, and his world had seemed to tilt off-center, teeter on its axis.

She'd slapped him, and his reaction had bordered on the insane. He'd wanted to pull her into his arms, kiss her senseless, kiss her and hold her until the entire world melted away and there was only the two of them, with only each other to care for, to hold on to; to bury himself in her, disappear into her, live in her, be the man he longed to be.

But the world still lay on his shoulders. He believed himself responsible for every man, woman and child in his orbit, had always believed that, even once he understood that Isabella's last words to him, her example of self-sacrifice, had made a larger impression on him, on his life, than she could ever have imagined.

He pulled his cloak closer around him against the wind and rain and made his way to the village. The clock had yet to strike the hour of eight, and he faced another long, restless, unproductive night.

His brothers laughingly called him a dull stick, and he probably was. Even when he'd ridden out as the Black Ghost to protect the local smugglers on their runs, he had done so out of a sense of duty, not one of adventure.

Although he knew, in his heart of hearts, that donning Ainsley's black silk cape and mask, leading nearly one hundred men across the Marsh by moonlight had stirred his blood, in spite of himself.

Only five years or so Chance's junior, Courtland had stood on the shore when the *Black Ghost* and the *Silver Ghost* had sailed away from the island harbor, out to sea, out to adventure. He had envied Chance, who had commanded his own ship before the age of twenty, standing on the deck, a cutlass pushed into his waistband, his hands on his hips, his legs spread wide for balance, his long, blond hair whipping around his face in the stiff, tropical breeze.

Vibrant. Adventurous. A young, vital animal, that had been Chance all those years ago. Capable, and yet daring.

While he, Courtland, had been the plodder, the silent one, always careful not to bring attention to himself, because that attention had always come in the form of a fist, or a whip slicing through the air over his head, ready to strike.

So was he wrong now, was it wrong now, to be almost looking forward to the inevitable battle with Edmund Beales? Was it wrong for his blood to sing with anticipation of the final struggle, the final victory? Was it wrong to want to think as a man of action, even of daring, rather than the safe, stolid, boring man he'd forced himself to be all these years?

Cassandra had a lot to do with what he was thinking now, how he wanted to envision himself…as she had always envisioned him.

She believed in him, trusted in him, did not find him to be boring or dull or unexciting. Still, he was more a man of thought than of action. He knew that, he understood that. When the family needed flash and dash, then it was Chance who was called upon, and Spence, and even Rian. Never him.

No, he had always stayed in the background, inventing a knife holder concealed beneath a jacket for Spencer to activate with a few squeezes of his arm muscles, devising a one-handed bootstrap device for Rian, plotting a better placement of signal fires along the Marsh, spending long hours with Ainsley, talking strategies, planning contingencies.

He was, he knew, as exciting and, well, as romantic, as a potted plant.

If Cassandra were free to go to London for her Come-out, and she was put into the company of men like Chance, like Spence and Jack and Rian and Ethan and Valentine? Handsome men, smart, witty, perhaps rich and titled? Would she realize that what she felt for him was a childhood affection that had no place in her life now that she was a grown woman?

He should let her go, *make* her go, once the confrontation with Beales was over. And, until it was over, keep his distance.

He'd rather tear off his own left arm.

"Court!" Rian called to him from the large table in the rear of The Last Voyage. "We were just coming after you."

Courtland shook off his uncomfortable thoughts, that weren't really productive anyway, and crossed to the table to see Spencer and Ethan also sitting there. "Why? You have news?"

"Possibly," Ethan said, and for the first time Courtland noticed that the man was wet, very wet.

"I thought you were upstairs with…I thought you and Morgan were…oh, hell, what's going on?"

Ethan grinned. "Well, we were, earlier, but all good things must come to an end, sooner or later, or we'd both be dead by now."

Rian, still in the throes of his rather recent honeymoon, threw back his head and laughed heartily…and Courtland wished he didn't have such a damn tendency to blush.

Ethan leaned forward on his chair, his elbows on the table, looking less a peer of the realm than a naughty boy about to tell a secret. "Morgan and I stopped in at a small tavern this afternoon, The Oak and Grapes, and the innkeeper pulled me aside, told me someone had been asking about the big house on the coast."

"Jesus, Ethan, why didn't you—"

"Why didn't we tell everyone immediately? Simple, Court. Because the man was gone. But the innkeeper described him quite well, so Morgan and I spent the rest of the afternoon searching for him, without luck. Tonight? Tonight, while all the rest of you were having dinner, I got luckier. Some of the gold pieces I spread around earlier today came back to me at The Oak and Grapes with the information I wanted."

"He's staying just this side of Dymchurch, at the Ship Inn," Rian added, and Courtland mentally measured the distance from Becket Hall to Dymchurch, deciding that, if they rode hard, they could be there in a little over an hour.

"We were just planning strategy," Spencer said, looking at Courtland. "What do you suggest we do? Rian's all for breaking down the man's door and hauling him out—but then Rian is always breaking down doors, isn't he? I said we should wait until morning, wait for him to leave the inn, so that we're not seen taking him. And Ethan? You agree, don't you?

Courtland rubbed at his short beard. "Do we tell Ainsley?"

"Not yet," Ethan said. "There's always the chance someone just wanted the promise of another gold coin, and gave us incorrect information. I think we have to go to the inn, see for ourselves, and then decide."

"We have to consider this man, whoever he is, to be one of Beales's men. If we don't, if we don't act sure, confident, he may be able to convince us of his innocence. No matter what the man says, we act as though we *know* he reports to Beales." Courtland got to his feet. "Are you ready?"

"*You're* going?" Spencer stood up, looked at his brother. "We thought…well, we thought you'd want to stay here. Somebody should stay here, don't you think, what with Jack always staying upstairs with Elly these days?"

"Fine. Rian, you're in charge here at Becket Hall."

"Now just wait a minute, Court," Rian said hotly. "Just because I have only the one arm is no reason to—"

"This has nothing to do with your arm, Rian," Courtland told him quickly. "I'm being entirely selfish here. You've all had…adventures. I've got lists of stores, and more lists of patrol schedules, and then more lists of— Hell, I'm not a shopkeeper. I'm going."

"He's right, Rian," Spencer said, clapping his brother on the shoulder. "It's probably time Court went out to play again. It's been a while since the Black Ghost was taken out for an airing."

"Exactly so," Courtland said, already turning over an idea in his head. "Now, here's what we'll do…"

CASSANDRA CAME DOWN the servant staircase, carefully balancing a small tray against her hip, and turned toward the study, thinking to ask her father if he'd like her to fetch him a pot of tea as long as she was heading to the kitchens with dirty dishes she'd taken from Eleanor's bedchamber.

It was already past midnight, but she knew her father never went to his bed before two.

She had her hand on the door latch when she heard voices coming from inside the room, and hesitated, as the door was already open a crack. If her papa and Jacko were having a private discussion, she wouldn't want to disturb them.

But it wasn't Jacko's voice she heard, or even her father's. It was Spencer's, and he sounded excited.

"It was all I could do not to laugh," he was saying, "even with a situation this serious. Court's a bloody genius."

"And with a career on the stage, if he wants it," Ethan added, and Cassandra pushed the door open just a little bit more, in order to see into the room.

Spencer was standing in front of her papa's desk, Ethan beside him, as her father sat behind that desk, looking at them, his expression unreadable. But where was Courtland?

Ah, there he was, sitting at his ease on the burgundy leather couch, one leg bent and propped on the other, dressed all in black from head-to-toe, and with something black tossed on the couch beside him. Was that…yes, it was. It was the cape he'd used to ride out as the Black Ghost. What on earth?

"How did you get the man out of the inn?" Ainsley asked, and Cassandra frowned, for the question made no sense to her.

"Easily enough, sir," Ethan explained. "We, um, we *borrowed* two of the uniforms you've so cleverly amassed. I presented myelf as Lieutenant Ethan of the Waterguard, and I had some questions about the man's whereabouts the previous evening, when a large cargo of brandy and tea had supposedly been landed only a mile from the inn. He blustered, he denied, but then became cooperative."

"Because I'd leveled my rifle at him," Spencer said, and Cassandra belatedly realized that both men had uniform jackets folded over their arms. "We marched him outside and into the dark, and Courtland took over."

"Courtland?" Ainsley inquired, raising one expressive eyebrow. "You'll explain?"

"There's really nothing much to explain, sir," Courtland said quietly. "What's more important is what he said once we'd convinced him to talk to us."

"Oh, no. No, no, no, Court, we're not skipping over the best part," Spencer said, crossing to the drinks table and pouring himself a glass of wine. "It was wonderful. Court was wonderful, just splendid. Comes out of the dark, all mysterious in the cloak, the mask, the slouch hat—all of it. Orders us to take the man inland, to the cliffs of Marshborough."

"I beg your pardon?" Ainsley asked. "And where, pray tell, are the cliffs of Marshborough? Indeed, where is Marshborough?"

"In Court's amazing imagination, sir, I think you'd have to say," Ethan said, accepting a glass of wine from Spencer. "We blindfolded the man, marched him about a mile, I would think, to a place Court knows, and started asking him questions. He wouldn't answer, not a word. Claimed not to know what we were asking him."

"So Court orders us to untie his hands and lower him over the cliff," Spencer said, then shook his head, laughed. "The fellow starts in to screaming, *'No, no!'* But our friend Court here is made of sterner stuff. We make the fellow get down on his belly, still blindfolded, and push his way back, back, until his body's over the side and he's hanging on by his fingertips. Then Court asks him his questions again. 'Who sent you? Who do you report to?' And the fellow answers every question, all the time begging that we pull him off the cliff, don't let him fall."

"Fall," Ainsley repeated, and now he was smiling. "Fall off a cliff, *inland,* in Romney Marsh. Obviously not a local resident. Go on, please. Did you let him fall, Court?"

"Yes, sir, that I did. I find that I am a mean, mean man," Courtland said, shaking his head to refuse a glass of wine.

"He ripped off the man's blindfold and shouted, 'Die, you bastard!'" Spencer said. "Then he stood there, his feet not a yard from the man's head, his hands on his hips just so, that damn black mask showing nothing but the fire in his eyes, and watched as the man slowly lost his grip and fell."

Cassandra's hand flew to her mouth in shock.

"Screamed like a stuck pig, he did," Spencer continued, "until he found himself standing upright now on solid ground two feet below the *cliff.* Then he really howled!"

Cassandra was glad she already had her mouth covered, for a giggle threatened to escape as she realized what Courtland had done. He'd hung the man over a small outcropping, dangled him only a few feet above the ground, and let the poor creature believe he was hanging over a huge cliff, soon to fall to his death. No wonder he'd told them what they wanted to know!

That last thought sobered Cassandra, and she held her breath, listening to what would be said next, hopefully a recitation of what they'd learned from their captive.

And that's just what Courtland reported to her father. The man obviously was in the pay of Edmund Beales, although he said he knew no names, and had been sent to find the best land route to the large house they'd earlier seen from the sea. He was to find out the name of the house, of the family that lived there, and report back to his master, in London.

Ainsley sat forward in his chair. "Where in London?"

Courtland shook his head. "Some nameless pub near Piccadilly. No great help to us, although we'll send the information we have along to Chance and he might have a better idea as to where to search. I don't believe the man we brought back here with us tonight will be any more help to us, unfortunately."

"Where is he now, Courtland?" Ainsley asked, getting to his feet.

"Jacko's got him, at the smithy. If he does know anything else, he'll be telling it to Jacko, chapter and verse, before Waylon can heat the irons. I told Jacko not to bother, the man knows very little, but you know Jacko. He likes to do things his own way."

"I'll go see the man personally, if anyone cares to

join me," Ainsley said, and Spencer and Ethan turned toward the door, so that Cassandra quickly stepped back into the shadows at the staircase until the three men had passed by her, on their way to the front of the house and the path to the village that was uncluttered with spikes and wooden balls of stakes.

Only when she heard the front door closing did she venture from her hiding place and walk into the study, saying, "Papa? I'm on my way down to the kitchens with this tray, and wondered if you'd like me to— Oh, Court. Where's Papa?"

He was already on his feet, the black cape slung over his arm, the black slouch hat sitting upside-down on the couch, the black silk mask evident inside it. He seemed to be mentally debating between picking up the hat or standing in front of it, as if she hadn't yet seen it. "He went over to the village with Spence and Ethan. You…you, um, just missed him."

And then he seemed to remember who he was, his supposed position in the household, and in her life. He looked at her sharply, his eyelids narrowed. "Why aren't you in bed?"

Cassandra rolled her eyes as she deposited the tray on a nearby tabletop. "Oh, for pity's sake, Court, you're not in charge of when I go to bed."

"Clearly," he said, at last turning around to pick up the hat and mask. "I am, however, in charge of when I go to bed, and that's just what I'm going to do right now. If you'll excuse me?"

But Cassandra, who had not advanced much beyond the doorway, stood her ground. "No, I don't think I will. I heard everything, Court. I was standing just outside this door, and I heard it all."

"Yes, I'd already figured that out on my own, thank you. And you'll be repeating nothing of what you've heard to any of the women."

"Another order, Courtland? What did you think I was going to do? Run through the house ringing a bell, telling everyone you went riding out as the Black Ghost again?"

"No, I don't think that. I apologize," Courtland said, looking at her curiously. "But what have you been doing, Cassandra? This past week, I mean. Why are you constantly following at Odette's heels? Because if that's in the way of a warning for me to stay away from you—"

"Or else I'll beg Odette to put a Voodoo curse on you? She doesn't do that, Court."

"No," he said, smiling. "She threatens to turn people into toads, remember? But she's never done it. The thing to figure out is that she's all bluster, and all loving. Even when she's chasing you with a spoon for disobeying her. It has been a long time since she chased me, but I remember those incidents well."

Cassandra returned his smile, but her heart ached. "She never tried to take my mother's place, but she did her best, didn't she? I love her so much."

Courtland put down the cape and walked over to

her, took hold of her shoulders. "Callie? What should I know?"

"Nothing. I'm tired, that's all. Eleanor seems to have slept so much in the past months, confined to her bed, that now she barely sleeps at all. She keeps making lists, and asking questions and refusing to ever take no for an answer when she asks if we know anything she doesn't know. Mariah and Morgan help, but they're busy in the nursery with their children, and Lisette still stays to herself most of the day, or with Rian. Being locked up inside with women all the day long, without so much as being able to ride Athena or walk on the beach? It's very tiring. You're probably right, I should go to bed now."

"Callie?" he asked in that way he had, using that special tone of voice she'd never been able to deny. "I'll say it again. What should I know?"

He was standing so close to her, his hands on her shoulders, his broad chest looking to be such a comforting haven. She took a step forward and laid her cheek against his black silk shirt. "It's Odette, Court. She's sick."

He was silent for a few moments, and then slipped his arms fully around her, rested his chin lightly on her head. "How sick, Callie?"

She kept her face hidden from his. "Papa said not to tell anyone, and I didn't, not for a full week, and I won't tell anyone else. But it's so hard, Court. I can see it, now that Papa told me. She walks even slower than before, and she naps in the afternoon in Elly's chambers. And she…she keeps touching her stomach when she thinks no one is looking, and biting on her bottom lip, as if she's in…as if she's in some sort of pain. I hugged her yesterday, and I could feel it through all those heavy clothes she wears. I could feel her bones. I think she told Papa that she's dying."

Cassandra lifted her head, her eyes filled with tears as she looked up at Courtland. "What can I do? There has to be something I can do."

"I doubt that we can do anything, sweetheart, not unless Odette asks us for our help. She's a proud old woman, and if she wants us to believe she's all right, then that's what we'll have to do. Can you do that, Callie? Can you look at her, and not let her see?"

Cassandra sighed, nodded her head. "I would never do anything to hurt her. And you have to pretend you don't know anything, because Papa asked me not to tell anyone."

"I shouldn't admit to this, but I'm glad you didn't listen to him, and honored that you chose me to be the one person you did confide in," he said quietly, pushing her slightly away from him, but not letting her go. "So we're still friends?"

She blinked, twice, and then glared at him. "Friends? What on earth are you talking about, Courtland Becket? *Friends?*"

He smiled. "A bad choice of words, I suppose. But you have been avoiding me for a week, ever since the night we caught sight of Beales's ships in the Channel. Was that because of anything Sheila Whiting said to you?"

"I'm not sure," she told him truthfully. "I've…I've missed you." He seemed ready to speak, so she put her fingers against his mouth. "But I don't want to go back to where we were before that night, Court. I *can't* go back to where we were. And neither can you. Do you see that?"

He touched his hand to hers, kissed her fingertips and then lowered her hand from his face. "Tomorrow, Callie. I'll take you riding tomorrow. I think we both could benefit from a few hours away from Becket Hall. We can't go far, but we will go, I promise. Exercise your Athena, and perhaps blow a few cobwebs from both of our heads."

She relaxed her tense shoulders, not realizing she'd been holding her body so stiffly, not aware of the tension between them until, at last, it was gone. "Thank you, Court." She stepped up on tiptoe and daringly placed a quick kiss on his mouth. "Thank you so much."

But when she went to step away from him his arms closed more tightly around her and he lowered his face to hers, sealing their mouths together.

Cassandra closed her eyes as the strangest feeling rippled through her body, and then raised her arms to hold them around his neck as he showed her that the kiss she'd given him had been far from what a real kiss should be.

She felt the tip of his tongue against her lips as he seemed to want her mouth open, and she complied, because saying no to anything Court had ever wanted from her was beyond her power.

"Callie," he whispered against her lips, withdrawing slightly, and then taking her mouth so completely that she could only sigh, and hold on to him for dear life. This was where she wanted to be. In his arms. This was where she was destined to be. In his life.

Only the sound of footsteps descending the servant stairs served to break them apart, and Cassandra found it difficult to look at Courtland as she attempted to recapture her breath, for it would seem that she had been holding that breath for quite a while.

He moved her to one side and closed the door halfway, to block them from sight from the hallway, and then took her chin in his hand, tipped up her head.

"You'd better go directly to your chamber, Cassandra," he told her, touching a finger to the side of her chin.

"Why?" she asked him, feeling close to tears because of the look in his eyes as he gazed down at her. As if she were infinitely precious to him.

He smiled slightly. "It would seem my beard and your tender skin are at odds with each other," he said. "We'll go riding directly after breakfast, all right?"

She nodded. Nodding was all she could seem to

muster, and she left the room, brushing past a frowning Sheila Whiting as she headed up the servant stairs, her face averted from Sheila's too-observant eyes.

CHAPTER NINE

COURTLAND HADN'T BEEN looking forward to entering the breakfast room, and he hadn't taken more than three steps into that room before he knew he'd been right to feel that reluctance.

"What ho! Who's this, a stranger in our midst? Stand just where you are, stranger, and identify yourself."

"Good morning, Spence," Courtland said, moving past him on his way to the heavily laden sideboard.

"Good morning, is it? And he even calls me by name. I say again, sir, who are you?"

Near the far end of the long table, her head lowered but her eyes raised so that she could peek through her lashes, Cassandra giggled.

"Oh, cut line, Spence," Rian said, taking his own seat, his plate fully loaded with eggs and slices of ham. "It's only our very own Courtland, his cheeks as smooth and pink as a baby's—"

"Rian Becket, mind your mouth," Lisette said, cutting him off, although Courtland was fairly certain his brother had meant to leave his observation dangling. After all, the joke was funny enough as it was, even if it was at his expense. "Court, I think you look very fine. Very handsome."

"Thank you, Lisette," Courtland said as he kept his back to the room, dishing coddled eggs onto his plate.

"You're welcome. And you'll look even more fine once the sun touches your skin and you, um, and you *even out?*"

Rian laughed so hard he choked on his bite of egg and had to take a drink before pointing out to his bride that her comment had been nearly as rude as his own, although he knew she was only attempting to be kind. "She just says whatever comes into her mind, Court. But she's right. A little sun on that face you've been hiding for so long will probably do wonders. Won't it, Callie?"

"Oh, no," Cassandra protested, getting to her feet, carrying her dirty plate over to the small side table, placing it with others ready to be returned to the kitchens. With half of Becket Village gone, and the other half spending long hours on watches and patrols, everyone had to do their own fetching and carrying, while thanking their lucky stars that Bumble had agreed to stay in the kitchens, preparing meals for everyone. "You won't drag me into this. Court? I have to go check in on Elly and Odette. Shall we meet at the stables?"

"Yes, that would be fine. In an hour?"

He watched as she left the morning room, her

head still curiously averted from his. Was she crying now? God, he was fairly certain she was.

"You're going riding?" Spencer looked questioningly at Courtland. "Do you think that's wise? Taking Callie with you, I mean."

"Wiser than staying here listening to your feeble jokes and eventually punching you in the nose, you mean? Then, yes, I do," Courtland said as he observed Rian work with the "knife" he had fashioned for him, a single sharp, curved blade attached in the middle to a wooden handle, the whole thing looking much like an anchor, so that he could rock the blade back and forth over his meat, neatly cutting it with one hand. Of all the things Rian could have complained about since losing his arm, and with good reason, it seemed that having to watch someone else cut his meat for him held the most embarrassment.

"How about I harangue you instead?" Rian asked before popping a bit of country ham into his mouth. "Why did none of you wake me when you brought that fellow back here last night? Jasper and I are very good at interrogating prisoners, you know. Mostly, my most wonderful giant has only to look at them. Oh, and perhaps growl menacingly."

"I understand that's just what he did, while holding a hot iron from the forge as Jacko asked his questions," Spencer told them. "Not that you weren't menacing enough last night, Court, in your pretty costume. Unfortunately, all Jacko was able to learn was that this man wasn't the only one sent to reconnoiter the area. We've caught him, but there were more. *Are* more. So I'll ask again—do you think it's wise to take Callie with you on your ride this morning?"

Courtland had already had second thoughts on the idea, especially knowing something Spencer and Rian still did not, but a promise was a promise. "We won't go far, and with the land as flat as it is, I'd see an approaching rider, or even a man out walking, while he's still a mile away, as you both know. Only a fool would come within several miles of this place in daylight unless he wants to be seen."

"True enough," Spence said, piling a fresh plate with food. "Very well, take your little ride, not that you need or want my permission. I'm going to fetch Mariah some breakfast and hope she can eat it. She's sick the moment she lifts her head off the pillow, which always makes me feel a complete monster for having put her in this condition."

Courtland grinned at his brother. "Mariah's increasing again? Lizzie's only a few months old! Have you two made it your mission to repopulate the Marsh?"

Spencer grinned sheepishly. "It was a surprise to us, too. And not Romney Marsh, Court, but Hampton Roads. We get this mess over with soon, and our third child will be born in America. I've argued that we should wait until the baby's born, but Mariah is adamant that we leave as soon as possible."

"Probably because she doesn't want to wait for the *fourth* to be born," Rian said, winking at Courtland.

"There is that," Spencer admitted, and then sobered. "But we are going, the moment I know I'm not needed here. Did I tell you I've bought land? My friend Abraham, Marianna Warren's ship captain, scouted out five hundred acres for me, promising it's some of the best land in a dozen miles. The house is already being built and will be ready for us when we arrive."

"No, you didn't tell me that," Courtland said, laying down his fork. "I've known you're leaving, you and Rian both, but I suppose I never considered it would be so soon."

"None of us did, not that any of us is ready to thank Beales for showing up now like a particularly bad penny," Rian said as Spencer left the room, taking Lisette's hand in his and lifting it to his lips. "Although she doesn't remember New Orleans, I'm taking Lisette home. It will be a grand adventure, won't it, sweetheart?"

"I only wish we could go now," Lisette said, her expressive eyes filled with pleading. "I don't want to see him. I can't see him again."

Rian squeezed her hand, looked across the table at Courtland, his own eyes showing the pain he felt for his wife. "Court, what do you think of this? I take Lisette to Brede Manor for a few days, to visit with Fanny and Valentine? We'd not be that far away, and Valentine and I could return as soon as needed."

"I think that's a very good idea," Courtland said, not adding that he'd be happier if all of his family would leave Becket hall until Beales had been dealt with, defeated. And that they'd take Cassandra with them.

"And I think I'm not such a terrible coward, Rian Becket," Lisette said sharply, pushing away his hand and getting to her feet. "I said I can't see him, but what I mean is that I can't *not* see him, either. I want to see his cold, dead body being lowered into a grave that will never know a prayer or a marker, and know he's really gone. I may spit on that grave. For my *maman,* you understand."

With that, Lisette tipped her chin in the air and stomped out of the morning room, leaving Rian to smile at Courtland. "Bloodthirsty little thing, isn't she, for being raised in a convent? I think that's her mother's blood in her, don't you? You know the Battle of New Orleans that ended so badly for us last year, Court? I've read that it was a pirate, Somebody-Lafitte, who helped turn the tide. Imagine, brother mine, I go to live with pirates. It will almost be as if I've never left here."

"We're going to scatter off everywhere once this is finally over, aren't we, Rian?" Courtland commented, carrying his own plate over to the small table, the plate not empty, but his appetite already fled. "It's almost as if it's Beales who has kept us a family."

"No, it's Ainsley's who's kept us a family, our love for him, our love for each other. We'll always be Beckets, no matter where we scatter to, either here in England, or in America, or wherever we might finally settle ourselves. Some things are thicker than blood, much as everyone discounts that as a romantic notion. No one save us has lived the lives we have lived, no one else has the special and sometimes terrible bond forged that day on the island."

"And Cassandra?" Courtland asked after a moment.

"Oh, so that's it? You're still telling yourself that Callie's your sister, that you're some perverted creature for loving her?"

"I've never said I—"

"No, you never have," Rian said quickly. "That day, Court, Isabella gave Callie to you. You'll say to protect her, and I agree. But if Isabella could whisper in your ear right now, I think she'd tell you that there are many different kinds and levels of love, and that, with you, her daughter will have the benefit of all of them. Callie sees it, Court, she's always seen it. So have the rest of us. Fate put you in Callie's way long before what happened on the island. Now, Lisette will tell you I'm *romantical,* and I am, but that's how I see it. You and Callie were destined."

Rian pushed back his chair and got to his feet. "And that's all I'm going to say about that. Go for your ride, Court. Blow the last of the cobwebs out of that thick head, and for God's sake, stop scowling and put a smile on that ugly face of yours. Your entire world is about to change."

Rian was right, Courtland knew, his world was about to change. Cassandra was going to hate him.

CASSANDRA WORE HER DARK burgundy riding habit because Courtland had once said he liked it. And because it was wool, and quite warm on this clear but chilly day. Although Cassandra wanted to look as fine as possible, she was also a practical sort, and she didn't wish to be cold.

She waited in the stable yard, pacing, rhythmically tapping her riding crop against her thigh, alternately smiling at the fact that Courtland had shaved off the short beard he'd worn since she was about thirteen and feeling tears sting at her eyes that he would actually have done that for her.

To protect her tender skin.

Because he was going to kiss her again.

She had her papa's blessing, but she would also wager her beloved mare, Athena, that her papa would still rather see her back in the nursery, playing with her dolls and dreaming only of fairy castles and sugarplums.

Growing up was difficult, but now Cassandra wondered if the transition was even more difficult for the parent than the child….

"And where do you think you're going, hmm?"

Cassandra turned about, to see Jacko lumbering toward her from the side of the stables. Like Odette, he was growing older, almost without her noticing, for Jacko, like Odette, had always been a part of her life; she'd never questioned their places in that life, had never considered that life without them in it, just as she would always like to believe that her papa would live forever.

But now she saw the weariness around Jacko's always oddly smiling eyes, and could hear his labored breathing while he was still a good ten feet away from her. He carried a lot of weight with him, seemingly more with each passing year, and it would appear that the load was becoming more difficult to bear. It was nearly impossible now to believe he'd once strode the deck as Captain before Chance had shared that duty with him on the *Silver Ghost,* and even more impossible for her to believe any of the stories they had all heard whispered to them by some of the crew; stories of a fierce, cold-hearted Jacko, who could spit a man on his sword as soon as look at him. Sometimes, they'd said, without worry about having a reason to do so.

"Court and I are going riding, Uncle Jacko," she told him, the only Becket child to address him as Uncle. She propped her fists against her hips and shook her head at him disapprovingly—the only Becket child save his true pet, Eleanor, who would dare do such a thing. "And where have you been, hmm? You look as if you haven't slept all night."

"It's true, then," Jacko said, grinning at her, "children should be seen but never heard. You've been with Eleanor? How is she this mornin'?"

"The same as she was last night, Uncle Jacko. Bored and testy and driving poor Jack to distraction. Why don't you go see her?"

Jacko shook his head. "She doesn't need to see the likes of me. It's enough she's fine. And how is the old woman?"

"*Odette* is also just fine," Callie said, shaking a finger at him. "And don't let her hear you calling her an old woman."

"The old woman's dyin', that's what she's doin', and her sayin' she can take care of Eleanor's lyin'-in is like askin' me to fly—we neither of us can do either thing. Damn fool woman. Why do ya think I made sure Sheila Whiting is still here, huh? The minute Eleanor starts her pains, you go fetch Sheila Whiting to her. Odette won't like that, but that's the way it's goin' to be, hear me?"

"I think everyone within a mile heard you, Uncle Jacko," Cassandra said, hiding her surprise that Jacko knew Odette was sick. "But if you're adamant that it must be that way, *you* go tell Odette. After all, she's an old, sick woman, and you can't possibly be afraid of her, can you?"

Jacko looked at her in that way he had, stretching his head forward on his neck, hunching his massive shoulders, skewering her with his eyes. And then he smiled. Laughed. "So it's true. All grown-up, aren't you? And full of sass for your poor uncle. Serves us all right, I suppose, lettin' you run free for so long."

His smile faded. "Just you mind what I said about Sheila Whiting."

Cassandra watched him go, lumbering along as if still maneuvering across a deck in a stormy sea. She sighed, knowing how Eleanor had come to be a Becket, and Jacko's role in the story. There were some who said Jacko loved no one, but Cassandra didn't believe that. He loved her papa, and he loved the petite, fragile Eleanor. He would probably gladly sacrifice himself for either one of them.

She began pacing once more, wondering what could be keeping Courtland, for he'd said an hour, and she'd been prompt. She looked over at Athena and to Courtland's new black, Poseidon, a gift from Morgan and Ethan, who now raised horses on their estate, many of them sired by Ethan's own Spanish stallion, Alejandro. They were both saddled and ready to go, Poseidon more than ready to go, it would seem, as he was dancing in place, tugging on the reins tied to a fence post.

Had Courtland decided it wouldn't be smart for them to ride out this morning? And, if so, he should at least have had the courtesy to— Ah, there he was. Walking toward her, making a leisurely journey out of it, too.

He looked so handsome, probably even more handsome than with his beard covering the bottom half of his face. Why, he had an almost square jaw, didn't he, cut so finely, so cleanly. Did he look younger now? Yes, he looked younger. Had he been attempting to appear older, was that why he'd grown the beard? A stodgy, hairy old man, much too old for her. Yes, that's what he'd been doing.

Silly man. As if a beard could change how she felt about him.

She could see a pistol tucked into his waistband beneath his dark blue hacking jacket, and she'd already seen the rifle attached to Poseidon's saddle, was fairly certain the bulges in a leather satchel strapped to that saddle contained more weapons. It wasn't as if anyone ever rode out on the Marsh unarmed, but this small arsenal seemed excessive.

"I thought you weren't coming," she called to him as she walked over to the mounting block, ready to climb on Athena's back and be gone before anyone else could wander by to say it wasn't safe out on the Marsh.

"There was a slight problem in the village I felt I needed to attend to," he told her, pulling on his riding gloves.

"But it's settled now? What was the problem?"

He held Athena's head as Cassandra mounted the block and lifted herself up onto the sidesaddle. Morgan may have shunned a sidesaddle for the most part, but Cassandra didn't feel the sidesaddle constrained her overmuch. After all, unlike the always hey-go-mad Morgan, she couldn't much see the point of attempting to sail over five-bar fences.

"Someone died in the middle of the night," he

said quietly, mounting Poseidon. "I was arranging the burial."

"Oh, no, who? I know Demetrious hasn't been well, but surely—"

"Nobody from the village, Cassandra," Courtland broke in, wearing an expression that told her he'd spoken without thinking the thing through, which meant he was definitely upset by this death.

She probably should let it go, not push at him for more information, but he looked a bit pale, and not just because his lower cheeks hadn't seen as much sun as the rest of his face for many years. "Someone came to the village, Court? But nobody comes here, not without an invitation, and we don't give out many invitations. Most certainly not now."

They walked the horses, side-by-side, out of the stable yard and headed inland, away from the Channel and the now dangerous, heavily defended beach. "Let's give them their heads, all right? Poseidon seems ready to run. Then we'll talk."

Cassandra rolled her eyes as Courtland urged the stallion ahead with his knees, leaving her and Athena to catch up as best they could. He would probably start up some other conversation once they'd drawn the horses back down to a walk, saying that they'd already spoken enough about the person who had died, but she wasn't about to be put off so easily.

Courtland was waiting for her beneath the tallest of the few trees in this area of the Marsh, an aberration that had somehow managed to avoid being bent nearly in half by the winds from the Channel as it grew.

She reined Athena in beside his mount and spoke as if they hadn't left the conversation behind them, in the stable yard. "If this person wasn't from the village, Court, where was he from? Did he say, before he died?"

"Callie, there are questions you simply shouldn't ask. Not right now. I shouldn't have said anything. It's my fault, but let's drop it now, please."

She tipped her head to one side, her curls bouncing as she knew they did—Courtland seemed to like her hair falling free, even as she hated the way it tangled—as if considering his plea. "No, I don't think so. I think I need to know who this man was, and why he died. It was a man, wasn't it?"

Courtland turned Poseidon and Athena simply followed, the two horses walking along beneath a thin November sun. "Yes, it was a man. One of Beales's men, sent to find the best way to approach Becket Hall. But you know all of that, thanks to eavesdropping outside your father's study last night."

Cassandra bit her bottom lip between her teeth. So, it was just as she'd already suspected, but she'd needed to hear Courtland tell her. "Uncle Jacko questioned him. Isn't that what happened, too? At the smithy? I saw Uncle Jacko just before you arrived. He looked awful, as if he'd been awake all night. Did he…did he kill the man?"

"Callie, please…"

"No! Tell me. Did my uncle torture and then kill this man? And my papa. He was there, wasn't he? Are we…are we barbarians now?"

"Jacko didn't kill him, Callie. Your papa had a plan," Courtland told her quietly. "We wanted the man to escape so that we could follow him, so Jasper tied him up very badly, and then pretended to go to sleep in the smithy. Hell, we even left the doors unlatched and tied a horse up just outside as if it was there to be shoed in the morning. We did everything save saddle the damn horse and point the man in the right direction. All of it your papa's idea, and a good one."

"But you said the man is dead."

Courtland nodded, heading the horses to the left, as if he had a particular destination in mind, although Cassandra wasn't paying much attention. "We followed him, simple enough to do when a dark silhouette against a flat landscape and a cloudy sky is easy enough to make out from a distance if you know what you're looking for. But we kept too much distance between us, and couldn't react in time when another rider came flying out of nowhere. The two horsemen met up and we—Ethan and myself—thought Ainsley brilliant, that our plan was working. Or we did, until the second rider got close enough, pulled out a pistol, and shot our prisoner in the face before galloping off again. The poor dumb bastard had served his purpose, you see, and wasn't needed anymore."

"That means someone else knew you'd captured the man in the first place, doesn't it?"

Courtland smiled ruefully, nodded. "Exactly. It also means that the man we captured was a fool, a dupe sent purposely to lure us out, and we shouldn't have been looking at him, but at whoever else was in the inn, watching him, hoping we'd take him. Which we did, allowing this second man to follow us straight back to Becket Hall."

"By the most direct route, as well." Cassandra shivered.

"And now Beales is certain that we *know* he's out there, watching, waiting. Ainsley says he's playing cat and mouse with us, and right now, the cat is winning. We're stuck here, waiting, while Beales is making all the moves."

For only a moment, Cassandra believed her father was not alone at wishing her back in the nursery, where she could still be innocent, unknowing. What she was hearing, what Courtland was telling her, might prove he no longer thought her a child, but his words were difficult to hear. "And Papa? Is he upset?"

"He's concerned," Courtland said, looking over at her. "There's a reason I'm telling you all of this. Ainsley said again this morning that he's begun to think Beales will never come at us directly, not in force, not the way he attacked the island. He wants you to go to Fanny, all of you women, even Eleanor.

Odette says no, Eleanor can't be riding these roads in a carriage, but your papa is adamant, and so is Jack. You'll all leave in the morning, before dawn, with half our men riding with you for protection. Two days of easy travel, possibly a little more, because of Eleanor, but by keeping to main roads once you're away from Becket Hall, Beales would find it impossible to launch an attack. You'll be safe."

"Will you be one of those men taking us there?" Cassandra asked as the horses approached a ruined stone cottage that was little more than a few broken fences around three half-walls and a chimney, open to the sky. A sad, abandoned place.

Courtland dismounted and came around to help Cassandra from the saddle. He held her waist once she was safely on the ground, looked at her closely. "No, Callie, I won't be going to Brede Manor. The only ones to remain at Becket Hall will be those directly connected to the island. We're what Beales wants, and that's who we're giving him. We're the only lure we have left. We can't let this stalemate go on much longer, and we won't."

She put her hands on his arms, dug her fingertips into his sleeves. "But the Red Men Gang was so large. Hundreds of men. How could you possibly fight them all, with half our men at Brede manor, protecting a few women?"

He smiled. "There were landsmen, carters, those that rode the ships. Beales's hired riders who protected them rarely numbered more than one hundred, and that was years ago, not now. Beales couldn't possibly amass that sort of small army in the time he's had since Lisette wounded him. And remember, we've got Becket Hall, all of our defenses in place. I'm not worried about Edmund Beales. I'm worried about you. I need to know you're safe at Brede Manor. So does your father."

"And if I refuse to leave you? If all of us refuse to leave? What will you do then, Court? Tie us up and throw us into carriages?"

"Callie, please—"

"No! Now you're going to ask me to be reasonable, aren't you? Because you're always so reasonable." Her voice had begun to quiver slightly, making her angrier than she already was, because she didn't want to cry. She wanted to yell, to scream, to shake him until he understood. Her place was here, with him. "I don't want to be reasonable, Court. I just want… Please…just hold me…"

"Callie, I— Damn it! Get behind me. *Now!*"

Cassandra obeyed him without question, even as Courtland drew his pistol free of his waistband and reached for the rifle at the same time.

She heard the hoofbeats now, and ventured a look past Courtland's shoulder, sure that Edmund Beales himself had come to kill them. But then she relaxed, just as Courtland swore under his breath and lowered his rifle.

"Rian," he muttered, shaking his head. "Rian! What in bloody blazes are you doing out here? I was about to blow your head off, you know."

Rian Becket pulled his horse to a plunging stop, grinning from ear to ear. "Interrupted you mid-wooing, have I?"

Cassandra, feeling her cheeks grow hot, stepped completely behind Courtland.

"We thought you should know," Rian said, remaining in the saddle. "A message just arrived from Chance. Beales has most definitely surfaced."

"What? Where?"

Rian lost his smile. "Chance had dinner at one of his clubs two nights ago and overheard two men talking about having taken dinner with Nathanial Beatty. I don't know—someone named Roberts, and a Sir Horatio somebody-or-other. One man said the name Nathaniel Beatty, the other told him to stifle himself if he knew what was good for him, and Chance now has men watching both of them, every move they make, in case they make contact with Beales again. We're getting closer, Court."

"Yes, and Beales is becoming bolder. So he's back to Nathaniel Beatty, is he? His given name, the name he gave to Lisette. He must feel very sure of his victory."

Cassandra watched Rian's face even as she slipped her hand into Courtland's. "Does this mean we can stay here at Becket Hall? If Beales is in London…"

"I don't know, Callie," Rian said. "Court?"

"I'd rather they still left for Brede Manor in the morning. After all, Ainsley will never go to London, give up our superior defensive position, so Beales still has to come here to us, sooner or later."

"And I agree," Rian said, nodding his head. "Before you ask, so do Spence and Ethan. Jack? He's starting to worry more about Elly, that Odette's right, and the journey could prove too dangerous for mother and child. When are you coming back to the house? We need to put our heads together."

"Soon," Courtland said as Cassandra squeezed his hand a little tighter. "We'll be back soon. We still have things to...discuss."

"Callie?" Rian asked, suddenly all brotherly concern. "Are you all right?"

"I'm fine, Rian," she told him, wishing him on the other side of the Marsh. "Tell Papa we'll be back soon. I want to give Athena another run."

"Court? Within the hour, yes?"

"She said she's fine, Rian," Courtland said tersely. "We'll be back by noon."

Rian nodded once more and turned his horse, took off at a gallop, as beautiful and competent a rider as he'd been before his injuries at Waterloo.

Courtland looked at Cassandra. "We could go back now, you know."

To answer him, she removed her fashionable shako hat, hanging it from the sidesaddle, and then turned away from him, to walk around the lowest stone wall, into the ruins of the cottage. What happened between them next would be up to him….

CHAPTER TEN

COURTLAND DAWDLED. There was no other word for what he was doing; checking that the horses were tied up securely, rechecking the pistols in the pouch, turning in a slow, full circle, his eyes on the flat, distant horizon broken only by the two church steeples he could see, one to the East, one to the West, although they were miles apart. The joke had always been that only a fool would think the Marshmen were so close to God—the steeples served as very tall, holy signposts on moonlit nights, and the churches often held more smuggled tea and tobacco than parishioners.

He'd brought Cassandra out here so that they could talk, away from the bustle and observant eyes of Becket Hall.

He'd brought her here to hold her, to kiss her, to perhaps even dare to talk about their future.

No, that wasn't true. That's what he'd thought he wanted to do, before sanity took over, knocked that idea from his head. He'd brought her here to say what had to be said, even if that meant he might be saying goodbye.

"Oh, sweet Jesus," he muttered beneath his breath.

When had it happened? When had everything changed?

When had she become his delight, his joy, the hope of seeing her smile the reason he woke up every morning, the sound of her voice, calling out his name, the only thing that could make his life complete?

For he knew that, in his eyes, his mind, his heart, she was no longer Isabella's child, Geoffrey's child. She was, simply, Cassandra. Callie. *His.*

And yet not his.

Stripping off his riding gloves and shoving them deep into his pocket, Courtland walked past the sagging length of fence, trailing his fingertips along the rough, weathered stone of the cottage wall, stopping just at the end of it. He leaned against the stone, looked at the young woman who sat primly on what was left of the fireplace hearth, combing her fingers through her thick, honey-colored ringlets that might be the bane of her existence but that so flattered her face; her sea-green eyes, her softly rounded chin.

She pushed her fingers into the hair above her ears, drawing it up and away from her face, lifting both her curls and her face toward the sun; a young, healthy animal enjoying the freedom of the Marsh after a long week of confinement. The movement exposed the sweet curve of her cheek, and then she let go, shaking her head so that the ringlets tumbled down past her shoulders once more, and a few soft corkscrew curls kissed at her forehead, blew lightly against her cheeks.

Courtland had a quick, sharp vision of those curls splayed across his pillow, and just as quickly suppressed it. Too fast. After so many years of an often uneasy status quo, things between them were now happening too fast.

"Callie," he said, still with his shoulder leaned against the damp stone, "we should go back."

"In a minute," she said, patting the hearthstone beside her. "I love the smell of the Marsh after rain, don't you? Some people might not, I suppose. I can't believe we'll be leaving here soon. Do you suppose Hampton Roads lies on a marsh? Probably not. At least we'll be near the sea, there is that. I don't think I could survive, living far from the ocean. I don't think Papa could, either."

"A sailor is a sailor," Courtland said, at last giving up the fight and joining her on the hearthstone, the two of them looking out over the waving grasses of the Marsh, watching white clouds scudding across an unusually bright blue sky. Where could he start? How would he say what he knew he must say?

"Yes, I suppose that's it. Although, except for a few short sails on the *Respite,* I couldn't possibly call myself a sailor." She turned to smile at him. "What is it like, Court, to command a ship? Sailing before the wind, nearly one hundred men waiting for your commands, outrunning the Waterguard? Your blood must *sing* with the danger, the adventure of the thing."

Courtland smiled, more than willing to keep the conversation in safer territory for a while longer. That probably made him a coward. "That sort of life is not all that romantic, Callie, and I'm glad we're done with such adventures, to tell you the truth. The Black Ghost, the smuggling runs, all of it. I know it cost Chance a lot, walking away from it all, but I'm not so adventurous. When I was younger, even as young as when we were on the island, I thought I wanted to be just like him, just like the others, like Ainsley. And you know what I discovered?"

She put her hand on his arm, looked at him curiously. "No, tell me what you found out about Courtland Becket."

He covered her hand with his own, sighed. Perhaps there was no safe conversation. Perhaps he simply had to say what must be said. "I realized that I'm a caretaker, a steward, a dull, boring man who wants nothing more of life than his family around him, safe, protected. The family who lived here, Callie? The father died on a smuggling run, leaving behind his wife and a dozen young children, one of whom was killed trying to bring his share of the booty from a smuggling run back to his family. I remember the terror in that woman's eyes, as we told her about her son, took her to see two more of her boys we'd brought to Becket Hall, one wounded, one simply a child again, sobbing for his mother."

"I know that story, so many of the stories. Papa says life has always been hard on the Marsh."

Courtland shook his head. "And it shouldn't be. If the government would pay a decent price for wool, if a man could feed his family with hard work alone. But we've been so isolated here, with the world, even the rest of England, believing Romney Marsh to be a country set apart, too different, too strange. It's why Ainsley chose this spot. Nobody looks too closely at the Marsh, not if he knows what's good for him, for we protect our own."

"You don't want to leave here, do you?" Cassandra asked him, turning to look toward the horizon once more.

"No, I don't," he said honestly, telling her what he'd been thinking, the conclusions he'd come to, not easily, but what was easy in this world? "I have to leave, just as your papa has to leave. Chance has rebuilt his life, he's safe, accepted. Jack is also safe, he and Eleanor, because Jack's only connected to the Beckets through his marriage, and his part in our actions always secret, behind the scenes. The girls are safe with their husbands. But the rest of us? We broke the King's law, Callie, we're known. We've been living on borrowed time for some years now, since I first put on that damned costume and went out to avenge Pike's death. Before the world comes here, we have no choice but to go. We've probably already waited too long. But we need Beales gone now that we know he's after us, no more ghosts to follow us, chase us away from wherever we go next."

"You're blaming yourself, Court? Because you rode out as the Black Ghost? That's ridiculous, you had no real choice. The Red Men Gang couldn't be allowed to control this area of the Marsh."

He smiled at her. It was as if she was helping him prove one of the points he felt he needed to bring home to her. "Now you sound like your papa. No, I really didn't have a choice, being the plodding, protective sort I am, the one who wanted only peace, only safety. I knew we had to risk that peace in order to preserve our safety. I'm only saying that I didn't like it, Callie, I didn't enjoy a minute of it. I'm not some brave, dashing hero out of a Pennypress novel. I'm only a practical man."

"And old," Cassandra teased, leaning her head against his shoulder. "No wonder you shaved all that fuzz off your face. It was probably going to turn gray at any moment. Why, you're nothing but a boring old graybeard, Courtland Becket, and I have no idea why we're here, and I'm hoping you'll kiss me again."

He slipped his arm around her shoulders. He shouldn't have, but some things couldn't be resisted, even for a sane, practical man. "So I haven't dissuaded you? You still think I'm what you want?"

She pushed away from him, leaving her palm pressed against his chest. "I still *know* you're who I want. Everyone knows. You, most especially. Now, unless I disgust you, or you have more arguments prepared for me, more examples like this poor ruined cottage to show me, would you please kiss me, Court? Kiss me now?"

He wanted to, he really did.

"No, Callie. It's time we went back."

She looked at him in clear astonishment. "No? But…but I thought…I…you don't want to kiss me? Is that it?"

"Callie," he said quietly, unable to put what he had to say off any longer, "sometimes…sometimes we only think we know what we want. We might even be surrounded by people—caring, kind people—who think they know what we want, believe they know what's best for us. What's right, what's natural, expected. But that doesn't make it true. It just makes it…convenient."

"Convenient?" Cassandra's eyes had gone wide. "You think I think you're *convenient?* Is that how you see me? As *convenient?* That…that you and I, together, would be convenient? For whom? You? Me? *Everyone else?*"

"Don't…" Courtland said, nearly begged. "I'm only attempting to—"

"Oh, I know what you're *attempting,* Courtland Becket. It's been obvious for a long time. But I thought you'd changed, that you'd finally realized that I— How can you think that I don't know my own mind! That's insulting, Court, it truly is."

This wasn't any easier than he'd imagined the moment to be. "I'm being practical, Callie. You've said it—you only know Romney Marsh. You only know the people here, life here."

"That's nothing but—but twaddle!" She narrowed her eyelids. "You don't want me, do you? You've let me chase after you all of these years, making a perfect fool of myself, but you don't want me. Not really. You kissed me, but you didn't want to kiss me, you only wanted to— Why did you shave off your beard if you didn't plan to kiss me again?"

It was a good question, but one he didn't want to answer, because he had wanted to kiss her again. Do more than kiss her. Much more. But somewhere between the act of shaving off that beard late last night and seeing her sitting at the breakfast table, so young, so innocent, he'd realized that his needs, his wants, had nothing to do with life as it truly was. It was a curse, being the practical one.

"I've given this—us—a lot of thought. You'll soon go to America with Ainsley. A whole new world is about to open up for you, Callie. I've decided to stay here a while longer, or perhaps travel on the continent. I'll…I'll visit in a year or two, and if you still feel the way you think you do now, then—"

"A year or two? No!" She got to her feet, glared

down at him. "Don't lie to me, Courtland. Don't put me off with promises about some vague *someday.* You can't wait for me to be gone, can you? God, what a trial I must be to you. Morgan *tarting* me up and pointing me at you the night we sang together, Spence and Rian and everyone teasing you, all but telling you that you have no choice but to— *God!*"

Courtland grabbed at her arm as he stood up, because she was about to run from him. He had to make her understand. Didn't he? Wasn't it important that she understood, even if he didn't quite understand himself? "Callie, wait. I never said I didn't want you."

"Really?" Her eyes were shooting green fire at him now, her chest rising and falling quickly. "Then prove that to me, Court. Prove it to me now."

He shook his head. "You still don't understand what I'm trying to say. I'm trying to protect you."

"Protect me? How? Make me understand, Courtland," she demanded as a cloud slid across the sun, throwing the Marsh into shadow. "You tell me to wait, even as you tell me you want me. Make me believe you. Make me believe you're not just saying you want me because you think that's what I want to hear."

His mind exploding, his heart still caught between demons pulling him toward her and away from her at the same time, he crushed her against him, brought his mouth down, hard.

She moaned against his lips, her hands grasping at him, her arms sliding up and over his shoulders, clinging to him as he deepened their kiss, at last gave into the temptation of her sweet curves, cradling her breast in his palm, sliding his thumb between two buttons of her jacket, to burn against the silk of her bare skin.

He felt her shudder, probably shocked by this new intimacy, but this was what she thought she wanted, and what he knew he desired more than breath, more than life itself.

With his free hand, he cupped her buttocks, pulled her against him, let her feel his arousal. He slipped his hand lower, easing it beneath her, between the split-leg fabric of her riding skirt, pressing into her softness, lifting her against his manhood, condemning himself to the frustration he would feel once he let her go.

If he let go.

He had to let her go…

"Court?" she whispered as he broke off the kiss and she was looking up at him once more, this time with a thousand questions in her eyes. And, perhaps, just a little maidenly fear.

"Enough, Callie," he said, stepping away from her, turning his back to her. "Don't…don't ever think I don't want you. But it may not be what you want, not really. It…*I* may just be what you feel you should want. The reality, what goes on between a man and a woman, may not be what you want at all."

She put her crossed hands to her breast. "You think I only want the dream? Is that what you're saying? That this reality is more than I might have bargained for?"

He turned to face her once more. "And was it?"

"I…I don't know," she said, and he could see that she was uncertain about her feelings for him, and with herself, perhaps for the first time in a life of thinking she knew just what and whom she wanted. "What I do know, Court, is that you've been lying to at least one of us all morning."

And with that she was gone, lifting her skirts and running back toward the horses. By the time he'd mentally kicked himself for being eight kinds of a fool, she had walked Athena over to a small pile of stones from the cottage and had mounted, ready to ride back to Becket Hall.

He lifted himself into the saddle. "Callie?"

"Leave it be, Court," she told him, her head held high. "I think we've done more than enough talking for now. I just want to go home."

Without another word, he turned Poseidon and led the way back to the beaten track through the tall grasses, feeling every one of the thirteen years that separated him from Cassandra.

Once the track widened, Cassandra urged Athena forward, and flew past Courtland at a full gallop, leaving him to follow, giving her some distance between them, until Becket Village was in sight and Athena slowed, Cassandra cooling the horse on the way to the stable yard.

He caught up with her and she turned to look at him. "I want to apologize, Court," she said, surprising him with her calm, even tone. "I don't know how you put up with me all of these years."

He attempted a smile. "You sound as if you're saying goodbye, Callie."

She smiled, and hers was a very real smile. "No, not goodbye. Oh, goodbye to the Callie you knew, definitely. The pest, I suppose. You…um…I was a little frightened. Back there? You were right. I never…I never felt that like before."

Courtland didn't know what to say, other than to tell her the truth. "If it makes you feel any less apprehensive, neither have I. I don't know what's going to happen, Callie. But you're definitely not a child anymore. No mere child could make me wonder what in bloody blazes I'm about, make me feel as if I'm in constant danger of my mind slipping its moorings."

Her smile disappeared. "Good. I think I like hearing that. Court? Am I a tease? Am I…have I been chasing after you, with no notion of what to do if I ever caught you? Is that what happened back there? Is that what you're afraid of?"

"I'm not afraid of— Yes, all right, I do worry about that. Do you know something else, Callie? We have the oddest conversations. Perhaps we know each other too well."

"Or we don't really know each other at all, but just what we suppose we know," she said, looking away from him, toward the huge, faintly ugly structure that had been their shared home and haven for so many years, now looking even more the fortress on its isolated beach, surrounded with overt and concealed defenses. "Court? Look, are those soldiers?"

Court urged Poseidon ahead on the track, motioning with one arm for Cassandra to remain where she was for the moment. Even from this distance, he could see the bright scarlet of the uniform jackets of at least a dozen soldiers, most of them on horseback, a few standing beside a plain, black, closed coach. It wasn't that unusual for the Waterguard to visit Becket Hall while out on patrol, but everything that happened now was looked upon as suspicious.

Even as he and Cassandra watched, one of the large double doors of Becket Hall opened and Ainsley Becket stepped out into the sunlight, a soldier holding on to each of his bent arms, his hands tied together at the wrist.

"Christ!" Courtland exploded, digging his heels into Poseidon's flanks, racing the remaining hundred yards or more, slipping down out of the saddle almost before the stallion plunged to a halt. "Ainsley!"

Jack Eastwood had followed Ainsley down the stone steps and quickly crossed to where Courtland stood, watching in disbelief as Ainsley was pushed into the coach, the door slamming behind him. "He's been placed under arrest, Court," Jack said quietly. "Don't say anything, don't do anything. He's charged with piracy and murder, crazy as that sounds. I tried to get the bastards to say more, but Ainsley warned me off, and Rian and Spencer had their hands full trying to restrain Jacko. They're taking him to Dover Castle, for trial. He wants us to— Christ Almighty, stop her!"

Courtland bounded forward, grabbing Cassandra around the waist from behind and lifting her up off the ground, turning so that her back was to the coach.

"Let me go! Put me down! Papa! *Papa!*"

"Callie, don't!" Courtland shouted as she struggled to be free of him, somehow managing to turn herself around in his arms. She was like a wildcat, kicking and scratching to free herself from a trap, beating on him with her fists as she strained to see Ainsley as the coach began to move off down the drive. "He'll be fine. I'll fix this. I promise, sweetheart. *I'll fix this.*"

She collapsed against him at last, her entire body trembling, sobbing as if her heart would break. "It's what you were saying out there. We waited too long," she whispered brokenly against his jacket. "We waited too long to go. *Oh, Papa...*"

Courtland slipped one arm beneath her knees and lifted her into his arms, close against his chest, and carried her into the house, Jack and several residents of Becket Village following right behind him.

"In the drawing room," Jack told him. "We're all in there."

Courtland expected to walk into a madhouse of

shouting men and weeping women, but the drawing room was silent, although all the Beckets save Eleanor were there, sitting or standing like statues. He put Cassandra down on the couch next to Mariah, who quickly grabbed her into a tight embrace, crooning to her as she would to one of her children.

Spencer stepped forward, a thick sheet of vellum in his hand. Courtland grabbed the thing, and could immediately see the seals marking it as an official warrant for the arrest of one Geoffrey Baskin.

"Baskin?" He looked at Spencer. "How did they— Why didn't he deny it? Tell them he's Ainsley Becket. He's been known as Ainsley Becket by everyone for nearly twenty years. They can't prove anything. Can they?"

Spencer pushed his fingers into his hair, grimacing. "We watched their approach from a good mile away. Ainsley knew. I don't know how he did, but he knew. He called us all in here, to wait, and warned us not to say a word, not a single word, no matter what happened. He…he even smiled—not a good smile, let me tell you—and said his greatest sin in life was that he'd always underestimated Edmund Beales. Jesus, Court, they're going to hang him."

"Pounded on the door like they were announcing Prinny himself," Rian said, picking up the story as the always volatile Spencer pinched his fingers to the bridge of his nose, Courtland fairly certain the man was wiping away tears without wanting anyone to know the depth of his concern. "Jacob let them in, just as he was told to, and the Lieutenant marched in here with five of his men, demanding Geoffrey Baskin and one Jacko—no surname known. Papa stood up immediately, said he was Geoffrey Baskin. That's when Jacko started cursing and threatening, and we had to drag him away before he damn well volunteered himself, as well. Ethan?"

The Earl of Aylesford kissed his wife's hand and left her on one of the couches to cross the room. "There really wasn't anything we could do, Court, after Ainsley said that. They were armed, we weren't. I think Ainsley was doing his best to protect the rest of us. I did demand to see the warrant you're holding now, but Ainsley acted as if he already knew what was written on it. And then…" he looked at Jack for a moment "…and then they asked if there was a woman named Eleanor in residence."

"Elly? In God's name, why? Were they going to arrest her, too?" Courtland asked, realizing the lines of strain on Jack Eastwood's face weren't confined to his worry about Ainsley. "That makes no sense."

"Yes, Court, it does," Jack said, sighing. "Ethan pushed at the Lieutenant, all the arrogant, important Earl, and the man finally told us that they had good reason to suspect that, after murdering the Earl and Countess of Chelfham during an act of piracy against the Crown, Geoffrey Baskin had either murdered or taken as prize their young daughter, Eleanor. We, of course, denied Eleanor's existence. Christ, I have to go up there. What am I going to tell her?"

"I'll go," Cassandra said, getting to her feet, and Courtland looked at her, sure she couldn't manage such a delicate task, not when she was so terrified for her father. But she looked deadly calm, resolute, even as she wiped a last, single tear from her cheek. "If she sees that I'm confident, then she'll be confident, too. Papa said I was to take care of Elly and Odette, and that's what I'm going to do. I'm going to do what Papa said. Morgan?"

Morgan immediately got to her feet, reached out a hand to Mariah, and then looked at Lisette, sitting very quietly, as if wishing to disappear. "Lisette? I think we'll need *all* of the Becket women for this one."

Lisette looked to Rian, who only nodded, and the knot of the curious parted to let them walk through, Cassandra waiting until they were all in the foyer to turn to Courtland. When she lifted her gaze to his, it was firm, sure, clear-eyed. "You said you're practical, Court, and I said I was all grown-up. So I'll be grown-up, and you be practical, because that's what Papa needs now, doesn't he?"

She turned in a full circle, eying each of the men one by one. "We'll do what we have to do here. Now you men go find some way to bring Papa home."

His brain reeling with half-formed plans, Courtland was silent until everyone else had left the drawing room before turning to his brothers, to Ethan and Jack.

"Home? We already know he can never come back here, and we've got to get most everyone who came here with us from the island gone, as well, as they hang the crew, as well as the captain. Jesus! Who thought we'd ever hear the name Geoffrey Baskin again? We've got to find a way to protect Becket Hall while we're also finding a way to get Ainsley out of prison and out of the country. Quickly."

"I already know what he wants us to do," Jack said on a sigh. "The frigate is fully provisioned. He'd tell us to bring the women and children back and load everyone from Becket Village who wants to go on it and send the ship off as soon as possible to Hampton Roads. But we need a captain, as Ainsley was going to fill that role himself. Court? How about you?"

"I'm not leaving until we get him back," Court said shortly. "I agree, though, we need to get these people gone before the soldiers return with warrants for everyone who sailed on the *Black Ghost* and the *Silver Ghost*. Will Jacko do?"

Spencer shook his head. "A November crossing? He's past it, don't you think? Besides, he won't leave here without Ainsley. My God, we're all going, aren't we?"

"No. Eleanor and I are staying here, at Becket Hall," Jack said quietly, looking slightly abashed. "That's also been discussed. And several dozen of the younger ones from Becket Village will remain, as well. Ainsley has written detailed instructions in case something happened to him, and shown them to me, believing I'd be objective, simply follow orders. It's…it's as if he had some sort of premonition. I'll go get them now."

"And I'll go right now to write a note to Chance, and another to Valentine. We're going to need every head we can muster to think up a miracle," Spencer said, already heading for Ainsley's study.

"Court?" Rian said as Courtland read the warrant a second time. "They'll move him from gaol to gaol, slowly, under heavy guard, giving us a couple of days, but that's all we've got. Once he's locked up in Dover Castle, it will be hell to pay to get him out."

Courtland was trying to decipher the signature at the bottom of the page. The Right Honorable Francis Roberts. Roberts? Hadn't Rian said that was one of the names Chance had mentioned? Edmund Beales had made his first move, and they were in trouble; they were all in deep, deep trouble. "Then the answer is simple, isn't it?" he said quietly, looking at his brother. "We can't let them get as far as Dover Castle."

CHAPTER ELEVEN

CASSANDRA CLOSED THE door to Eleanor's bedchamber a full hour after midnight, lifting her exhausted gaze from the hallway floor to see Courtland leaning against the wall, his arms crossed, looking at her. Simply looking at her.

He appeared as tired as she felt, his hair mussed, his neck cloth askew, his eyes shadowed. She'd never needed to see him more than she did now.

Without a word, she went to him, pressed her cheek against his chest as he wrapped his arms around her. Held her close.

For long moments, they didn't speak. There was no reason. They both just held on.

"How's Elly?" Courtland asked at last, guiding Cassandra down the hallway, toward her own bedchamber.

"Still angry," Cassandra told him. "She still seems to believe she somehow can make a difference, go to Dover Castle and plead Papa's case, or something like that. Jack has his hands full with her, we all do, especially once Jack pointed out that, mistake or not, misled thanks to trickery by Edmund Beales or not, Papa did sink an English ship. Did you know that Jacko killed her mother? Morgan told me when Elly was at last taking a small nap."

"Yes. I'd rather you didn't know about that, though. He had reason to do what he did, but his life's never been the same. There's not going to be a trial, in any case. We won't let it go that far."

She looked up at him hopefully. "You've decided on a plan?"

"We have a few plans, some already set in motion. But there's time for all of that in the morning. You must be exhausted."

"No, no I'm not," Cassandra lied quickly. "I'm angry, Court. I'm as angry as Elly, even more than Elly. At first…at first I just wanted to die, seeing Papa with his wrists shackled like that, being pushed into that horrible black coach. But now I'm angry. How dare they! How dare Edmund Beales be able to have the Crown do his bidding like this?"

"Money is a powerful weapon, I suppose. We'd hoped for a private war, a final settlement of old hurts, but Beales obviously didn't want that." Courtland depressed the latch, pushed open the door to her bedchamber. "How's Odette? Sheila Whiting told me she's not with Elly, that she's retired downstairs, to her own rooms."

"Oh, Court, it was terrible," Cassandra said, not entering her chamber. "She had no idea, none, for all her supposed powers. She listened to what we had to say, and then just sat in her chair, rocking back and forth, keening quietly, like a woman in mourning, I suppose. The way Madge Everett did when her little Johnny drowned. I think she's even more ill than she let Papa know."

"Damn. This poses yet another problem we hadn't thought of on our own," Courtland said, as if talking to himself. "If she's that sick, and with Elly needing her at any moment, I suppose, Odette won't be able to leave Becket Hall. Rian and Spencer and I are going to try to visit with him tomorrow at the garrison in Dymchurch. I don't know that your father will agree to leave England, though, not without first coming back here, to say his farewells to Elly, to Odette. But that's going to be dangerous."

Cassandra slipped her hand into his, drew him into her dark bedchamber, and then left him standing there, lost in thought, as she lit a few candles. He didn't seem to even notice that he'd followed her. "They aren't taking him directly to Dover Castle? Why?"

"We left that one up to Jack, who seems to know more about such things. The law moves slowly, and Ainsley will be kept in Dymchurch, and then even paraded through Hythe and Folkestone for some days before the final move to Dover Castle. Jack said each garrison enjoys showing off a captive as dangerous as a pirate or murderer, share in some of the credit. It's all meant to impress the populace with the idea that crime is never rewarded. I'm afraid we're in for a circus."

Cassandra thought of the secret drawer and its contents. "And Edmund Beales? You all think he will be content with this, seeing Papa humiliated, put on trial? Hanged?"

"No, we don't. We've also sent a good dozen men following after the coach, with orders to surround the gaol at all times. Rian's already gone to join them, taking Jasper with him. None of us believes we'll be the only ones who will attempt to free him. It's genius, actually. Why attack us here, when moving Ainsley to a place where he's more vulnerable makes everything easier? Especially when you control the magistrate, and probably the judges."

"I don't understand most of this. Deviousness, I suppose. I just want Papa to be safe."

"And that's all you need to worry about, Callie," he told her.

She climbed up on her tester bed, tucking her legs beneath her. She'd been thinking about something for most of the day and night, and had come to the conclusion she was sure her father wanted. "I don't think so. We have to protect Becket Hall, be just as vigilant as we've been this past month or more. If Beales can't get to Papa, and even if he does, he will still have to come here."

"*Have* to come here?" Courtland joined her,

leaning against the side of the bed. "And why do you think that, Callie?"

"Because he wants the Empress," Cassandra said quietly. "Beales has always wanted it."

She saw the confusion in Courtland's eyes and knew that her father hadn't confided in him about the emerald. Jacko and Billy knew, Odette, but he'd never told anyone else but her, never shown anyone else the secret drawer. She felt rather special, knowing that her father had so trusted her. But it was time everyone else knew what she knew.

She slid down off the bed, held out her hand to him. "Come downstairs with me. I have something to show you."

They passed by the drawing room on their way and Cassandra turned into the room, Courtland still holding her hand as they walked to the fireplace, to the portrait hanging above it.

"I hate Edmund Beales, with everything that's in me. I didn't know I could hate like this," she said, looking up at the portrait, at her mother's young, beautiful, smiling face. "He took my mother from me, Court," she said fiercely, "but I'll be *damned* if he'll have my father, as well. Whatever I have to do, I swear this right now, he won't have him!"

She used her free hand to wipe at the tears stinging her eyes, and squared her shoulders as she looked at Courtland. "I'm a part of this, Court. I know what I said earlier, that we'd all take care of Elly, and you men would find a way to rescue Papa. But we've all talked about this—Morgan, Mariah, Lisette and I—and we can't just sit here, waiting, not knowing. Whatever you do, whatever you decide, we're going to be a part of that plan. And I'm sure Fanny and Julia will feel the same."

"We can't have you involved," Courtland told her, shaking his head, "not with the rescue. Breaking into a gaol, possibly shooting some of the King's own men, if it comes to that? It's too dangerous. We need you women here, protected behind these walls. If we can deal with Beales away from Becket Hall, fine, but if he has gathered enough men to make an assault here, we have to know you're all safe."

"I'm going to see Papa tomorrow in Dymchurch," Cassandra told him doggedly, pulling her hand free of his. "Either I go with you, or I follow you, but I will see him."

"No, absolutely not. You look too much like Isabella. If Beales sees you, he'll come after you directly. He'll use you against Ainsley," Courtland told her as she turned on her heel and headed back to the foyer, turned in the direction of Ainsley's study. "I won't put you in harm's way like that."

"Morgan says we're just as able to aim a pistol as—"

"I don't care what Morgan says, she's not donning breeches and racing off like some wild-eyed Boadicea, much as I'm sure she sees herself in that role. Right now, Ethan's probably informing Morgan that the two of them are leaving for Brede Manor at first light to tell Fanny and Valentine what's happened. The plan is to have them all then travel to London as quickly as possible, to argue your father's case on its merits, to petition for a pardon before there's time for a trial. Both men have friends in positions of power—Valentine's friends with Wellington himself, and Ethan feels there's a fair chance a pardon could be possible. For Ainsley, for Jacko, for the entire crew, with the provision that they all leave England. What we've got to do is keep your father alive long enough to get that pardon."

Cassandra crossed her arms, gripped her elbows tight in her frustration. "That's…that's probably a wonderful idea. But…but I have to do more. I can't just stay here, Court."

"You told me Ainsley asked you to take care of Elly and Odette."

"I *know* what he told me," she said as they entered the study. "But that…that doesn't count, now that he's been arrested. Mariah and Lisette will still be here for Elly. I'm going to stay in Dymchurch, or Folkestone, or wherever Papa is. You men probably shouldn't be too obvious in any case, visiting Papa, not with Beales or his cohorts watching the gaol, correct?"

Courtland shoved his fingers through his hair, leaned against the desk. "Correct. We thought we'd use Sheila Whiting to take him food and fresh clothing, pass him messages."

"But Sheila has to stay here," Cassandra said quickly, feeling she was now employing her trump card. "With Odette so unwell, Sheila will be the one to deliver Elly's baby when the time comes. Which, since you've sent all the other women away, means that I'm still the logical choice. I'll wear my cape, keep the hood over my hair, careful to keep my head lowered as I go in and out of the gaol straight from a coach pulled up just outside the doorway, so no one can see my face. Jacob Whiting can escort me, and the rest of you can watch from hiding to make sure no one approaches us. I'll be safe as houses. Please, Court? *Please?*"

"I'll speak to the others about it, give you our decision in the morning," he said after a few moments, exasperation, as well as fatigue evident in his voice. "If you're going to go with us, we'll be leaving at dawn, along with Morgan and Ethan. But I'm not promising you anything, do you understand? Now show me whatever it is you think I need to see, and then get to bed."

Cassandra decided not to push him. She'd simply be dressed and ready to go, before dawn.

She went over to the map table and bent down, for she had only opened the drawer twice while her Papa was in the room with her, and neither time had been without having to first fumble her fingers along the wood to find the small latch. It took a full minute, during which Courtland kept attempting different arguments as to why she should remain at Becket Hall before the latch depressed and the small drawer slid open on its own.

"What in bloody hell—?" Courtland said, pushing away from the desk.

"Hold out your hand," she said, much as Ainsley had said to her. "And it's small, I agree, and fragile, but heavier than you might think, so be careful."

She opened the strings of the pouch and poured the Empress into Courtland's hand, then held her breath as she waited for his reaction.

It wasn't long in coming. "Sweet Christ Almighty," he said, picking up the large stone, holding it to the candlelight, so that the majority of the emerald, emerging from the surrounding stone, glowed a bright, grass-green. "*This* is the Empress? All these years and he's never…this is what Beales wanted? No mercy, no quarter, until it was his? That's why he tortured everyone, to find out where this damned piece of stone was? He killed babies for *this?*"

Cassandra grabbed Courtland's wrist as he pulled back his arm, as if to throw the priceless stone against the nearest wall. "No! We need this, Court! It's what Beales wants. We can—"

He lowered his arm, sagged back against a corner of the desktop. "We can use it as a bargaining chip. Yes, I understand. But a rock, Callie. A damned piece of pretty stone. How many people died for it? Your mother, more than one hundred more. I—is the man insane?"

Jacko spoke from the doorway. "That stone's got powers, that's what Edmund said. A man filled to the brim with superstition, that's Edmund. Free her from her moorin's, polish her up all pretty like, and release the power. To live beyond your time. For wealth beyond your imaginin'. Good luck not just followin' you all the days of your life, but chasin' after you, to shower all your dreams over your head. Own a stone like that and rule the world. Should have seen it when the Cap'n showed the thing to him. Never looked at a woman with that much passion, Edmund didn't, not even your mother, Callie."

Courtland turned to watch Jacko lumber into the room, collapse his bulk onto the couch that seemed like the man's second home for these past nearly twenty years. "So it was Ainsley who found it?"

Jacko nodded, let his chin remain lowered on his broad chest. "Luck of the draw. Two Spanish ships. Edmund took the one, we took the other. Ainsley got the Empress."

"We can give it to him, can't we, Uncle Jacko?" Cassandra asked, having come to that decision on her own, hours earlier. "We'll give it to him, and he'll go away. And it will all be over. No reason to want Papa dead, no reason to come here to Becket Hall. It's as Papa told me, the stone's never done him any good. Why not just give it to Beales, if he wants it so badly?"

Jacko chuckled, looking at Courtland. "Women, eh? And shall we invite him for tea while we're about it? All nice and civilized? Are you daft, girl?"

Cassandra looked to Courtland.

"We want to be free of the past, Callie," he told her, "and so does Beales. It's clear he wants to move in London society, but how can he do that when we're still alive? Any one of us could come forward, brand him a pirate, just as he has already done to us. We're...we're each other's dirty linen, I'm afraid."

"Not to mention that he hates your papa with the hate of ten thousand men," Jacko told her, pushing his hands down on his knees as he levered himself to his feet. "I wouldn't trust Edmund Beales as far as I could toss Becket Hall itself. He measures the world by his own yardstick, so he won't rest until we're all dead and buried, and his past along with us. Because, even if our word is good, he won't believe it, as his own word never has been good for anythin' save foulin' the air as he gives it. I'm for bed. Put that trinket away—it offends my eyes."

Cassandra waited until Jacko had left the room before opening the pouch so that Courtland could slip the Empress back into it, and then returned it to the secret drawer. "I had hoped..."

"I know. I was already thinking of a few different ways we could use the Empress before Jacko came into the room," Courtland told her pulling her into his arms. "But I think we have to defer to Jacko on this,

Callie. All seeing that stone tells me is that Beales will definitely come here."

She slid her arms around his waist, closed her eyes as he held her, gently stroked her hair.

He kissed her temple, put her from him as he walked to the drinks table, poured himself a glass of wine. "What did your father say about the stone?"

"Only that it never brought him good luck. But I don't think he wants Beales to have it, not now." She summoned a small smile. "While he was teaching me how to work the secret drawer he said that bad luck has to wear off at some point. I think he wants the Empress to remain with the family. He said we'd certainly paid a high enough price for it. I don't think he wants to turn it over to the Crown, in any case, or he would have done so long ago."

"At the moment, I'm for shattering it to bits with a hammer, and then sprinkling those pieces so the sands can swallow them. When you see Ainsley tomorrow, you can ask him what he wants us to do with it."

"Then you've decided I can go?" She ran into his arms, nearly knocking the wineglass out of his hand. "Oh, thank you!"

This time when his arms went around her she lifted her face to his, waited for his kiss. Longed for his kiss.

Waited in vain.

"Good night, Callie," he said quietly, releasing her.

Another time, she would have argued with him. Teased him. But not now, not tonight. Whatever was growing between them, whether it was a new and different bond or an unanticipated division they might never be able to breach, wasn't important right now.

Frustrating. Maddening. But not important.

She could only hope that they'd be given the gift of time to sort out their feelings, and the chance for a future, here, or in America.

"Good night, Court," she said, and left the room.

She was almost at the front stairs when she heard the sound of a glass shattering against a wall, the sound definitely coming from the study, and for the first time since riding back to Becket hall that morning, Cassandra smiled.

CHAPTER TWELVE

THE PRACTICAL ONE. *The steady, dependable one, counted on to keep a clear head no matter what the crisis. He prided himself on that, believed himself to be a sober, reasonable man. Had made it his mission in life to be the one everyone else turned to, the one who protected them all.*

So what in hell was he doing, sitting beside Cassandra in the coach on their way to Dymchurch, wanting nothing more than to hold her, kiss her, take them both away from all this madness? To go someplace where the past meant nothing, where they could build a future for the two of them.

"Court?"

He shook himself free of what had to be traitorous thoughts, and smiled at her. "For the third time, Callie, no. I will not give you a pistol so that you can attempt to smuggle it inside your father's cell. Sulk, pout, refuse to speak to me completely, but don't ask me that question again, all right?"

"I wasn't going to ask you again," Cassandra told

him, coming very close to a pout, but then smiling at him. "I was only going to ask you if you have any other questions for Papa."

"No, I don't think so. What's most important is that you assure him that we're all safe, that Jacko is still at Becket Hall and not under arrest, and that Odette is taking good care of Elly, who is also fine."

"Odette has taken to her bed, and Elly is driving Jack around the bend, demanding that she be allowed to speak to the authorities, prove that she is no more a captive than is the King of England."

"Considering that Farmer George spends most of his time in a straight waistcoat, mumbling to himself or having lively conversations with potted ferns, I don't think that's quite the comparison we want to use," Courtland told her, smiling at last. "But we have no choice but to lie to him, Callie. What good would it do to tell him the truth?"

"He must feel so helpless," Callie said, sighing. "I hate the thought of seeing him locked up in a cage."

He took her hand in his. "A sight he and I, everyone, wishes to spare you. It's not too late to change your mind, Callie. If Beales is somewhere close, watching, he'd recognize Rian, and perhaps Spencer, as well, but he wouldn't know me. I was too withdrawn from the crowd, too much in the background, to have gained his attention on the island."

"No. I'll do this. I won't promise that I won't cry, but I will do this. Where will we go…afterward?"

"There's a small inn we know, just a mile outside of Dymchurch. Rian was instructed to rent every available room. The innkeeper, Fairchild, has benefited from the Black Ghost's assistance a time or two over the years, and we've asked that he close the inn to other travelers for as long as we need it."

"Your plan, I suppose."

He nodded. "We'll take a circuitous route each time we go to the inn, although we'll surely be followed once you've made your first visit to the gaol. With any luck, we'll be able to not only see who is following us, but capture a few of them, ask them some questions. Damn, I still don't believe I'm letting you do this."

"You're not allowing me to do this, Court. I'm doing it because even the cruelest gaoler wouldn't deny a daughter's wish to see her papa."

He looked at her, her resemblance to Isabella so startling inside the dimness of the coach. "Just keep that hood covering your face. It's not beyond belief that Ainsley has more than one daughter, but if Beales knows you're also Isabella's daughter, that you weren't killed in the raid, there's going to be hell to pay."

"He believes he killed everyone, doesn't he?"

Courtland shook his head. "He has to know that Odette escaped the slaughter. The more I think about this, the more I know you shouldn't be seen, even if you keep your hood up on your way from the coach to the gaol. Morgan would have been best suited for this, but she's friends with the wives of some powerful men in Parliament, so she's needed in London as much as Ethan, or Fanny and Valentine."

"And Mariah is best suited to stay with Elly, and Lisette is—well, surely not Lisette. She can't be within miles of her horrible father. Why are you still frowning? It's my hair, isn't it? It's so much lighter than Mama's, but just as curled." She lifted her hands to her head, pushed her hair back straight from her face. "Here, look at me now. Do I still look so much like her?"

He looked at her, felt his heart turn over. She was so exquisite, like a porcelain doll, with her rounded chin and cheeks, the slight blush to her honeyed skin, the pouting fullness of her mouth. All she'd managed to do, pushing her curls out of the way, was to emphasize her youth, her innocent beauty. Isabella had been more slender, her cheekbones slightly sharper, her eyes darker. But there was no denying the resemblance.

"That might be worse," he said, attempting to remain rational, while he tried to tamp down another realization—that Cassandra was all grown-up. She was showing him a woman's face. The last of the child had left her eyes yesterday, as she watched her father being carried off to prison. "I should have stayed with my original plan and brought Sheila Whiting."

"Then *I'll* be Sheila Whiting," Cassandra said, grabbing his forearm. "Really, Court, why can't I be her? A servant from Becket Hall, come to fetch her master some meat pie and fresh linen?"

Again, Courtland shook his head. "There's a chance the officer in charge will then just take the bundle of clothing, eat the meat pie himself, and not let you see him at all. That's really why I decided that you could do this. They won't refuse a daughter. Sheila, bless her, couldn't have passed herself off as a daughter of the house if we had months in which to school her in how to behave. To say nothing of the fact that she's missing one of her top front teeth."

Cassandra giggled, laid her head against his shoulder. "Why, Courtland Becket, anyone would think you're a snob."

Unbelieving that he could find something amusing in this entire mess, Courtland found himself smiling again. "Yes, I suppose I am. After all, we're all so civilized now, aren't we? Real Englishmen."

"Soon to be Americans, some of us," Cassandra reminded him. "You are coming with us, aren't you? You can't plan to remain here, not once we break the law again, taking Papa from the gaol. Isn't that another reason you've told Jack he cannot be involved with anything you do? So that he and Elly can remain at Becket Hall?"

"Chance, Valentine and Ethan will be able to keep Jack away from any problems, or at least that's what we're hoping. But, no, I probably won't be able to remain in England."

She actually looked smug. "So you'll be sailing to America with Papa and me."

He looked at her for a long time, and then nodded. "Yes. I'm coming with you. I don't know why I ever thought I wouldn't."

She launched herself into his arms and he held on tightly, pressed a kiss against the side of her neck.

He wanted to say so much more. Warn her that nothing was really settled between them. She was still so young, had seen so little of the world, not that he was exactly a world traveler himself, having rarely left Romney Marsh, and then only to cross the Channel for a night or two at a time as the Black Ghost.

But she'd never danced with anyone but her brothers, never had been flirted with by some handsome young fool twice as clever as he; no one had ever stolen a kiss from her in a dark garden.

"Do you love me, Court?" she asked against his ear.

"I've always loved you, Callie," he answered, putting a bit of distance between them as the coach wheels began to roll over the cobbled streets of Dymchurch. "From the moment you were born."

She rolled her eyes at him, blew an errant lock of corkscrewed curl up and out of her face. "That's not what I asked, and you know it. Morgan said you'd say something stupid and vague like that if I asked you, and you've just proved her right. Are you *in* love with me?"

"Now's not the time to begin such a lengthy discussion," he told her as the coach turned a corner and came to a halt, none too soon to save his sanity. "Once your father is free, once we're in America…"

"I see," she said, all the sparkle leaving her eyes. "Shall we then make an appointment to have this *discussion?* After all, you're such a *practical* man."

"Callie—"

But she held up her hands, warning him to silence. "No. Not another word, Court. I shouldn't have pushed at you, I know that. I knew that before I asked the question. I shouldn't have said anything. But don't you ever wish to *not* be so solid, so dependable? So—so unselfish? To not think first of Papa, or of anyone else for that matter, but just of *you?* Of *me?*"

"I think we're here," Courtland said in what he hoped wasn't obvious relief, lowering the shade on the off-window and looking out onto the street.

The very crowded street.

"Who are all those people?" Cassandra asked, giving up her argument to lean in close beside him, and he quickly pushed her away from the window before anyone could see her face.

"I don't know. We're still a good block away from the gaol," he said, raising the shade once more. "Stay here. And *don't* look out the window again."

"Yes, yes of course. I'm sorry. I won't look out again. Just come back, all right?"

He touched his fingers to her cheek reassuringly. "I'll be back for you, I promise." Then he opened the door on the other side of the coach and jumped down onto the cobblestones, saw that theirs wasn't the only conveyance brought to a halt in the congested street. He walked to the front of the coach to look up at Jacob Whiting and Waylon who sat on the box holding a nasty-looking blunderbuss balanced across his knees.

"Can't go no closer, Court," Waylon said, spitting tobacco juice onto the ground not a foot from Court's boot. "Want us to give a blow on the tin, push the horses through 'em?"

"No, I'd rather not call attention to us, not with Callie inside the coach. Wait here. I'll go see if I can find out what's going on, although I already have some idea. They may have Ainsley on exhibit, like an animal from the Tower Zoo. We can't let Callie see that."

"True enough. Not much for seein' such a sad, sorry thing m'self, not the Cap'n," Waylon said, his long, hound-dog face looking even more sad and world-weary than usual. "A proud man, the Cap'n."

Courtland nodded his agreement and walked toward the rear of the crowd made up of mostly men, although there were a few women also there, holding on to the hands of young children brought to the gaol to learn an edifying lesson about what it means to break the King's laws.

He nudged, and excused himself, and kept on moving, on the lookout for Rian or any of the men from Becket Hall, who had damned well better be standing close to Ainsley if he was on show. Ignoring anyone who cursed him for pushing in front of them, he only stopped when he was finally near enough to see Ainsley standing on a wooden box on the raised flagway in front of the gaol, still dressed in the now rumpled clothing he'd worn the day before, both his wrists and ankles chained now, his posture straight, his chin high, his look as he gazed out over his fellow men one of mingled pity and disdain.

The man was magnificent, even in chains, ten—twenty—times the man of any other man in all of Dymchurch, in most of the known world. And this was how he was being treated!

"Jesus," Courtland breathed under his breath, his hands squeezing into fists when he realized that Ainsley's left cheek was bruised, and there was a small cut over his eye. Perhaps from a fall, his steps confined by the irons, or perhaps from a push that sent him flying against a stone wall of the gaol.

"They'll pay for this, whoever is behind this show," Rian said, stepping up beside Courtland, who turned to see that Rian was dressed in rather nondescript clothing, a rough woolen seaman's jacket hung over his shoulder, concealing the fact that half his left arm was missing, which could have identified him to Beales. "My money's on the blond one holding the whip—see him? Lieutenant, but with the look of a bully."

Courtland scanned the half dozen soldiers standing guard on either side of Ainsley and quickly saw the man Rian had pointed out to him. His uniform fit him badly, and he wore the self-satisfied smirk of a man who would find petty torture a fine entertainment. "I see him."

"Good. But don't worry about him. He's mine," Rian said tightly. "Damn, now what?"

Courtland looked toward Ainsley once more, in time to see a tall, painfully thin man dressed in funereal black from head to toe and holding a Bible stepping up onto another wooden box. He also noticed the man's white collar, gaping badly around a curiously long, stick-thin neck. "A man of the cloth? I think we're about to be treated to an edifying sermon on seeds that fall on shallow soil or some other such rot. Yes, look—Ainsley's smiling, enjoying the joke. He wouldn't be so amused if he knew Callie was here."

Rian's head whipped around to Courtland's. "What? I thought you were bringing Sheila Whiting. What in hell's name is Callie doing here?"

"It was my decision," Courtland said, his jaw tight. "My fault."

"Damn straight it's your fault. The only thing I can think of that would be worse would be to bring Fanny. Christ, or Morgan. Where is she?"

"Back there," Courtland said with a slight movement of his head, "safe in the coach, with Waylon and Jacob Whiting watching her, several others on horseback, as well. What's that fool saying?"

Both men looked toward the front of the gaol, and listened.

"Here he is, good citizens. You see before you Geoffrey Baskin. Spawn of the devil. Remember the name—Geoffrey Baskin, *murderer,*" the skinny black crow was shouting, waving the Bible in the air as he spoke. "You see before you the wages of sin! Blackguard!" he yelled, pointing the Bible at Ainsley. "*Murderer! Traitor!* Daring to walk among us, among God-fearing people who follow in the footsteps of Christ, while he dances with cloven hoof in the company of devils! Look at this man—this devil! Look at his fine clothing, the *arrogance* of the creature!"

The man paused, and there were several angry shouts from the crowd, most of them coming from the very front of the crowd.

Courtland leaned closer to Rian. "They're calling him Geoffrey Baskin. I don't know if that's lucky for us or not. Would you like odds that those are Beales's hirelings, taking up the cry the loudest?"

"No need to wager. You're right. Look at Ainsley—he's staring down at one of them, isn't he. Recognizes him, I'll bet. Look—did you see that? He said something to one of them. God's teeth, Court, someone could put a knife in his ribs before either of us could move. We have to put a stop to this."

The minister had gotten the bit between his teeth and was even louder now. "And now he dares—*dares!*—to speak, to mock us, sure his money will save him, his *arrogance* will save him. Do we stand here and let that happen? *No!* Do we allow him to sit safe at Dover Castle, laughing at us, to be perhaps transported or even freed to kill again? This murderer of women, of a helpless child? Yes! A child! *No,* I say, he will not escape justice! He is in Dymchurch, and in Dymchurch he will stay, buried in ignominy, justice meted out by you good citizens who will not allow his sins to go unpunished! Take him! Take him now! Show him the swift, vengeful sword of the Lord, show him the justice of good and honest men!"

"Bloody hell," Courtland breathed as the crowd seemed to surge forward as one, arms reaching up toward Ainsley as the soldiers were curiously slow to react. Even as he and Rian shoved their way forward, Ainsley disappeared into the mass of reaching, grabbing hands, dragged down from the box, unable to defend himself.

Courtland saw the men from Becket Hall pushing into the crowd, to protect their Cap'n. He knew they were all armed, with pistols, with knives, with belaying pins tucked beneath their jackets—and were now exposing their presence to anyone who was watching, counting noses, trying to identify anyone from Becket Hall, from the island. The riot could turn deadly at any moment.

The Lieutenant finally barked out orders and the soldiers quickly affixed their bayonets and leveled their rifles at what was now a mob intent on blood, even as more soldiers emerged from the gaol, also pushing themselves forward, their bayonets slowly inching back the mob as they formed a phalanx around Ainsley, who lay still on the cobblestones, his knees drawn up as if he had been fending off kicks from wooden clogs and heavy workman's boots.

"Bastards!" Rian shouted as the crowd began to disperse and, remarkably, the minister had vanished. "Bloody cowards!"

Courtland grabbed Rian by the shoulder and pushed him to the side of the street, where they blended in with the others who watched, but were now silent, whatever had pushed them into acting now warning them that the day could end with more than Geoffrey Baskin in chains.

"Let go of me, Court. God, is he all right?"

"We'll find out soon enough," Courtland told him. "But we can't chance going to him now, exposing ourselves. Look, there—they're getting him to his feet. Jesus, he doesn't look good, does he? Come on, we'll take this alleyway, circle around, back to the coach, find a doctor and have Callie take him with her into the gaol."

Rian took one last look toward the gaol as Ainsley was being half marched, half pushed back up the few steps to the flagway, and through the doorway. "What in hell were they thinking? Parading him out there, all but asking for something like this to happen. Beales. You had it, Court, he had to have planned this—the humiliation, and probably that beating as well, keeping his own hands clean. It's cowardly, underhanded, just the sort of man he is."

"I think you're right, and I think I also understand what he's trying to do. Just as Ainsley always taught us, cut off the head and the body dies. With Ainsley dead, Beales must think the rest of us will fold like a bad hand of cards, leaving him to—well, I'll tell you about that later. Beales wants more than to see us all dead. Right now, let's find that doctor."

Rian looked at him curiously. "You'll tell me about what? Don't tell me something else is going on. And nothing else matters anyway, not now. We've got to get him out of there, Court. Because we were right when we discussed all of this yesterday, even if we didn't understand what we were saying—one way or another, he'll never make it to Dover Castle."

CHAPTER THIRTEEN

CASSANDRA KEPT HER head down as she descended from the coach, the good Dr. Fletcher taking her hand and helping her up the few steps to the door of the gaol. Jacob Whiting followed, carrying the portmanteau holding fresh clothing and food from Bumble's kitchen.

A red-jacketed soldier stepped in front of her, in front of the door. "No entrance, miss. I'm sorry."

She said what Courtland had instructed her to say. "I'm here to see Geoffrey Baskin," Cassandra told him quietly. "As his daughter, that is my right."

"*He* ain't got no rights," the soldier said, snorting. "No visitors. Now take yourselves off before there's trouble."

Courtland had also said that, if she should meet resistance, she should climb back into the coach and drive away. They didn't need another incident.

"Come away, Miss Callie," Jacob Whiting warned quietly.

But Cassandra was going to see her father, and no smirking idiot was going to keep her from him.

She lifted her head, her heart pounding, and skewered the young soldier with her eyes, mimicking Eleanor, who could be as quietly imperious as a queen. "It saddens me, but I fear I will have to report this rudeness to your superior. What is your name, please?"

The young guard's watery blue eyes turned suddenly fearful. "M'name? I ain't givin' you m'name. I don't have to do no such thing."

"His name's Thomas Cobby," the doctor told her wearily, "and I brought him into this world, for my sins, but it wasn't me dropped him on his head and rattled his brains. Tommy, you've got an injured man in there and I'm going inside to tend him. You want me to go fetch your Ma?"

Cassandra ducked her head once more so young Thomas Cobby couldn't see her smile.

"I'll…I'll go ask the Lieutenant," Thomas said quickly and retreated inside the building while a second soldier, who had been watching and listening, grinned at the doctor. "Got him good, Dr. Fletcher. His Ma'd have his ears, and that's a fact. Bad business, this, Dr. Fletcher. Almost had us a hangin'."

"So I heard," the doctor said as Thomas Cobby opened the door once more.

"The Lieutenant says you can come in, but he's to inspect the bag and all, so as to see you didn't bring no pistols or nothin'. Goin' to do it hisself, he says. It's a bad man we got in there, no mistake. A real pirate, so I heard it said. Can you imagine that? A real honest to goodness pi—"

"Thank you, Tommy, that will be enough," Dr. Fletcher said, gesturing that Cassandra should precede him into the gaol house, and Cassandra quickly complied, before anyone inside had a change of heart and denied her.

"Ah, Miss Baskin, or is it Miss Becket?" a large soldier with a pockmarked face and a leer like a loon said as she stood in the dimness, fighting the urge to cover her nose with her hand, for the smell was not unlike a stable that hadn't been mucked out in weeks. "I apologize for the misunderstanding. Of course you may see your father. Although I will warn you. He's had a small accident. Fell on some boots—fell a couple of times, didn't he, boys?"

Again Cassandra fought the urge to lift her head, to speak to this man the way she wished, which would not be with kindness in her heart. "Thank you," she murmured quietly. "I'd like to be taken to him now."

"Not until you're searched. No end to the weapons and such some seem to think they can slip to a prisoner. But don't worry, I won't leave that to any of these bumbling idiots. It will be my pleasure to search you, personally. You'll like it, you'll see. I'm real thorough."

She couldn't help her reaction this time. Her head came up, the hood of her cloak falling back, exposing her face, her tumbling curls.

There was an audible intake of breath from the darkest corner of the room and Cassandra turned that way, unable to see anything but a vaguely human shape in the gloom.

"Leave her."

The lieutenant also turned toward the corner. "But I have to—"

"I said, leave her. You play the boorish buffoon to new heights, but you are not indispensable to me, Lieutenant Tapner." A chair scraped against the stone floor and the shape grew larger, became recognizably human as the man stepped out of the darkness.

He was dressed in black, from head to shiny black Hessians, his linen crisply white. He was tall, slim, like her papa, his hair black, his eyes blacker. He slowly lowered the scented, snow-white linen square he had lifted to protect his nose, revealing that he was almost a handsome man. Almost. But there was something about his eyes that edged him into the world of the terrifyingly sinister. He smiled at her, and Cassandra did her best not to shiver as his ice-cold stare raked her to her toes before settling once more on her face.

She wanted to look away. She wanted to attack him, rip his face with her nails. But it was as if her shoes had been nailed to the floor. She couldn't move. She could barely breathe. *Please God, that You didn't allow that face to be the last thing my mother saw before she died.*

"Well, well, well," the man said, all but purred. "And what is your name, hmm?"

"Sheila," Cassandra said quickly, probably too quickly. "My name is Sheila Whiting."

"No, it's not. Let me think. I knew the name, once. Oh, yes, I remember now. Cassandra, the prophetess whose beauty enslaved men, who warned that Troy would fall but, alas, was not believed. Poor doomed Cassandra. That's why we couldn't find Odette. She hid you. Naughty woman, but I think now I should thank her before I turn her over to her loving sister who so longs to see her again. And how you must ease my dear friend Geoff's heart, little sweetheart."

He stepped closer, bent to whisper in her ear. "Tell him. Tell him you saw me. Tell him how delighted I am to have seen you. Tell him you're mine. You, *and* the Empress. Everything that's owed me. No mercy, no quarter, until it's mine. And there's not a blessed thing in the world he can do about it but to die."

And then, before she could move, he put his lips to her cheek, kissed her.

She raised her hand to slap him, but Jacob Whiting, who had never moved quickly in his life, grabbed at her arm and pulled her away, held her arms at her sides as Edmund Beales smiled one last time before leaving through a door that led deeper into the gaol.

"Are you all right, Miss Callie?" Jacob asked her. "That was him, wasn't it? The one what caused all the troubles on the island. I have to go right now, tell Court. We got him, Miss Callie, stuck right here. All we have to do is wait for him to take himself outside of the—"

"Yes, all right. Go, tell Court. I have Dr. Fletcher here with me, and Waylon's just outside. Go."

But Lieutenant Tapner had another idea, and that included pointing a pistol in Jacob Whiting's direction and cocking it. "He didn't say anything about not touchin' *you,* now did he? Stand where you are."

Cassandra waited, her mind whirling with what she would say to her father, what she would keep from him, as the portmanteau was inspected, as the lieutenant checked the black leather bag Dr. Fletcher had brought with him. But, finally, they were ushered back through a thick, barred oaken door as Jacob remained where he was, and led down some damp stone steps, deeper into the bowels of the gaol.

They passed several empty cells and, Cassandra counted, a half-dozen armed guards who came to attention as the lieutenant led her past them, bayonets affixed to their rifles. There were small, smoky torches hung on the walls every twenty feet or so, with darkness in between that concealed at least a few puddles Cassandra found with her slippered feet and tried to tell herself were composed of water, just water and nothing else. No windows, for this was a cellar, dank and dreary, a place where hope could be very easily abandoned, to be replaced by fear, which could always grow quite well in the dark.

At last the lieutenant stopped in front of another thick oaken door guarded by two more soldiers, and motioned that it should be opened. The key one soldier took from his pocket was larger than any key Cassandra had ever seen, and the last of her optimism about breaking into the gaol, easily freeing her papa, disappeared at the sight of it.

"Ten minutes, no more," the lieutenant said as the door creaked open and Cassandra rushed inside.

"Papa? Papa!" She could barely see anything in the dark, until Dr. Fletcher entered behind her, carrying a candle in a tin holder. "Oh, God, Papa!"

Cassandra went to her knees beside the low straw pallet her father lay on, his arms wrapped about his waist. At least he was no longer in chains.

"Here now, that does him no good. Stand back, girl, let me see him."

"Cassandra?" Ainsley attempted to push himself to a sitting position, but Dr. Fletcher put his hands on his shoulders and pushed him back against the moldy straw. "Oh, no, no. You shouldn't be here. You shouldn't be anywhere near here. And who, sir, are you?"

"Josiah Fletcher. I'm the doctor your sons ordered to take care of you or they'd have my liver on a spit, that's who I am, not that I've ever had to be told my duty to my fellow man. Here, let me open that shirt, see what they've done to you. Your sons said you were kicked."

"I've been kicked before, thank you, by better men than I saw today. I'll be fine," Ainsley protested, this time managing to get to his feet. He looked at Cassandra. "You have even more power over Courtland than I supposed," he said, unbuttoning his shirt so that the doctor could press against his ribs. Even in the weak light of the candle, Cassandra could see livid purple bruises forming on his skin. "Nothing broken, you'll agree, Doctor?"

"Doesn't mean you don't hurt like a bitch—your pardon, Miss," the doctor said, opening his bag and pulling out a rolled up white bandage he then wrapped tightly around Ainsley's body while Cassandra held the shirt up and out of the way. "I'd give you some laudanum, but you won't drink it, will you? No, I thought not. Then that's all I can do, sir, save to remember you in my prayers. I'll leave you two your privacy. From what I can see—and I see much but say little—you have a lot to talk about."

Cassandra waited until the doctor was gone before she put her arms around her father, hugged him gently, stood on tiptoe to place a kiss on his cheek. "We don't have much time, Papa," she then said quietly, looking to the door that remained slightly open, bending down to hike up her skirts, exposing the knife she had strapped to her thigh. "The lieutenant wanted to search me, but…but he didn't," she adjusted quickly, having decided not to tell him about Beales.

Ainsley also had his gaze concentrated on the

door. "Ah, one of Bumble's best lemon tarts, always with a nice, sharp sting to them," he said loudly as he took the knife from her, smiled, and slipped it beneath the straw. "Now what are you doing?" he then whispered to her.

She had turned her back to him and was in the process of unbuttoning her gown. "The harness Court made for Spencer. You remember it, Papa. He's since made several more. Court strapped one on me, so you could see just how it works." She turned back to him, stripped to her waist save for her chemise, the harness belted to her, running down over her shoulder, her arm, to where the deadly stiletto that could be extended by flexing her muscles just so was exposed.

"And you'll give my best to Courtland, to everyone? Tell them not to fear for me or be so foolish as to attempt a rescue," Ainsley said as he slipped out of his shirt. Again, he smiled, his voice dropping once more to a whisper. "All that seems to be missing is our new friend, Jasper's fine French cannon," he told her as he narrowed his gaze, looked at the straps, and then signaled for her to undo them so that he could don the clever invention.

Cassandra rebuttoned her gown before reaching into the pocket of her cloak and extracting a small bible, opening it to show Ainsley its hollowed-out center that held a small velvet bag heavy with gold pieces. "Court said you my have use for this prayer book, as well."

Ainsley nodded, placed the coins beneath the mattress with the knife. "There's always a use for prayer in a gaol. Again, please give Courtland my compliments. He seems to have thought of everything a poor, tortured soul might need. Now, tell me about Becket Hall. Jacko? Eleanor? Odette?"

Cassandra hastened to tell him that everyone was fine, and that Courtland, Rian, and a dozen men from Becket Village were never going to be far from the gaol. She told him Chance would probably ride all night and day to get to him, as well, and what Ethan and Valentine were about to do in London. She spoke quietly, quickly, as she emptied the portmanteau onto the crude bed—alternating her hushed words with bits of idiocy meant for the guards—unwrapped the food Bumble had prepared for him as Ainsley shrugged into a clean shirt and a jacket that would help conceal the harness.

He listened, asked no more questions, and then took hold of her shoulders, looked intensely into her eyes. "Now, here is what I've decided. Retrieve the women we've sent away. Gather everyone who wishes to leave, and have them boarded on the frigate in three days, waiting for the evening tide. Three days exactly, Cassandra, no more, for then I will be moved from here to Dover Castle. But I am confident I can buy us those three days. Court, along with Jacko, is completely capable of handling the ship, and Kinsey can captain the *Respite*. He's done it before although, granted, only in the Channel. I have left Becket Hall only once, to come here, and I will never see it again. Do you understand, Cassandra? I will never see Becket Hall again."

She nodded, too overset to speak.

"Jack has everything else, my instructions, the location of the land I've purchased in Hampton Roads. I want you to go first to Marianna Warren, until Courtland can oversee the construction of a suitable home on the property. Not that on the waterfront, but the acreage inland. You'll have a fine living there, all of you. And the Empress, Cassandra. Bad luck wears off, eventually. It stays in the family, hidden, to surface again when fate decides. Edmund will not have it, you understand?"

Cassandra listened carefully to everything her father said, and then shook her head. "No. We're not leaving you, Papa. None of us. We're going, yes, but you're coming with us."

He nodded his agreement even as he said more loudly, "My crime, Cassandra, my punishment. I'm willing to face those facts. You're grown now, all of you. There nothing else left for me to do but to know you're all safe."

"Yes, Papa," she said, agreeing with him only because she didn't know if he was really speaking to her, or to the guards listening outside his cell. She committed his every word to memory, to repeat it all to Courtland, let him decide what was important. Three days. The evening tide. Everyone who felt it necessary to leave was to be aboard the ships.

"I'll tell Court what you said. But there could still be a pardon."

Ainsley smiled. "Yes, there's still that chance, isn't there?"

"But you don't think you'll live long enough for it to arrive," Cassandra said, echoing Court's words to her earlier. "Papa, perhaps you didn't always adhere to the King's laws, but that was all so long ago."

"But the Black Ghost still rides," Ainsley pointed out to her. "I've already volunteered a confession that I am also the Black Ghost, and everyone seems quite delighted with the coup of catching such a nefarious creature." He lowered his voice again. "Once the Black Ghost is hanged, Jack and Eleanor, anyone who remains in England, will be safe."

"You confessed? Oh, Papa, how could you have done such a thing? Even if Valentine and Ethan procure a pardon for Geoffrey Baskin, they'll still hang him for a smuggler." Much as she loved him, all she wanted to do now was to shake him, make him see reason. "How much penance must one man do? Isn't what happened on the island enough? What happened to my mother? Wasn't that enough?"

"Time to go, missy."

She whirled about to see the lieutenant standing

there, leering at her. "No! I need more time. Just a few more minutes. Please?"

"I won't allow her to return to this hellhole, Lieutenant. Give a father a moment to say his final goodbyes to his child."

"Oh, she'll see you again. If she comes to the hanging, and again, when your body is gibbeted and hung up in some nearby village until it rots. One more minute, that's all," the lieutenant warned, stepping outside the cell once more.

Ainsley kissed her, held her close for a moment, for one last whispered conversation. "Just go, sweetheart, and don't come back here. It's too dangerous. Do you remember everything I've told you? You'll do as I say?"

She looked up at him stubbornly. "You haven't given up hope, have you, Papa? Some of what you said wasn't for me, was it, but for that horrible man. I must ask you something else. Outside, when they were…when they had you outside…Court said he thought you recognized someone in the crowd, and spoke to him. It was one of Beales's men, wasn't it, from the time in the islands."

Ainsley's eyes went flat, dark. "Liam Doone, yes. He was there."

"What…what did you say to him?"

"I wasn't polite, let's just say that, all right?" Her father smiled, some of the light coming back into his eyes, and then whispered into her ear. "Fathers and daughters shouldn't have such talks as these, not in a perfect world. But I'm flattered that you believed my sad story of hopelessness. I feel more confident now that my gaolers, with their ears pressed to the door all of this time, also believe me a beaten man, accepting of his fate."

Cassandra's knees nearly gave out on her as she sagged against him in relief. "Why, you old pirate, you," she said quietly. "You almost had me thinking you were—what are you planning?"

"I did mean one thing, Cassandra, you're not to come back here. If Edmund were to see you? It's just too dangerous." He pressed a much folded piece of paper into her hand and then motioned that she should leave him. "The guards who searched me didn't bother to take the paper and bit of pencil I'd slipped into my pocket before the soldiers arrived at Becket Hall. Give this to Courtland, with my compliments. He doesn't believe it, but he makes a fine Black Ghost."

She smiled, laughed. "Oh, Papa, I love you."

He pulled her close, whispered into her ear. "Tell Courtland I want the frigate christened before I take her to sea. We've neglected to do that."

She looked up into his face, memorizing his features. "Certainly. Do you have a name in mind?"

Ainsley smiled, and suddenly she was looking at a young man, the young man her mother had loved, strong and sure, exuberant, daring—even here, beaten physically and locked in the bowels of the Dymchurch gaol. "That I do, my darling daughter, that I do. She'll be called the *Isabella.* We take her with us, to freedom."

CHAPTER FOURTEEN

"I SAW HIM. Oh, Court, I saw him. It was how it must be to look into the eyes of the devil himself."

Courtland led her to a chair in the small bedchamber assigned to her. He'd been all but out of his mind while she was gone, even knowing she was well protected. He'd watched over her from a distance, he and Rian, following the coach and its heavily-armed outriders out of Dymchurch, keeping back far enough to be able to intercept anyone who might decide to follow them.

They hadn't seen anyone, but that didn't mean they hadn't been followed. It also may have meant they'd been followed very well.

He sat down beside her at the small table, pulled a plate of fruit in front of her. "Here, eat something. Are you saying that you saw Beales? Inside the gaol? I didn't think he'd—he didn't see you, did he?"

Cassandra picked up an apple, put it down again. "He saw me. My cloak hood fell back and he—that doesn't matter. That horrible man is here, Court. Here, in Dymchurch."

Courtland began rhythmically patting his mouth with his fist, sure Cassandra wasn't telling him everything, considering what Beales's presence meant to them. "And Ainsley said nothing?" he asked a few moments later. "He doesn't know Beales is this close?"

"No, I think he knows. He was worried that Beales might see me if I returned to the gaol." She reached into her pocket and withdrew the note her father had given her. "We had to be careful not to be overheard by his guards. He's written instructions to you. And he told me three days, Court. In three days, on Tuesday, we sail on the evening tide. After that, they move him to Dover Castle. He said he will never see Becket Hall again—he was quite adamant about that—and yet he will escape. Was he saying that we should—?"

"Bring the ships here, to Dymchurch, yes," Courtland agreed, reading the closely-written but legible hand of Ainsley Becket. "And he's right, Callie. Once he's at Dover Castle, the chance of freeing him becomes much more difficult, and we'd have to rely on that pardon. Not that he'll ever live to get there."

"Don't say that, Court, please, not ever again," Cassandra begged him. "He can't die in that atrocious cellar."

"And he won't," Courtland said, getting to his feet. "Tomorrow, you and I ride back to Becket Hall, to meet with Chance. But tonight Rian and I have much to discuss concerning how we will protect the gaol. We can't have another incident like the one we saw today. It will be a long evening, Callie, and a longer day tomorrow and every day until we're at sea. I've ordered dinner for you, and a hot tub."

"I smell like the gaol, don't I?"

Courtland smiled. "I would have said a stable. One with a middling-size family of cats in residence. When you've eaten, a maid will take you to your room. Try to sleep."

"You'll come see me later? Tell me what you're planning?"

He shook his head. "It would be better if—"

"Please, Court," she said, looking up at him, fear and fatigue in her beautiful eyes.

Yes, he could see that. They were all frightened. But at the same time, those who had survived the massacre on the island were also excited, believing they would at last have their revenge. And that's how he and the others had to think of the next few days; as if they were back in the islands, those fairly lawless islands, not in staid, civilized England.

No mercy. No quarter.

They couldn't have done much anywhere else, would have had to stand back, rely more on Ethan and Valentine and even Chance. But this was Romney Marsh, a land that had seen centuries of smuggling, shipwrecking, pirates and violence. It was its own small country, physically attached to the rest of England, but often a land and a law unto itself, loyal, sympathetic first to its own. The violent Hawkhurst Gang had once ridden here, the Groombridge Gang, the Addington Gang and so many others, and the wool laws and the war with Bonaparte had resurrected the owlers once more. The populace, even many of the Waterguard, had learned to look the other way when the gangs rode out, for to pay too much attention could prove fatal.

The fact that the Black Ghost gang had aided much of the population feed their families for several years could also play a large part in the success of Ainsley's bold plan.

The trick would be in protecting Becket Hall, as well as effecting Ainsley's rescue.

"I may be very late," he told her at last.

She nodded. "I doubt I'll be able to sleep, in any case. Oh, I forgot—Papa wants you to christen the frigate."

"Bloody hell." He shook his head. "We don't have time to—"

"She's to be called the *Isabella.* Papa said…he said we take her with us, to freedom."

Courtland felt as if he'd been punched in the stomach, all his air gone from him. "I'll see that it's done."

"And Mama's portrait? He'll want that, too, won't he?"

"I'm sure we'll all want many things, Callie, eventually. For now, most of them remain here, with Elly and Jack. We can have them shipped to Hampton

Roads. For now, every inch of available space will be needed for human cargo."

"And the Empress?"

"That damn stone? Callie, I don't know. It'll end up somewhere. Maybe Ainsley plans to toss it into the sea. That's what I'd do with it."

Cassandra smiled, stepped closer to him. "So unflappable, Court, that's how I've always seen you. Yet this stone seems to unleash something in you, doesn't it? Toss it in the sea? Papa says it's priceless."

"It's had its price, Callie," Courtland told her, a muscle working in his jaw. "I've seen it on the island. Its victims are already buried in the sea, so why shouldn't the damn thing join them?"

Callie's smile faded. "I know, Court. I'm sorry I teased you. The world's gone mad again, hasn't it? Hold me for a moment before you leave, please?"

How could he possible resist her? "It's going to be all right, sweetheart," he said, pulling her against his chest. "I promise. I'd wager my life on our success."

"Don't die for me, Court," she said passionately. "I need you to live for me. I need you to be with me. I need you to hold me, not just to keep me safe, but to share with me, the good times and the bad—to treat me as the woman I want to be. Your woman, Court. Please."

The tensions of the last days pulled taut, snapped, and he crushed her against him, bringing down his mouth to meet hers, seized by an almost overwhelming passion he'd never felt before, not for anything, anyone, any hope, any dream he could dream.

He wanted her. God, he needed her.

"Don't go, Court, not yet. Stay here with me," she whispered as he kissed her hair, the slender stalk of her throat. "Can you do that?"

"More than anything…I want to…"

She put her hands against his shoulders, looked up into his face. "But you can't, can you? You've got your…duty. I understand."

"I wish to hell I did," he told her, cupping her chin in his hand. "Not that I don't understand. In my mind, I understand." He closed his eyes for a moment, trying to marshal his words. "It's…it's my heart that doesn't want to be anywhere but here, with you."

"Oh, Court," Cassandra said, standing on tiptoe to kiss his mouth again, and the innocent gentleness of that kiss forced him to close his eyes against the sudden, stupid burning of tears. "Go…do what you have to do," she said, clasping his hands in hers. "But then come back here to me. I'll be waiting, no matter how late the hour."

Court wanted to say no, to tell her that there was a time and a place and a— "Are you sure, Callie? You're afraid for your papa, for all of us. It's natural you should feel…are you sure?"

"I've never been any more sure of anything in all of my life, and I've been sure of my feelings for you for all of that life. Don't make me be alone tonight, Court, not if you care for me."

He squeezed her fingers, and then slowly, reluctantly, let her go. "Lock this door behind me," he said before kissing her one last time.

"You lock it from the outside," she told him, handing him the key. "And then you can open it again."

Courtland smiled, shook his head. "One of us is crazy, Callie. Or maybe both of us…"

He left her then, heading for the common room, knowing that only those from Becket Hall now occupied the inn, and that two dozen good men from Becket Village and volunteers who had been protected by the Black Ghost and had already heard of the trouble stood guard around the perimeter at all times.

Rian met him with a tankard of ale and a quizzical look. "Well? How is she? How is he?"

Courtland quickly flashed on how Cassandra had looked when he'd left her, so soft and willing, doubting Rian would want to hear any of that, so he forced himself to concentrate on Ainsley. He pulled the folded note from his pocket and tossed it on the scarred tabletop. "See for yourself. We have a busy three days ahead of us. But I will say this, brother mine, for all that Beales made a first strike none of us expected, Ainsley Becket is still a bloody genius. And one thing more, Rian. Edmund Beales is in Dymchurch—and within our grasp. Chance is going to arrive just in time for the fun."

"THE ENGLISH REFLECTION of her mother, isn't she?" Edmund Beales asked as Ainsley, once more with his ankles and wrists bound by shackles and chains, was pushed roughly into a chair in a small office in the gaol. "Last we spoke, you failed to mention her. Little Cassandra, all grown-up, nearly the age Isabella was when you first brought her to your pretty little island. I was quite startled—pleasantly so—to see her, and thought immediately of Isabella. So beautiful, so foolish. I would have treated her as my queen."

Ainsley looked at his onetime partner, unblinking, as Edmund slipped a few small, dark green leaves into his mouth, between teeth and cheek. Lisette had told him, in great detail, of everything that she remembered of her father, his actions since removing her from the convent. "An idle question if you will, Edmund. Are there any teeth left in that side of your head? Any brains left, as well, or do the coca leaves do all of your thinking for you now? Not to be insulting, but you really don't look well. Perhaps a recent wound has done more damage than one would suppose?"

Edmund Beales only smiled. "That's the best you can do, Geoff? Fling words at me? Fling my daughter's traitorous action at me? Yes, I suppose it is. We can't all be lucky in our daughters. The mother of mine was clearly unsound. The shackles. Do they chafe?"

Ainsley said nothing. He'd first been shackled and dragged into Edmund's presence the previous evening. The man had offered him a glass of wine, which

Ainsley threw into his face, at which time Liam Doone, who Edmund now called Thibaud, had run him face-first into one of the stone walls, rendering him unconscious. Ainsley wouldn't make that same mistake in his second conversation with his former partner. He was no good to himself or anyone else injured, and it was time to set his plan into motion.

"You weren't very cooperative last night, Geoff," Beales continued from his seat behind the desk. "And it's been so long since we've last had ourselves a pleasant chat. Too many years. Let's see, whatever shall we talk about, hmm?"

"How you would prefer to die?" Ainsley suggested, earning himself a sharp poke in the back from the belaying pin Thibaud had already threatened to use to smash both his knees.

"Leave us, you fool. He's wearing more chain than an anchor. Brute force is unnecessary. My good friend Geoff wishes to speak about death, and I'm inclined to oblige him. Did you know, Geoff, if the knot isn't set correctly, a man can slowly choke to death for long, painful minutes, rather than have his neck neatly snapped by the drop? Oddly enough, the hangman is known to me, his instructions already given as to where to position the knot. You'll do a fine dance, Geoff, and a quite lengthy one."

Thibaud mumbled something and quit the room.

"Not your so-loyal Jules, is he, sharing your delight in the sound of your own voice?" Ainsley said, smiling as he mentioned the man Spencer had seen and destroyed in London. "Also quite painful, I would imagine, being burned alive. My men told me he screamed for a long time."

Beales shrugged. "He failed in his most important mission. He would be dead, screaming, if he'd returned to me. But you're correct. Our friend Liam is a sad disappointment. They grow old, Geoff, and weak. We're the only strong ones left. And how is our good friend Jacko?"

"Dead these last two years," Ainsley lied, looking at Edmund levelly. "Did you really arrange this charade so that we could reminisce? If you have, I'd like to be returned to my cell. It smells better there."

Edmund leaned his elbows on the desk top. "Oh, but I so long to speak of the old days, one in particular. How did you escape? There were three warships escorting those merchantmen. You should be dead."

"I was dead, for many years. Odd that the man who killed me now gives me new life."

"Ha! That's good, Geoff, very good. I should almost be afraid, were it not that you're sitting here in chains, waiting to be tried and hanged and—well, and I'm not, am I?"

"You were always overly confident, especially for a man of your limited talents."

Edmund's smile left him. "Oh, you'll be hanged. While I watch you dance, your legs vainly stretching to feel solid ground beneath them. I won't be cheated a second time, the way your ungrateful wife cheated me."

Ainsley felt every muscle in his body tensing. He could release the stiletto, fling himself across the desk, stab the blade deep into Beales's throat. Except that the chains would slow him, and Beales had a pistol lying close beside him on the desktop. He would gladly die if he could take Beales to Hell with him, but the odds, at the moment, were against that happening. So Ainsley remained silent, tried his best to look unimpressed.

Beales tapped at his own cheek. "You've got a tic, Geoff, working just here. Feel it? How dare I speak of your beloved wife? Your dead wife? Your *stupid,* wasteful wife."

"You killed her," Ainsley said, unable to stop himself. "And now you blame her for what you did?"

Beales sat back against the chair, shook his head. "You don't know, do you? Perhaps that's best. After all, the insult was to me."

"Knowing you still breathe, Edmund, is an insult to humanity at large."

Beales leaned forward once more, and Ainsley could see the hatred in his dark eyes, the spittle born of the juice of the coca leaves forming at the corners of his mouth. "I told her—told her how it would be with me now that you were dead. She'd be mine, my wife, my consort in all things, as we conquered England together. I was offering her the world, Geoff!

Any other woman would have been *honored* to have been so chosen. But not that stupid Spanish strumpet. If you—her so wonderful Geoffrey—were dead, then she would die, too, though it damned her to Hell. I damned her to Hell—that's what she meant."

"What are you saying? In Christ's name, Edmund—tell me what you think I need to hear and have done with it."

"She jumped," Beales said baldly, striving for bravado, but even Ainsley could hear the frustration in the man's voice. "She broke free of me and ran up the staircase, to the railing, while I chased after her like some lovesick fool, begging her to stop." He put out one hand, formed it into a tight fist. "I nearly had her…I almost had her as she lifted her leg over the railing, calling your name, over and over again, until she fell."

Beales slammed his fist against his chest. "She dishonored me, in front of my own crew. After that, everyone had to die. Everyone! I would not be made to look the fool!"

Ainsley slowly closed his eyes, traveled back in his mind to the moment he'd burst into the nearly destroyed house and seen Isabella, his darling Isabella, lying on the marble floor like a beautiful, broken doll. "Oh, God. Oh, my God…*Isabella.*"

He flinched as Beales brought both his fists down hard on the desktop. "Enough! The Empress. Where is she? You can't save yourself, Geoff, you'll understand that I want my pound of flesh, but I am willing to bargain."

"I would have given you the emerald," Ainsley told him dully, raising his head once more. "I was going to give it to you before we left for England. Christ, Edmund, it's just a pretty piece of rock, that's all. Not flesh and blood, not half so precious..."

"So say you. I know differently. In the right hands, in *my* hands, the Empress is *power!* You can still save the others, Geoff. They're nothing to me, anyway. I'm a civilized man now, a gentleman, and the island a lifetime ago. Why, I'm not even going to personally bloody my hands on even you, for those violent days are gone. Just give me the Empress and it's over, my revenge ends with you. You have my word on it."

Only an idiot would believe the man. An idiot, or a man Edmund believed to be desperate, broken, totally without options. Edmund's flaw, his failing, like Machiavelli's, had always been in overestimating his own brilliance, underestimating the resolve of his opponents. Like Machiavelli, Edmund adored the twists and turns, the intrigues, the machinations...forgetting that one too many twists and you've tied yourself in a knot.

Ainsley reluctantly nodded his head, and then launched his own plan, his own twist and turn. "Very well, I agree, as I can see no other option than but to trust you. I can...yes, that's what we'll do. Tuesday evening should give them enough time. I'll need to speak with someone from my family again, to arrange matters, and that someone will bring the stone to the gaol on Tuesday evening. I need that much time to have the stone retrieved from its hiding place and brought here, as long as you promise whoever brings the stone safe conduct, along with the rest of my family and crew. You can manage to have me kept here for three more days before moving me to Dover Castle, can't you, Edmund? A powerful man like you?"

Edmund looked at him for a long time, his mind working, his intelligence competing with his greed. With Edmund, Ainsley knew, greed always won. And then Beales nodded. "I've waited nearly twenty years, Geoff. I can wait a few more days. Very well, I'll arrange to have you kept here, in Dymchurch, until then. Have your daughter bring the Empress."

"No," Ainsley said, outwardly panicked, inwardly elated, looking at Beales and seeing a dead man. "You gave me your word, Edmund. Unless you promise to leave my daughter alone, the Empress stays where she is, forever out of your reach. My daughter will not be involved. Give me your word."

"Given. And as the fine English gentleman I have become, my word is, of course, my bond," Edmund purred, getting to his feet, crossing to open the door leading to the hallway. "Congratulations, old friend.

You've saved a great many lives. Just not your own. That was always your failing, Geoff, your Achilles' heel. Unselfishness is *not* a virtue. Thibaud! Take him back to his cell!"

COURTLAND SLIPPED INTO Callie's room shortly after midnight. His heart was pounding but his hand, thankfully, was steady as he turned the knob.

He stepped inside, closed the door, locked it behind him. Took a deep breath, told himself yet again that he could leave at any time, that he wouldn't pressure her if she'd changed her mind, that sometimes circumstances caused people to think things, believe things, they wouldn't ordinarily…

"Court?"

He turned to see her standing in the middle of the small chamber; barefoot, wearing a virginal white dressing gown, her masses of curls falling loose past her shoulders, looking darkly golden in the candlelight. The room was warm, a fire burning in the grate, and it smelled of violets and spring on this chilly November night.

"Cassandra."

No. He wouldn't be leaving. Some things just weren't possible.

He walked over to her. "You're so beautiful." He raised a hand to her face, cupped her cheek.

She turned her lips against his palm.

The world was outside, clamoring for his attention. And the world could wait. His world was here, with Cassandra.

He slid his fingers into her curls, put a hand to her slim waist, drew her closer. He could feel the rapid beating of her heart.

She sighed, closed her eyes.

He bent his head, kissed her temple, trailed his lips down the side of her face, to the silken skin of her throat. Whispered the words into her ear. "I would die before I hurt you."

Cassandra raised her head, her eyes open now, and clear, without a shred of fear in them, without a whisper of doubt. Now it was she who traced her fingertips down his freshly-shaven cheek. "I know," she answered quietly. "I know…"

He lifted her against his heart and carried her to the curtained bed in the corner, where the covers had already been turned down for the night. He laid her down on the fresh sheets brought with them from Becket Hall, his breath catching in his throat as her curls spilled across the pillow. As she smiled, raised her arms to him.

Damning himself to hell, Courtland reached for Heaven….

CHAPTER FIFTEEN

CASSANDRA ROUSED HERSELF slowly, the warmth of Courtland's body, so close against hers, bringing a small smile to her face as she realized she felt very near to purring, like a contented cat.

So this was what it felt like to be a woman.

She could think of worse fates.

Courtland put a finger beneath her chin and lifted her head from its comfortable spot, pressed in the small dip just below his bare shoulder. How very considerate of him, to have that lovely little hollow, fashioned just for her comfort.

"Callie? Are you laughing or crying?"

"Hmm?" she said, pushing against him so that she could lever herself up higher and look into his wonderful face.

"I felt your shoulder shake there for a moment," he explained, pushing himself up also, so that he was now sitting with his head and shoulders against the pillows.

"Oh. I wasn't laughing, not really. I just was thinking of how well your body fits mine."

He raised one eyebrow as she felt hot color run into her cheeks. "I beg your pardon?"

"No, no, I didn't mean *that,*" she said quickly. "I only meant that you…you make a lovely pillow."

"My one aspiration in life, fulfilled," Courtland teased back at her. "To be a lovely pillow. Are you all right?"

She settled herself against him once more, her arm across his waist. "If you ask me that question again, no, I won't be all right. I'm fine, Court. Wonderful."

"The first time…it isn't always…pleasant for the woman."

Cassandra rolled her eyes, although she was careful not to let him see her. "It was very…*pleasant.*"

And it had been. Very…pleasant. Yes, there had been some pain, but she felt certain that Courtland had felt it more than she. What it hadn't been was what Morgan had said it would be. Magnificent. Explosive. Incredible.

But it had been lovely. Courtland had been so… gentle.

Morgan had never mentioned *gentle…*

Courtland cherished her. Cassandra knew that. As he'd said, he would die before he hurt her.

Well, the *hurting* was over, wasn't it?

"Court…?"

He kissed the top of her head. "Uh-oh. I've heard that tone before, and ignored it to my peril. What impossible thing are you going to ask me for now?"

She pushed herself up and onto her haunches, holding the sheet against her breasts, for the candles still burned, low in their holders, and the fire still cast a soft glow over the small room…and she'd only just become the woman Morgan had told her she'd be once she'd been taken to her marriage bed, and not the *wanton* Morgan had advised her to become for her husband.

Not that this was her marriage bed…

"I…what we *did*…and it was wonderful, truly," she said, wishing she could stuff the sheet in her mouth and not say anything else. "Well…isn't there *more?*"

"More?" Courtland repeated, looking at her rather owlishly. "By God, I think I've just been insulted."

"No! I didn't mean…I certainly wasn't saying that— Oh, stop laughing at me!"

"Truly, Callie, I'm not laughing at you," he told her, and then laughed again. "Why do I sense the fine hand of the Countess of Aylesford in this conversation, hmm? Mariah might give you advice on how to get me to do whatever she thinks is best for me, and Julia would encourage me to tell you my every secret. Eleanor, dear Elly, would explain that a man must be provided every comfort—which is why Jack is always smiling, I think. But Morgan? I imagine her advice, whispered in her youngest sister's ear, has always been more…earthy."

"Yes, but you'll notice that Ethan is always smiling, too," Cassandra said, allowing the sheet to slip, just a little bit.

Courtland's gaze slipped a bit, as well, to her half-exposed breasts. "You know, Callie, I still can't believe I've…I always promised myself that I'd…would you for God's sake keep a grip on that sheet?"

Her heart had begun to pound. "So there is…more."

"Callie, I'm not teaching you how to ride a horse, or sail a skiff in the Channel, or— Yes. Yes, all right. There's…more. But I knew I'd hurt you, might even frighten you, and I only wanted to be—"

"Gentle," Cassandra finished for him. "But now you've been gentle, and I thank you for that. Could you please not be gentle now? Morgan smiles all the time, too, you know."

And she let the sheet drop just as Courtland took hold of it and ripped it down toward the bottom of the bed.

He sat up, laid his hands on her shoulders, looked deeply into her eyes, and she felt something vaguely familiar begin to curl, low in her belly.

She lifted her chin, waited for his kiss.

But he didn't kiss her. Instead, he slowly trailed his hands down her arms, then moved them to her waist before inching upward, cupping her breasts, lifting them, running his thumbs across her nipples until she involuntarily arched her back, slowly moving her head from side to side, imagining she could actually feel her blood beginning to heat.

He teased her then with his mouth, his teeth and

tongue. Slipped a hand between her thighs, touching her in a way that told her this might be her body, the one she had lived with for all of her life, but she'd never really known it. Known what it meant to be a woman, to be touched like this, brought to the brink of something that kept building inside her, this tension that couldn't possibly be sustained, not without her heart exploding inside her.

Courtland took her to that unknown brink, that precipitous cliff, and with a final touch flung her over, to fall, fall, fall…

…but then catching her as she fell, catching her cry of surprise and delight with his mouth, pressing her back against the pillows and then covering her, becoming a part of her as she held on tight, as he moved inside her. Faster, deeper.

Gentle became a memory to cherish, a testament for how much Courtland cared for her. But this? This! This was how he *felt* about her!

A rainbow of brilliant colors seemed to burst behind her closed lids when he thrust one final time and their bodies sang together, making the most beautiful music in the world.

Now, she thought, as he held her tightly, as she clung to him, her breathing as ragged as his, her body still singing…*now* I am a woman.

COURTLAND WOKE JUST AS the false dawn replaced the glow of the now dying fire, to feel Cassandra's hands on him, her lower body covering his as she explored him with her fingertips, lightly tracing over his skin, the sprinkling of hair in the center of his chest.

"Callie, what are you doing?" he asked, looking down at her, seeing her tangled curls as they tickled his skin in delightful ways.

"I couldn't sleep," she said, lifting her head, blowing away the corkscrew curls that had fallen into her eyes. "And…and you're very interesting. What's this?" she asked before pressing her lips against a scar low on his hip.

It was a hell of a thing, blushing like some callow youth, but he could feel the heat rising in his cheeks as she bent her head once more, to continue her investigation. "A gift from the man some would have called my father. It's old now. Faded both on my skin and in my memory."

She shot him a quick look, her expression as pained as if his father had inflicted the wound on her instead of him, and then traced the scar over his hipbone, along his side. "How far does it go?" she asked him, tears welling in her eyes.

"Leave it be, Callie."

But she was pushing at him now, urging him onto his stomach. "Please, Court? Let me see."

He turned onto his side, his back to her, and closed his eyes. The whip had crisscrossed his back so many times that new scars had built upon older scars. His skin crawled slightly as Cassandra traced some of the worst of them, silvery lines against his tanned skin.

She pressed her lips against his shoulder blade, and one of, he knew, the worst scars. "Oh, Court…"

He rolled onto his back once more and she laid her head against his shoulder, held him tightly as he felt a tear slide onto his chest. "It's all right, sweetheart. We all carry scars from our time before we were Beckets. Mine just happen to be visible."

"You loved my mother very much, didn't you, Court?"

He nodded, her question momentarily robbing him of speech. "She didn't care that I was…different. I didn't speak, not for a long time. I kept waiting to be sent back to my father, unable to believe that I was safe, that I wouldn't put a foot wrong, a word wrong, and be banished from this glorious place where no one hit me or called me stupid or— Again, Callie, it was a long time ago. It's enough that I finally realized I was loved, that I was safe." He ran his fingers up and down her arm, not even realizing he was doing so. "And then you were born, and everything else…everything else just seemed to fall into place. I had a *reason* to be on that island, a reason to have been saved. You."

"Oh, Court…"

"You were everything to me, Callie, from the moment Isabella urged me to touch my finger to your palm and you closed your fingers around mine, held on tight. I really have no idea how old I am, what my age was then—twelve, thirteen? Ainsley just guessed, as he had to do with most of us. In any event, I promised myself then, young idiot that I was, that I would spend my life protecting you, seeing that no harm ever came to you, the way it had come to me. That you'd never know pain, never be hungry, never face a night alone and frightened…"

"You've always kept that promise, Court," Cassandra told him as she reached up, kissed his cheek.

"Have I? I don't know that being here with you now is keeping my promise. I've taken something from you that I can never give back. I'm a selfish man, Callie. Selfish, and probably foolish."

She held out her arms to him as he climbed from the bed, searched out his clothing. "You took nothing I didn't all but beg you to take, Court," she said as he slipped into his clothes, reached for his boots.

"And I picked one hell of a time to do it," he said, pushing his fingers through his hair as he looked around the room, searching for her dressing gown, and then tossing it onto the bed. "Here, put this on while I go find the innkeeper and have some hot water sent up to you. We leave for Becket Hall in an hour."

"But I'm coming back with you?" she asked as she shoved her arms into the sleeves of the dressing gown. "Because we leave from the docks here, correct?"

He nodded, his mind working through all the plans he and Rian and Chance had discussed last night. It was easier to think of them than to think about Cassandra, and how much he wanted to crawl back into the bed behind him and forget the world for just another hour, another day.

At last he turned around, to look at Cassandra as she stood behind him, buttoning the dressing gown. "God," he said, feeling as if an unseen hand had just swept his legs out from him. He opened his arms and she ran into them. He kissed her hair, her eyes, her sweet, willing mouth, clasped her tightly to his body, as if she might disappear even as he held her in his arms.

"I have so much to say to you," he whispered against her ear once he'd reluctantly broken their kiss. "So much I long to hear you say to me."

"We have time, Court," she told him, and he could hear the fear in her voice once more. "Don't we? All the time in the world."

Of course they did; all the time in the world. If the gods were kind, if the wind was fair…if Ainsley's plan was as brilliant in practice as it was in its conception…if they all survived these next days.

CASSANDRA ENTERED Becket Hall and went directly into the drawing room, to stand beneath the portrait of her mother. Her smiling mother. A woman wrapped in beauty—because she was loved, because she loved.

"Oh, Mama, how I miss you right now," she said, wiping away fresh tears. "But don't you worry, Mama. We'll keep him safe, I promise."

Then she sighed, untying the strings of her cloak as she realized that it was terribly quiet in this usually noisy, bustling household.

Courtland entered the drawing room, his expression closed, and held out a hand to her. "Upstairs, Callie. It's Eleanor."

"Elly?" She put her hand in his and began to run toward the staircase. "What? Is it the baby? Oh, God, Court. Is it the baby?"

They stopped outside the closed doors to Eleanor and Jack's bedchamber, exchanging looks, and then Courtland pushed open the door and they stepped inside. All the quiet that had been downstairs was even more quiet here, even though the room was fairly full of people.

Mariah saw them and, a finger to her mouth, motioned for them to step back out into the hallway as she followed. "She's all right," she said hastily, as Cassandra squeezed Courtland's hand. "Odette gave her something, some foul drink, and she's sleeping now, the pains lessening."

"She's laboring?" Cassandra asked quietly. She'd helped Odette in small ways when Mariah's daughter was born. Holding Mariah's hand, putting cool cloths on her head. But she really knew little about childbirth, other than the fact that Eleanor had already miscarried twice, and that this baby wasn't supposed to be born until Christmas. "That isn't good, is it?"

"No, it's not," Mariah said, sighing. "Court, could

you please get Jack out of there for a while? He's been at her side all night and all of this morning. He needs to eat something, get some sleep."

"In a moment, Mariah. What happened?"

Mariah rolled her eyes. "Eleanor is a stubborn woman, that's what happened. She waited until everyone was at dinner last night, and then got up out of bed, tried to dress herself so that she could go to Dymchurch, prove that she's alive, and tell whoever would listen the truth about the day Ainsley sank that ship. She got as far as the head of the stairs before Jack saw her, catching her as she fainted. My God, she's been off her feet for months now. How did she expect to just get up, dress and be driven all the way to Dymchurch?"

"She loves Ainsley very much," Courtland said, absently rubbing Cassandra's back.

"We all love Ainsley, Court," Mariah said, sounding as if she, too, had not eaten or slept in some time. "That doesn't mean we go running off to slay dragons, not in Elly's condition."

"You ran off to France when little William was only six weeks old," Cassandra pointed out, feeling protective of Eleanor. "And then, if I'm not mistaken, to London only a few days after that."

Mariah smiled, her shoulders losing some of their stiffness. "Yes, I did, didn't I? I was so sure Spence couldn't manage without me. I'm sorry. Everything is at sixes and sevens here, and has been since Ainsley was taken. What news have you?"

"I saw Papa yesterday, in the gaol," Cassandra told her as Sheila Whiting approached from the servant staircase, carrying an armful of towels, and entered the bedchamber. "They've hurt him, but he's all right."

Mariah looked to Courtland.

"We'll discuss it later. Where's Spence? Chance is downstairs, in Ainsley's study. We need to put our heads together, Mariah, we're rapidly running out of time and there's a lot to do. Are you sure Elly's going to be all right?"

"Are we safe here?" Mariah asked, without answering Courtland's question. "Spence assures me we could hold off Bonaparte and his entire Grande Armeè, but Beales won't bother with us now, will he, now that he has Ainsley?"

"Divide and conquer, Mariah," Courtland said, and Cassandra inhaled sharply at the seriousness of his tone. "Beales has made sure that our strength is divided between protecting Becket Hall and protecting Ainsley. No, we're not out of danger here, not when we're dealing with a man as vindictive as Edmund Beales. I don't think so, and neither does Chance. Now, where's Spence?"

Mariah waved a hand in the general direction of the village. "Jacko's taken himself off to The Last Voyage, after drinking here all night. You know how he is about Elly, as if she's his daughter, I suppose. Spence went to bring him back here. Nobody's supposed to be in the village anymore."

Courtland swore under his breath and went off to the village, and Cassandra followed Mariah back into Eleanor's bedchamber, to see Lisette sitting at the head of one side of the bed, running rosary beads through her fingers, as Jack sat on the other side, holding one of Eleanor's hands in both of his.

"Odette?" Cassandra asked, approaching the woman who was rocking in the chair that had once been in Fanny's bedchamber. She bent to kiss the old woman's cheek. "How are you?"

"She's close," Odette said quietly.

"Eleanor's close? Close to having the baby?"

"No, child. Loringa. My twin. She's close, and getting closer. I can't hold her away any longer." She looked at Cassandra, smiled knowingly. "Ah, you're a woman now, are you, sweet baby? You'll give him strong sons and he'll give you beautiful daughters. You tell them about Odette, and about your fine mama. Don't let us die, not in your heart."

Cassandra dropped to her knees, laid her head in Odette's lap. "You're coming to Hampton Roads with us, I promise. Now you promise me that. Please, promise me."

"Odette!"

At Jack's panicked cry, Cassandra quickly got to her feet and helped Odette out of the rocking chair, then stood back, watching the bed, for Eleanor's eyes were open now. Wild and searching.

"Odette?" Eleanor said, reaching up a hand to her.

"Something's…something's happening. I feel wet… between my legs. I'm tired…so tired. Odette, what's happening?"

The old woman threw back the covers and Cassandra's hands flew to her mouth. The sheets were red beneath her sister.

"The afterbirth—it is coming too soon," Odette said as Sheila actually leapt onto the bed beside Eleanor, to throw up her nightgown, push Eleanor's knees into the air. Eleanor, their lady, their refined, modest lady amongst so many savages, as they all said, didn't protest, made no move toward covering herself. "Everyone—leave us!"

"The hell I will!" Jack shouted as Eleanor slowly closed her eyes. "Eleanor, hold on, darling. It's fine… everything's fine. I'm here, I'm not going anywhere. I love you, sweetheart. Eleanor? *Eleanor!*"

"Mariah!" Odette shouted, no longer an old woman, weak and maudlin. "My bag—now! Lisette, hold her other hand, hold her down. Cassandra—out! This is no place for you!"

Cassandra didn't argue, but simply stood her ground. She was a woman now, and this was the lot of women. To carry the children, to give them life, to sometimes give their own lives in the process.

But not this time. Odette had lived long enough to be with Eleanor, to be there for her when she was needed, if it took her last bit of strength.

Cassandra picked up one of the large white towels

from the pile Sheila had brought into the room earlier, waiting as Odette barked orders and Jack begged Eleanor to open her eyes and Sheila Whiting advanced on Eleanor with what looked to be a huge, twisted set of spoons.

She hugged the towel to her breasts as she moved her lips in prayer. When Eleanor's baby was born, it would need to be wrapped up in something warm.

CHAPTER SIXTEEN

COURTLAND STOOD IN the dimness inside the quiet bedchamber, a hand to his mouth, looking toward the bed, the figures on that bed.

Jack, his friend, lying there, fully clothed, his long body curled close against that of his wife. Eleanor, his sister, so small, so still beneath the covers, her face ghostly pale.

Courtland dropped his hand to his side and, reluctantly, approached the bed, laid a hand on Jack's shoulder. "I'm sorry, Jack. I wouldn't do this...but we have to talk. Ainsley told you things we need to know."

Jack turned his head to look at Courtland, and then nodded. "Give me a moment, and I'll join you downstairs, in Ainsley's study."

Courtland stepped away from the bed, taking one last look at Eleanor. God, he had to watch closely to see her chest rising and falling ever so slightly beneath the covers to convince himself she was still alive.

He hadn't seen the baby. No one had, except for the women. He'd been bundled up and carried into the dressing room, where a roaring fire now burned and the old Indian woman who had accompanied Mariah from Canada sat holding the child, ceaselessly chanting to him in her own language. According to Cassandra, who he'd seen earlier in the hallway, Odette had put Onatah in charge of young John James Eastwood, and it would probably behoove everyone else in Becket Hall to keep their distance.

Odette had retired once more to her bed—Jack had actually carried her there—and a tearful Cassandra had told him she doubted the woman would ever leave it again.

"How's Elly now?" Courtland asked once Jack joined him in the hallway.

"Still alive," Jack said, looking as if he'd aged ten years in the past day and night. "God, Court, there was so much blood. Odette has given all sorts of instructions, including one that will keep Eleanor in that bed for at least two weeks, no matter how she might complain. Christ, how I want her to wake up, even if it's just to complain. She hasn't even seen young Jack yet."

"But Odette says she'll be all right?"

Jack nodded. "And the baby. In time. She promised, and after the miracle I saw in there a few hours ago, I have to believe her. But Ainsley will never see either of them, will he?"

"That's what he told Callie, but it's not what he wrote in his note to us—at least not the timing of each of the orders he gave her. Clearly he doesn't want Cassandra to know just what he's planned, in order to keep her from returning to the gaol," Courtland said as the two men made their way down to the study. "Chance and Spence are waiting for us. Rian's still in Dymchurch, keeping watch there, in case no one told you. You can tell us what Ainsley wants you to do, and then we'll tell you what he wants us to do. We don't have much time, you know."

They entered the study and Chance got up from behind Ainsley's desk, to clasp Jack close, the two of them heartily patting each other's back, as men are prone to do. Chance was still the golden boy, for all that he was the oldest of them all, and now a sober, law-biding citizen of the Crown. The devilish pirate was in his eyes tonight, though, beating back the fatigue of being in the saddle almost day and night to get to them, and Courtland was damn glad that when he fought, Chance would be fighting with him, not against him.

"Here, now," Spencer said as he poured them all glasses of wine, "you'll have me blubbering like a baby myself if you don't all stop that. Time to get down to cases. But first let's drink a toast to young Jack, and to his splendid mother."

They'd all taken a glass and Chance was about to offer a toast when Jacko walked into the room, his normal swagger replaced by slowly dragging feet, badly slumped shoulders. "I need to see her," he said simply, looking at Jack. "I won't go close…I won't bother her none…I just…I need to see her for myself."

Jack looked to Courtland, who nodded his head almost imperceptibly. They all knew the story, knew that Jacko's life hadn't been the same since the day of the mistaken raid, the day Jacko had rescued Eleanor…by killing her mother. Life was choices, and Jacko had chosen the child over the mother. It was that simple, and that complex. And Jacko, the man who would swear he loved no one, needed no one, had lived with that choice for too many years.

"Of course, Jacko," Jack said, putting down his wineglass. "I'll take you to her. She's sleeping, but you can stay as long as you like. Sheila Whiting's there with her, but she won't bother you."

Courtland averted his gaze as Jacko's eyes turned bright with tears. He looked to Chance, who had been on the doomed English ship that day, had been the one to grab Eleanor and run with her to safety. Chance only shook his head, shrugged.

They were quiet for long moments after Jack, his arm around the older man's shoulders, quit the room, before Spencer said quietly, "I never thought I'd live to see the day Jacko would— Well, there's all kinds of love, aren't there?"

Courtland immediately thought of Cassandra. *God.* He'd never said the word, had he? What sort of idiot was he, anyway? "I—it might be some minutes before Jack returns," he told the others. "I'll be right back."

Before Spencer could do more than look at him curiously, Courtland left the study and headed for the drawing room, hoping to find Cassandra. But she wasn't there; the large room was empty. Which, he realized, made some sense, as everyone was probably exhausted after the hours spent worrying about Eleanor and the new baby.

He stood there, considering going upstairs to Cassandra's bedchamber, to say precisely what he didn't know, when he felt eyes on him and looked across the room to Isabella's portrait hanging over the fireplace.

Slowly, he walked forward, until he was standing no more than six feet away from the portrait. "I love her, Isabella," he said quietly as she smiled down on him. "And I'll keep her safe for you, I promise. She's my life…"

He stood there for another few moments, until he began to feel silly, before turning around, figuring it was time he returned to the study and the business of putting Ainsley's plans into motion.

"Was she as wonderful, as perfect, as we remember her," Chance asked from the doorway, looking toward the portrait, "or have we and the years turned her into a saint? What do you think, Court?"

Courtland took another look at Isabella's young beauty. "She was little more than a child," he said at last. "A beautiful, brave girl just stepping into womanhood, a brilliant creature of light Ainsley loved with a fierceness that, looking back on it, was almost frightening. To love that much, and then lose that love in such a terrible, senseless way? How did he survive it? Are we fools, any of us, to dare to love that much, dare that much pain?"

"Jack's probably asked himself that question a time or two these last months, and a thousand times in the past twenty-four hours. But now he's learning something else, something I learned most definitely the day that bastard took my little Alice out onto the sands. You remember that day, Court?"

"I think of the good lieutenant from time to time when I pass by the sands," Courtland said quietly. "And then I spit on him."

"I never think of him. I think only of Alice, and what it would have been like to lose my daughter to that man and those shifting sands. That's where Jack is now, in two separate hells full of fear for both the mother and the child. Love *is* fierce, Court, and often frightening. And the more you love, the more you realize what you have to lose."

Courtland smiled wryly. "You make love sound like something to be avoided at all costs."

"On the contrary, safe, practical brother of mine. Love is something you embrace with both hands, because love, loving someone else, is the only way a man knows he's alive. A man's wife, someday, his children, as well. Now, is there something you want to tell me?"

"Not until I tell her, no," Courtland said quietly

as Jack entered from the foyer, looking tired, but also happier than he had looked a few minutes earlier. "Jack?"

"Eleanor's awake," he said, pinching at the bridge of his nose, probably to wipe away a few tears. "Well, she was, for a few moments anyway. Long enough for me to tell her about our beautiful son and, bless her generous heart, long enough for her to smile at Jacko, tell him she loves him. She's sleeping again. I want to go back up to her, but I'll leave Jacko to sit with her for a while. Let's go back to the study, get this done."

"Good idea, Jack," Chance said, clapping his arm around his brother-in-law's shoulders. "Court's got a few other things to do once we've set our plans into motion. Don't you, Court?"

"You know, Chance, just when I wonder why I ever wanted to knock you down, you remind me," Courtland told him, and then smiled. "Thank you."

Chance flashed him a grin. "You're welcome… and God help you."

CHAPTER SEVENTEEN

CASSANDRA WAITED FOR hours for the sound of Courtland's footsteps outside her chamber, but finally gave in to sleep some minutes after three o'clock, not waking until the sunlight coming through the windows crept far enough across her bed to find her eyes, waking her all at once, Courtland's name on her lips.

She threw back the bedcovers even as she looked at the clock on the mantel, realizing that it had already gone nine, and the entire world, save her, must be up and bustling, preparing for the days ahead.

Her first thought was of Courtland, but her second was of Eleanor and the baby, so that she quickly splashed cold water on her face and then threw on her dressing gown before running down the hallway to Eleanor's bedchamber.

Once inside the chamber, she stopped, took a deep breath and smiled. Eleanor was sitting propped up against a mountain of pillows, and Mariah was feeding her porridge. Eleanor was opening her mouth like a little bird. And Eleanor hated porridge.

"Good morning, Callie," Mariah said, looking at her for a moment as she dipped the spoon into the bowl. "Would you be so kind as to go into the dressing room and tell Onatah that Miss Eleanor would like to see her son now that she's eaten six whole bites of porridge like a good girl?"

Callie laughed as Eleanor pulled a face and said quietly, "Spencer says she should have been a general, and now I see why. Bring me my son, Callie, please?"

"You want me to...*carry* him?" Cassandra had seen the baby, watched him be born, and she had been amazed at how strong he'd been, how little he was, and how...how slippery he'd seemed. Not that he had been all that lively, not at first, not until Onatah, who had slipped into the room unnoticed, had taken his bluish body from Sheila Whiting, dug into his small mouth with her finger, and then blown her breath into his small face. Then? Then he'd drawn in a huge breath and begun to cry, and when Onatah laid him on his belly, the remarkable infant had managed to get himself up on his hands and knees, as if ready to crawl, even as Onatah laughed and said he wouldn't do that again for months and months. "I don't know that I—"

"I'd be happy to do it," Lisette said, entering the room to stand behind Cassandra. "Courtland was looking for you, Callie, downstairs. He said if I saw you that he'd be at the stables for a while, and see you back here at the house sometime before luncheon."

Cassandra nearly hugged Lisette for saving her and quickly ran back to her own chamber to finish washing and dress for the day. She chose one of her riding habits, just in case Courtland wished to return to Dymchurch, for she was not going to be left here to wait and worry, not when all the action would take place in Dymchurch. Snatching up her blue woolen cloak, she headed down the wide, curving staircase.

She stopped off in the morning room to grab an apple from a lovely tower of fruit on the sideboard, and then stepped outside into the chill breeze of a sunny November day. Her second to last day in England at Becket Hall.

The realization hit at her unexpectedly hard and she walked over to the balustrade to look out over the Channel that had been out there every day of her life at Becket Hall; unchanging, steadily pushing unceasing lines of small waves into their sheltered harbor. Seagulls wheeled overhead, squawking and arguing with each other. The sunlight turned the waves almost silver, brilliantly reflecting off the water and stinging at her eyes. The entire world lay beyond this shore, and she was about to become a part of some new place, some foreign scenery that she knew she would grow to love as much, if differently, as she did the view from this terrace.

Because Courtland would be with her. Wherever they went, wherever they landed, wherever they built their lives together, that place would be her home.

She lingered for a few more minutes, until she heard Sergeant-Major Hart's voice sharply calling out orders and turned to her right to see the differently dressed but perfectly aligned troops marching onto the one cleared area of shingle beach for their morning drill, Clovis Meechum dancing about the lines, shouting into faces, shifting a rifle more firmly onto a shoulder. Even Bumble, their cook, who had a peg for a left leg below the knee, was marching this morning.

But hadn't Papa all but assured her that they'd all leave from Dymchurch, and that Becket Hall need not fear an attack?

Holding on to the edges of her cloak, Cassandra set off for the stone steps leading down to the beach, intent on finding Courtland and asking him a few pointed questions. She had to jump back quickly, though, when another troop came marching from the side of the house, this one much more ragtag, and composed of faces she didn't recognize. Men. Women. A scattering of children.

"Here now, Miss," a large man in a butcher's apron asked her in a booming voice, "where would be Mr. Courtland Becket, hmm? We was all told to reconnoiter at that village over there, but there ain't nobody there, so we come lookin' here. That's all right, ain't it? Comin' here instead?"

"I...um..." Cassandra stammered, wondering how this large group had gotten past the Becket Hall defenses. "He's probably at the stables. I'm going there now, if you'd like to—"

"That I would, Miss," the man said, turning to the people behind him. "Silas? Head on back down the road, to show the others where to come to, hear? I'll go see Mr. Becket, get us all straightened out. Long ways to Dymchurch, you know. When are those wagons goin' ta be here?"

Still wondering what on earth could be going on, and beginning to believe that Courtland had been hiding something from her, Cassandra motioned for the man to follow her, and set off at a near run toward the stables.

She saw Courtland just outside, unsaddling his own horse, for all the men who were usually working at the stables were now marching on the shingle, being yelled at by Clovis and the Sergeant-Major. "Court? This gentleman wishes to speak to you," she said once she was close enough for him to hear her. "And then, Mr. Courtland Becket, if you don't mind, so do I!"

Courtland's smile faded at the tone of her voice and he looked past her to the man who seemed to slowly have come to the conclusion that he may have done something wrong. "George Gummer, beggin' your pardon, Mr. Becket," he said quickly. "Rode with the Black Ghost a time or three, I have, and m'sons, as well. At your service, sir."

"Why, yes, thank you, George," Courtland said as Cassandra crossed her arms and glared at him. "If you'll excuse me for just a moment?"

Cassandra turned on her heel, sure Courtland would follow her, and stopped a good twenty paces away from the uneasy George Gummer. "Well? Why would Mr. George Gummer and his friends need wagons to take them to Dymchurch, Court? Would you like to explain that to me?"

"And a good morning to you, too, Callie. Did you sleep well?"

"After waiting up half the night for you to— No, I did not sleep well. And you look as if you haven't slept at all, and your poor horse looks like he's been ridden hard all night. And then there's the matter of the Sergeant-Major and Clovis drilling troops on the beach. If nothing is going to happen here, then why is there any further need for them to—"

He took her by the elbow and walked her over to the fence overlooking the paddock. "Forget everything your Papa told you at the gaol, Callie, please. His orders to me were very different, and they've been set into motion."

"Yes, I think I can see that much on my own. When were you going to tell me?"

He looked away, ran a hand through his hair. He had the beginnings of a beard this morning, proving to her that he had been up all night. She longed to wrap her arms round him, comfort him because he looked so tense and yet so fatigued. But, stupidly, at the same time she found that she was angry with him for, clearly, whatever her papa had told him to do, Courtland had not wished to let her in on the plan.

"We're kidding ourselves if we think there won't be a battle. Some sort of attack, that is. Here, at Becket Hall. Beales made the first strike, removed your father—which serves to divide both our forces and our attention, making it easier for him to attack us here. You understand that?"

"I'm not a simpleton, Court. Yes, I understand that. But we have no choice, do we, as long as Papa is in that gaol."

"Exactly. Which is why we're going to go get him *out* of that gaol. Tonight."

"But…but we aren't leaving until tomorrow night. Tuesday night, correct? We're taking everyone on-board the *Respite* and the *Isabella,* and we're leaving directly from—" She stopped, shook her head. "Why would Papa lie to me like that?"

Courtland finally smiled. "So that you'd agree to come back here, busy yourself packing up your belongings, and then board the *Isabella* without argument?"

"Because once I was aboard ship, then I couldn't do anything if I saw you riding off back to— How dare he! And how dare *you,* Court?"

"It was a moment of madness, I assure you," he told her, touching a hand to her cheek. "But we hoped, all of us, to have you and Lisette and Mariah, all of the women, all safely aboard the *Isabella* until we returned from Dymchurch on the *Respite.*

Eleanor's confinement upset our timing some, but that was still the hopeful plan."

She put her hand on his and pushed it away from her face. "And, now that your plan has failed, what are Lisette and Mariah and I going to do, hmm? Sit here at Becket Hall, tending to our knitting or some such nonsense, while you all go hieing off to Dymchurch with Mr. George Gummer and his friends? To do *what?*"

"Not all of us. Our own people will remain here, to defend Becket Hall."

"Or to keep us pesky women confined and out of the way?"

He was beginning to look exasperated with her, not at all loverlike. Cassandra knew that for she'd seen that particular look on his face many times over the years, when she'd gone too far, said too much, pushed his laudable patience one step too many. But she stood her ground, her chin lifted, glaring at him. Waiting for him to speak. They were equals now, man and woman, not protector and child, and it was time he figured that out!

"And Mr. George Gummer and all his friends?" she asked when he kept his silence. "What, exactly, will they be doing in Dymchurch?"

"Look, Callie, as I keep saying, a divided army is a vulnerable army. That's always been the case. So, we're going to get Ainsley back. Yes, tonight, not tomorrow. Becket Hall is a deceptively clever fortress, we know that, and we need to be the ones who choose the field of battle. Ainsley has chosen Becket Hall, and that Channel out there. Dymchurch Gaol can't be allowed to figure into our confrontation with Edmund Beales."

"So we're getting Papa out of Dymchurch Gaol and bringing him back here. *How?*"

He took in a long breath, let it out slowly. "If I tell you, you'll promise to stay here, wait for us to bring Ainsley home?"

"No, of course not," she said, actually smiling at him. "Whatever you're planning, Court, I will be a part of it. Mariah and Lisette, too, if I tell them what's happening, and I will. How dare you think to exclude us? Mariah will have Spence's ears, and Lisette will rain French all over Rian, and you know it. Look at Elly, what she risked, trying to get to Papa. We can't do any less."

He opened his mouth to protest, but she cut him off.

"Court, think, please. I saw the people who have come here with Mr. Gummer. There are women with him—children. People who owe Papa so much, owe the Black Ghost so much, and are offering their loyalty to help him now that he needs help. More people are coming, and I can only assume there will be more women, more children among them. That day on the island, I was too young to know anything, but I've heard the stories. While you were carrying me deeper into the island to hide me, everyone else was running *toward* Edmund Beales and his men. Old men, injured men, women heavy with child. Children. With pistols and pitchforks or only their bare hands as weapons, they ran *toward* the fight, Court. They didn't hide from it. I won't hide from it. I won't, and neither will Mariah nor Lisette. We're Beckets. This fight belongs to all of us."

Now she held her breath, waiting for his answer, marshaling new arguments if he didn't see that she was right.

"You make a compelling argument, much as I hate to admit it. I knew my duty that day, but I wished I could have stayed, fought alongside the others. Beckets stand, they stand and fight. Very well, Callie," he said at last. "Gather the ladies and inform them that we'll be leaving in little more than an hour if they wish to accompany us, whenever Spence comes back with the wagons we'll need."

"And what do I tell them?"

"Tell them…" he said, at last smiling in a way that told her he forgave her, "tell them they're going to a hanging."

GEORGE GUMMER AND HIS companions numbered only thirty, but the Beckets were joined by another thirty, and then twice again that many as the wagons made their way toward Dymchurch. Each small village they passed through along the way, already alerted that the Black Ghost needed them, sent along some of their own, piling into the empty wagons. Men, women, children. Even a few dogs. By the time they neared Dymchurch, it was as if half of Romney Marsh was on the move.

Cassandra, Mariah and Lisette rode in the very first wagon, where two of the men who loved them could watch them, shake their heads over them and plan for ways to keep them safely in the wagons once they'd arrived in Dymchurch. None of their plans, offered to each other as they rode along together on their horses, would mean anything, but at least they occupied the hours.

A mile from Dymchurch, Spencer turned his horse, to ride back along the line of wagons, to speak to some of the men, thank them for their assistance, warn them to keep their weapons handy but uncocked.

Courtland sat his horse alongside the road, waiting for the wagon carrying the women to approach him, and then guided the horse alongside to speak to Cassandra.

She was sitting with her back to him, watching Billy fiddle with the stout rope he'd formed into an impressive noose, her eyes wide even though she knew the rope was simply for show, like some prop in a play performed at Covent Garden.

"Callie?"

She turned around, put her hands on the board side of the wagon, and lifted herself carefully to her feet. "I'm in my habit, let me ride with you," she asked him, already holding on to his arm and slinging one leg over the side of the wagon, aiming it toward Poseidon's hindquarters.

"For God's sake, be careful," he warned her, grabbing on to her as the wagon wheel hit a rut, and he had to quickly pull her sideways in front of him, hold her as he moved Poseidon away from the wagon. "What was that in aid of, may I ask?" he asked as he reined the horse to a halt as the rest of the wagons rolled past them.

Cassandra, her arms wrapped around him, laid her cheek against his chest. "I'm sorry. I just wanted to…be near you, I guess. You were looking so stern and solemn, and Billy keeps fiddling with that noose, and we're getting closer now and— Is this going to work, Court?"

He urged Poseidon forward once more. "It nearly worked for Beales when he tried it the other day," he pointed out. "And, frankly, it would have, if he'd really wanted Ainsley dead at that moment. But happily for us, it gave Ainsley an idea, reminded him of something he'd heard about—an incident not that many years ago, somewhere on the Marsh."

"Yes, Billy told us about it, but that was years and years ago, and that horrid Lieutenant Tapner doesn't seem the sort to turn and run," Cassandra said, tightening her hold on Courtland. "When…when can we…see each other again?"

"When can we be alone again, you mean," Courtland said, smiling. "That's a question I've been asking myself, knowing that it damns me to admit that I'm concentrating on the wrong thing at the wrong time. You're a corrupting influence, Callie, and I seem to be more than willing to be corrupted."

"I know," she answered, sighing. "I feel so selfish, and at the same time I want to just wish the world away so that you and I could be alone. Take a walk on the beach beneath the full moon tonight, ride out onto the Marsh one last time before we leave for Hampton Roads, sit in the dark and talk…"

He leaned in, kissed her cheek. "I do need to talk to you, that's true. This isn't the time or the place, but you need to know that I want to tell you something I should have told you before we ever— Damn, now what!"

Spencer came riding up to them, a huge grin on his face. "Interrupting something, am I?" he asked, and then sobered. "By my very cursory count, there are more than two hundred of us now, Court, damn near a full contingent of owlers and landsmen we've dealt with over the years, and all champing at the bit to help. We won't go to the gaol before full dark. How in bloody blazes are we going to feed all of these people?"

"A better question, Spence. How are we going to keep them from drinking the tavern dry before we move off? We need to be able to control our own mob, correct?"

Cassandra pressed her face against Courtland's chest, obviously the only one of the three of them to see any humor in that statement. But then she had an idea. "Put Mariah in charge of everything," she told Spencer. "If your wife can't make everyone behave, we're past all hope."

Spencer's highly strung horse danced in a full circle as he attempted to keep his gaze riveted to Cassandra. "Christ. I think you're right, Callie. My beloved wife just assumes everyone will obey her—and damned if they don't think so, too."

As he rode off, Cassandra whispered, "You're welcome," and smiled up at Courtland. "Oh, don't frown so. This is going to work, I'm sure of it. Feeding people is the least of our problems, in any case. Do you think Chance and Kinsey are in place yet?"

"We can only hope so," Courtland said, urging Poseidon off the roadway, into the trees. He didn't rein in the horse until they were a good hundred yards from the wagons that had all nearly passed them by at that point. "Now, how long has it been since I last kissed you?"

Cassandra made herself more comfortable as she sat sideways in front of him on the saddle, slipping her fingers into his hair as she brought her face up to him. "An eternity, I believe."

"That matches my own conclusion," he said just before he caught her mouth with his, sliding his arms around her as his tongue invaded her sweetness and she moaned low in her throat, feeling the now more familiar stirrings of passion deep inside her.

Poseidon danced in place a bit as Courtland held the reins loosely in one hand, moving his other to the flatness of Cassandra's stomach, and then skimmed over the jacket of her habit, to cup her breast. She smiled against his mouth as he began to open the covered buttons of her jacket, at last able to push the jacket off her shoulder, lower his face to between her breasts. She clung to him, holding on to his head in order to keep her precarious balance as he traced over her with his tongue, suckled at her through the thin lawn of her chemise.

Cassandra tipped back her head, looked up at the fading sunlight drifting down through the gnarled trees in the small copse, so dizzy with sensation that she nearly forgot to hold on to Courtland, and was in very real danger of falling from the horse.

But Courtland had her. He'd never let her fall. She'd always known she'd be safe with him. She hadn't realized that he could also fill her with a delight past all understanding.

He lifted his head, looked at her with an intensity that made her shiver, and she watched as he used his teeth to pull the leather glove from his hand, let it drop to the ground. She leaned her head against his shoulder, held on tight once more as he gripped her waist with one hand, lowering his uncovered hand to fist her divided skirt in his fingers, slowly inch it up, up, until he could slide his hand beneath the hem, touch her bare thigh.

"Stop me now, Callie," he whispered hoarsely against her hair, "because I believe I've just lost my mind."

To answer him, she moved on the saddle, shifting her weight so that she could wrap one leg around his muscled calf as he sat in the stirrups; anchoring herself, opening herself to his touch. His touch, that she wanted more than anything, needed more than anything she had ever needed in her life.

"Please. Touch me, Court…touch me the way you did before…*oh!*"

He'd slid his fingers between her legs, pushing aside the scrap of material that was all that kept him from finding her, spreading her, beginning to stroke her…stroke her faster…harder.

She bit at the side of his neck, why, she didn't know, as he slipped a finger inside her, using the sweet moisture he found there to work his magic on her, ignite a liquid fire inside her that grew, and grew, and, at last, consumed her.

Cassandra could feel herself convulsing around him as he pushed his hand against her, held her still so that they could both experience the intensity of her release.

She held on tight, even as she began to cry.

Courtland eased down her skirt once more and put his arms around her, kissed her hair. "Shhh, sweetings. It's all right…it's all right."

"No…it's not. You're so good to me, and I'm so selfish…"

He disentangled himself from her embrace, smiled at her. "Oh, I don't know about that, Callie. I think, in my old age, I'm still going to look back on this moment as one of the most wonderful, and daring, of my normally boring, staid existence. However, practical man that I am at heart, I'm going to put you down for a moment, to retrieve my glove."

"I gave those gloves to you last Christmas," she said as he carefully lowered her to the ground and she bent to pick up the glove. She handed it up to him and then rebuttoned her jacket. "I didn't want Papa to pay Ollie to make them, so I swept out his store every day for a month. Did you know that?"

"We keep secrets very well at Becket Hall. No, Ollie never told me. They're doubly precious to me now. But come on, let's get moving, before Spence comes riding back to find us. He isn't really as amusing as he thinks he is, and I don't want to have to punch him in the nose."

She raised her crossed arms to him and he lifted her onto the saddle once more in one fluid motion. He kept hold of her hands, lowering them around his neck as he bent in to kiss her, a gentle kiss that nearly had her crying again.

"There was something you wanted to say to me?" she asked him as he urged Poseidon back toward the roadway.

His intense look had her toes curling in her riding boots. "I do, but it'll keep. Contrary to the evidence of what just happened, sweetings, there's a time and place for everything. For now, just promise me one thing."

Still feeling more than a little mellow, Cassandra agreed, but then quickly added, "...as long as it doesn't include waiting at the inn while the rest of you go into Dymchurch."

"No, I won't ask the impossible, Callie. You were right when you said that Beckets go toward the fight, not run from it. But, since we kept the crew in readiness back at Becket Hall, you, Rian, Billy, and Spencer and I are the only ones who've seen Edmund Beales and might recognize him. If you see Beales tonight, pretend you haven't."

"I still don't understand why, if he's at the gaol, we can't take him then—kill him then. And, no, I'm not sorry that I wish him dead, and just as quickly as possible."

"Normally, I'd agree. Better a swift end to things. But Ainsley has other plans for our old enemy. And if they work, the Beckets, here or anywhere in this world, will never have to look over their shoulders again, worried that their past will come back to destroy them."

CHAPTER EIGHTEEN

"WHERE'S MARIAH?"

"You don't want me to answer that, Court," Spencer said, lifting a mug of homebrewed ale to his lips as the Beckets gathered around the table in the only private dining room in the small inn. "Suffice it to say, by the time my beloved wife is through bullying her way through the kitchens and taprooms of this small village, that business of the loaves and fishes will have paled in comparison. Of course, our dear Lord was not equipped with three fat purses filled with gold pieces, but we'll take our miracles any way we can find them, correct?"

"Now I wonder, Lisette," Courtland asked, smiling. "Would that be blasphemy or sacrilege our friend Spencer has just uttered—or both? In any case, if a white-hot bolt of lightning comes crashing through the ceiling in the next few moments, Spence, please have the courtesy to stand up and deflect it from the rest of us."

Courtland held out a chair for Cassandra and then

sat down beside her, looking to the convent-educated Lisette, who merely shrugged in that graceful Gallic way of hers as she buttered a warm biscuit for Rian. Lisette was a beautiful young woman, all pale and golden, but at the moment she was too pale, knowing that her father was close by.

"Tell me again about this Empress," Rian said after taking a large bite from the biscuit. "Ainsley was rather vague when I saw him this afternoon and we played at how I am to deliver it to the gaol tomorrow evening. What does it look like?"

"I think it's beautiful," Cassandra said, reaching beneath the table for Courtland's hand, and squeezing it, "but it's only a stone, nothing to have caused so many deaths."

"Well, whatever it is," Rian continued, "Ainsley won't let Beales have it, not now that we know that damn thing is the real reason Beales attacked the island. Isabella was only a part of his madness. It's still difficult to believe so many people died because he thinks the stone is—what? Magical?"

"The stone is bad luck," Cassandra said, her appetite gone. "Papa says bad luck wears off, but I know I don't want to so much as touch the Empress again. How can anyone know when the bad luck is gone? I wouldn't risk it. Perhaps in a few hundred years it will have lost its curse, or whatever it is, but until then it can sit where it is, as far as I'm concerned."

There was general agreement around the table as

Mariah walked into the room, dusting her hands together and looking more than a little satisfied with herself. "Everyone has been fed—including the horses and oxen—thank you very much for doubting me, husband, and in case no one else has noticed, it is almost full dark out there."

Cassandra watched as Courtland grabbed one last forkful of mutton and shoved it into his mouth even as he got to his feet. "And Chance and Kinsey are in place?"

Rian nodded. "They've been here for several hours now. Kinsey's staying with the *Respite,* but Chance has positioned himself just outside the gaol, as a part of the guard from Becket Hall."

"In that case, let's do what we came here to do, before Mariah has to feed everyone again, and allow our friends to return to their homes and families," Spencer said, also getting to his feet. "But first," he added, lifting his mug, "to success."

"To success!" they all agreed, and the drained mugs hit the tabletop all together, so that Cassandra involuntarily flinched, and realized that her nerves were not as steady as she would like Courtland and everyone else to believe.

To hide her concern, she quickly rose and led the way out of the dining room, Courtland throwing her cloak over her shoulders as Rian walked past her to open the door to the innyard.

She stepped outside and gasped at the sight that

greeted her. Over two hundred people, all of them waiting quietly, solemnly, a scattering of bright, smoking torches casting strange shadows on all their faces. They hadn't looked to be so many, not piled into the wagons. Now they were very impressive indeed. And at the very front of the crowd stood Billy, still holding the noose.

"You remember the plan, friends. Our sheer force of numbers will be the road to our success," Courtland said, standing behind her, his hands resting on her shoulders. "At the most, there are a dozen soldiers assigned to the gaol. The remainder are either sleeping off their dinner at the garrison or out on patrol—looking for some of you, yes, gentlemen?"

That brought a few laughs and cheers from the assembled company, most of whom had most probably had to outrun the Waterguard at some time in their lives.

"Ah, but tonight we are upstanding citizens of Romney Marsh, set on not allowing the dangerous Black Ghost to escape justice, isn't that right? Tonight we march on the gaol, righteously indignant, demanding Marsh justice, not Dover justice, that is too often not as harsh as we would like. Transportation? No! Death! We demand death for the crime of smuggling, do we not?"

"Not so's you could tell by me, thank ya kindly!" someone called out from the back of the crowd, and everyone laughed this time.

"So much for your inspired speech, Court," Cassandra teased him, turning to look at him and his suddenly confused expression. "Perhaps we should just go? They already know what they're to do."

His expression softened and he smiled down at her. "We need Chance here, I suppose. He's much more eloquent, and I'm beginning to remember why I like to remain in the background, sweeping up after everyone else."

"You make yourself sound so dull," she scolded. "Wasn't it you who first rode out as the Black Ghost?"

"Don't remind me," he said, pulling her cloak hood up over her hair before addressing his audience once more. "He's in the cells in the cellars and there will be guards there unless they're called upstairs to deal with us. No violence, not if our numbers are sufficient to encourage the soldiers to abandon their posts. We find the key, we get him out, we surround him as he makes his way into the shadows, and it's over. Understood?"

Again, that voice from the back of the crowd: "Just a quick stoppin' off to deliver a kick or three, sir? Nothin' too fatal?"

This time Courtland laughed with the crowd, and then he raised his arm high and held it there as he turned, began the mile-long march into Dymchurch.

Cassandra fell into step beside him, Rian and Lisette, Spencer and Mariah flanking them. The Beckets, united, leading the way because, as they'd all heard Ainsley say so many times, no one should be asked to do what a Becket wouldn't do for himself. Behind them, walking ten abreast, the crowd followed, the light from the torches helping to light their way, as did the full moon.

Soon enough those torches were reflected in the windows of houses and shop windows lining the streets of Dymchurch, and the evening silence was broken only by the sound of several hundred feet, many clad in wooden clogs, striking the cobblestones.

People began opening their doors, most of them just as quickly shutting them, for to see a mob on the move had to bring back memories of the old days, when freetraders marched openly through the streets, rough, defiant, daring anyone to look at them crookedly.

Cassandra believed her heart was now beating in time with those marching feet, and she squeezed Courtland's hand tightly as they turned one last corner and began advancing directly toward the gaol house.

"Drop back now, Callie," he said. "Stay with Mariah and Lisette."

She didn't argue. She was excited. She was terrified. She was not, not at this moment, about to disobey orders.

She held out her hands to Lisette and Mariah as the men moved ahead and, arms linked together, they followed, their steps never wavering.

Rian yelled out, "You! You in the gaol! Give us

Geoffrey Baskin! We've no quarrel with you! We come for Geoffrey Baskin!"

Spencer cupped his hands around his mouth and shouted, "The Black Ghost! Scourge! Murderer! Bring him out! Bring him out!"

The crowd, on cue, took up the cries, repeating the demands, raising their weapon in the air as they continued to advance on the gaol house.

The pair of guards flanking the door, both of whom Cassandra recognized, leveled their rifles at the crowd. At Courtland's chest.

"Oh, God," Cassandra whispered, and just for a moment, she thought she might faint.

"Women and kiddies up front!" Billy yelled, waving the noose above his head. "Fine boys up there, what knows what's what! Not goin' to shoot women or kiddies! Come on now—step lively!"

It was unbelievable. The men all stopped and allowed the women to push past them. And the women, if it were possible, seemed more formidable than the men. They carried brooms, pitchforks, lengths of stout wood they held high in the air as they demanded entrance to the gaol house.

"I wish I had a weapon," Mariah said beside her. "My God, Callie, they're magnificent, aren't they? Come on—don't let them lead the way when it's Becket women who belong up front."

Their arms still linked at the elbows, the three women arrived once more at the very front of the crowd—the noisy, highly belligerent mob—just in time to see the heavy door close behind the two guards. Cassandra could hear a stout wooden bolt shooting home.

"*Merde,* what do we do now?" Lisette asked. "This is all a fine show, but that's a prodigiously large door."

"Pardon us, misses," someone said behind them, and they stepped to one side to see a half dozen short, brawny men holding a freshly-cut tree trunk and heading straight for the door.

"Well," Mariah said, clapping her hands as if at a party, "I guess that answers that question!"

But the battering ram wasn't necessary, because the door opened once more and there was a moment of congestion as the soldiers, all local youths who knew on which side their bread had been buttered for many a year, all bolted outside and then ran off in every direction. After all, their own mamas could be brandishing one of those pitchforks.

So they retreated—ran away like rats deserting a sinking ship, in truth—leaving the door open.

And then Chance was there, without Cassandra realizing he had been anywhere near. He leapt up onto the raised flagway, light spilling over him from inside the gaol house, a wicked-looking sword in his hand, his long, blond hair flying loose in the stiff breeze coming off the Channel. He stood on the wooden flagway as she felt certain he would look on the deck of a ship, his legs spread, one hand on his hip, his chin held high, defiant. "Men! You allow your women to fight for you? To me! Now! We're here for Marsh justice!"

"A man men follow," Courtland said in some admiration as he slipped his arm around Cassandra's shoulders, pulled her off to the side as the crowd surged forward once more.

"But you said no weapons drawn," Cassandra reminded him, biting her bottom lip.

"Sweetheart, there's only one person left inside that gaol, and that's your father. Chance knows that, but we still need the crowd to cover our withdrawal, as at least one of those soldiers fled to the garrison house. Passion rises quickly and fades just as fast. We don't need our friends all wandering off to the nearest tavern before we're safely aboard ship, now do we?"

"Oh, no, I suppose not. You'll excuse me. I've never assaulted a gaol before. You'll stay here?"

"And that's what I do, yes. I stand and stay, attend to all the boring details while they delight in the glory. Plodding and practical, Callie, that's who and what I am. I did warn you, remember?" Courtland said as Spencer and Rian joined the stream of men pushing into the gaol, the two of them grinning like fools because they lived for this sort of adventure.

Mariah and Lisette smiled, for they were, at heart, adventurous women. They weren't afraid for their husbands because, if given the choice, they'd be right there, beside them.

Cassandra admired them all, even as she thought they might all be just a little bit crazy.

"I'm glad you're the way you are, Court," Cassandra said sincerely. "It's often more difficult to stand, I think. What if Beales is in there?"

"I'm sure he's long gone, watching from somewhere safe. They've had to know for at least ten minutes or more that we were on our way. I wonder if he has begun to recognize his mistake. Let's hope not."

"His mistake? You still haven't explained that to me," Cassandra said as they both continued to watch the doorway, waiting for Ainsley to appear. The worst was over; it was all now just a matter of time before her papa was with her again.

"Yes," Courtland told her, slipping his arm around her waist. "Beales had the arrest warrant written for Geoffrey Baskin, not Ainsley Becket. Your papa was quick to recognize the opportunity that gave him, and immediately confessed to being the Black Ghost, which—"

She turned to look up at him when he stopped speaking, to see that Lieutenant Tapner was standing directly behind them, an armed soldier on either side of him, his sword drawn and pushing into Courtland's back.

"We'll take the young lady off your hands if you'd be so kind as to release your hold on her, thank you," the lieutenant said. "Someone is very anxious to see her again."

"Oh, God, no," Mariah whispered, grabbing Lisette's hand.

Courtland closed his eyes for a second, and then looked at Cassandra. "And here I thought I could safely leave all the derring-do to my adventurous brothers. Hell of a thing, for a practical man. But then, a practical man prepares himself for most any eventuality…"

And, before Cassandra could even open her mouth to scream, Courtland had turned on his heel, a stiletto magically appearing in his right hand, winking in the light from the torches before disappearing into the very center of Lieutenant Tapner's chest, reappearing again, red with the soldier's heart's blood.

"Everyone—follow me!" Courtland yelled as the two soldiers, not quite up to anything more than supporting their dying lieutenant, lowered their weapons.

Within moments they were swallowed up by the crowd, Cassandra nearly tripping on the cobblestones as Courtland aimed them all at a nearby alleyway, Mariah and Lisette close behind them.

They didn't look back, Courtland urging them on, seemingly already knowing where he was heading. But then Mariah stopped, and Lisette and Cassandra stopped with her.

"I'm sorry, you go ahead," Mariah said, leaning against the wall of a building at the side of the alley. "The baby, you understand. I think he'd prefer I walked."

Cassandra's hand flew to her mouth. "But you're all right?"

"I'm fine," Mariah assured her. "There's a lot to be said for coming from good peasant stock."

"Court?"

"Yes, I'll carry her," Courtland said, but it wasn't necessary. They all looked back down the alley as they heard more racing footsteps, and a moment later Cassandra saw Spencer running toward his wife, scooping her up without a question and taking off down the alleyway once more.

"Rian!" Lisette shouted, holding out a hand to him, and then they were also gone, disappearing into the darkness.

Cassandra waited, afraid to breathe, until her father's beloved face was revealed by the moonlight, and then she launched herself into his embrace.

"Well met, sir," Courtland said. "But we might want to move on now. We're only another block or two from the wharf."

Ainsley took Cassandra's cheeks between his hands and kissed her forehead. "I should have known better than to believe you'd be any less the woman your mother was," he said quietly. "Court? Lead the way, if you please."

"Yes, sir, but where's—"

"Looking for me, Court?" Chance asked, advancing toward them, what looked to be Billy's legs and hindquarters folded over his shoulder. "It took some convincing to get our friend here to believe he'd conked enough heads. What a party! Some two dozen or so of the Waterguard have arrived on the scene, and it would seem a lot of old grudges are being settled back there, God love every last one of those people."

"Put me down, you misbegotten whelp of a sea dog!"

Chance deposited Billy on his feet, the bandy-legged man looking none the worse for wear, although it was rather disconcerting seeing the noose strung around his throat as if it were a neck cloth he'd donned for the evening.

"Amusing as all this is, I believe I might enjoy being on the water, preferably in the next five minutes," Ainsley said, and Courtland nodded. Taking Cassandra's hand he led the way toward the wharf and the longboats that would be waiting there to row them out to the *Spectre* and the *Respite* for their return to Becket Hall.

"One small, niggling matter, Ainsley," Chance said, his tone even, conversational. "There are two other sloops anchored in the harbor, new to the port as of a week ago, I'm told. If we're lucky, Beales is even now being rowed out to one of them."

"We're not," Ainsley told him. "Beales left this afternoon, after I convinced him that Rian would retrieve the Empress from Becket Hall and bring it to the gaol tomorrow evening, as we'd agreed—just as he agreed, on his honor, to not attack my home or family. Edmund being Edmund, I imagine he's very close to Becket Hall right now, considering strategy for his attack and capture of the Empress, leaving me to hang at Dover Castle. Just as I don't believe him, he doesn't believe me—a sad testament to the friendship I once thought we had between us. If either of the sloops follows when we up anchor, we'll have to eliminate it, quickly."

Cassandra shot a sharp, worried glance at Courtland, who squeezed her hand reassuringly, and quickened their pace toward the beach.

COURTLAND LIFTED Cassandra above the small waves running up on the sandy beach and carried her to the longboat to deposit her alongside Mariah and Lisette, Spencer and Rian. They'd be rowed out to the *Respite* while Chance would rejoin his own crew from Becket Hall on the *Spectre*.

They'd already seen men climbing the rigging of one of the sloops anchored a few hundred yards from their own two ships, and as it was a strange hour to be setting off on a voyage, it was simple to assume that the sloop belonged to Edmund Beales.

As Courtland rejoined the rest of the men on the beach, Ainsley was giving last minute instructions to Chance. "The most efficient way to eliminate her is to simply sink her. We have no time to play cat-and-mouse, and no reason to want anyone aboard her to survive. Agreed?"

"If there's a chance Beales is aboard…" Chance said, and then shrugged. "No, you say he's not, and I believe you. We'll certainly know one way or another, in any case, once the sloop makes its first move. The bastard was brilliant on the water, if ruthless."

"True," Ainsley agreed. "But Jules is dead, which leaves only Richard Oakes, who never understood the nuances of eluding contact until in a prime position to strike. For all we know, Oakes may also be dead. But let's hope he still lives, and still sails with Edmund. If the sloop's first move is to try to evade using a starboard tack, it's most probably Oakes, as he never had any imagination. And then we'll have him."

"Have him where? We can't be chasing him all the night long," Chance asked, shaking his head. "Tell me what you're thinking, Ainsley."

"This is no time for a warning across the bow, Chance. I heard of a daring maneuver accomplished many years ago by the one the Americans called Blackbeard. We open with full broadsides," Ainsley said matter-of-factly, heading toward the already loaded longboat. "We lead him out, lull him into thinking we're allowing him to follow, and then turn, both of us—you to port, me to starboard—mindful of his penchant to evade by tacking hard, starboard, and flank him. Roll out the guns and eliminate him."

Chance threw back his head and laughed aloud.

"Full broadsides? From both of us? That story? It must be some fairy tale. Hell, Ainsley, if we miss, we'll damn well sink each other."

Ainsley was already in the water, making his way to the longboat, but he took a moment to turn about, grin at Chance. "Then, son, I most sincerely suggest you don't miss."

Chance laughed again, more of a short explosion of breath, and looked at Courtland. "That wily bastard. Good to have him back, isn't it, Court?"

Courtland watched as the longboat carrying Cassandra pushed off into the deeper water. She was holding on to one side, looking back at him, and he waved to her, as if to tell her that he'd be right along. "It is, yes. Can you use an extra hand on the *Spectre?* I have this sudden need to personally take charge of the aiming of the guns."

"I'd be honored, brother," Chance told him, resting an arm on his shoulder as they headed for the second longboat. "Have you talked to her yet? Said what needs to be said?"

"Not really, no," Courtland admitted as the longboat seemed to disappear into the darkness. "She saw me kill a man tonight, Chance. God knows what else she'll see before this is over. I always wanted to protect her from this part of our lives. Hell, I just want this part of our lives over…a new beginning."

"You'll have that new beginning, Court, soon. She

knows that. Now come on, we've a ship to send to the bottom."

"Two ships," Courtland pointed out tersely as they each grabbed an oar from other crew members, and Chance cursed as they both watched the sails being run up on the second sloop. "I don't want to sound worried, but it has been a long time since either you or Ainsley did this sort of thing. Are you sure we shouldn't just outrun them and lose them in the dark?"

"And hazard a combined attack on Becket Hall from both land and sea? No, Court. This is our chance, a golden opportunity to lure Beales's crews into deep water and be done with them. Now, if you please," Chance said, grinning wickedly at his brother, "which way is starboard again?"

With those joking words, Courtland laughed out loud, nearly losing his grip on the oar. "My God, I'm beginning to think I may be as mad as the rest of you!"

"You were always a slow starter, brother mine," Chance told him, "but we all knew you'd catch up, eventually. There's the rope ladder. You first, brother."

CHAPTER NINETEEN

CASSANDRA HAD BEEN out on the water on the *Respite* several dozen times, but only in daylight hours, and only to watch as the crews practiced their seamanship, for her father believed in keeping their skills fresh.

She'd never been out on the Channel at night, and she certainly had never even dreamed of being caught up in a sea battle.

She and Mariah and Lisette would be ordered below decks before the beginning of the battle, but for now no one seemed to notice that they were still above decks, standing in the shadows, watching the flurry of organized chaos as the sails were manned, as the anchor was hoisted, as Ainsley Becket calmly, even politely called out orders.

Courtland had gone with Chance, she knew now, while Rian and Spencer had boarded the *Respite* with them. Cassandra believed this to be an equitable division, keeping husbands with their wives, the father with the daughter—but that didn't mean she was happy with the arrangement.

She would be less than useless as they engaged the enemy, she knew that, but to watch the *Spectre* and not know if Courtland had been injured? How was she going to endure the next hours?

"The only time I've been to sea was when Rian brought me to Becket Hall. What are they doing now?" Lisette asked as two of the crew walked around the decks, spilling buckets of sand onto the boards.

"It's…it's so they won't slip in the blood of the injured," Cassandra told her, remembering her lessons, many of them told to her by a laughing, winking Jacko. That information no longer sounded quite so exotic, so exhilarating.

Spencer came down from the quarterdeck, grinning as he handed Mariah a long glass and pointed aft. "We've got them both after us now, lambs being led to the slaughter. Ainsley thinks they'll keep their distance, follow us home, thinking to trap us between them and Becket Hall as they attack from both land and sea. In fact, it was probably their plan all along. Squeezing us in the middle, sinking our ships before we could run up the sails and get free of the harbor. Now they're hanging back, trying to figure out what to do now that we're already free of the harbor. Ainsley says we sink one, the other will run, consider it a good day's work to have survived, and take Beales's ship as their prize."

"You cannot buy loyalty," Cassandra said quietly, remembering yet another lesson learned at her father's knee. "What happened tonight, all those people coming to help Papa the way they did, without asking for any reward? It never occurred to Edmund Beales that anyone would come to Papa's aid, storm the gaol to release him. Because he couldn't have hoped for such support, could he?"

"Edmund Beales," Spencer said, his jaw tight, "would probably have to think twice before asking his own mother to help him. Fear and respect are two very different things. He probably has his own captains on those sloops, but the crews? A sloop going into battle can't boast size, so it depends on its swiftness, and its skilled crew. Ainsley said that if Beales is running true to form, he's hired the dregs of the earth for his crews. We're hoping for a quick fight, a quicker victory. Now, we need you all to go below decks, to Ainsley's cabin, all right?"

"Not yet, please," Cassandra begged him.

Spencer looked to his wife, who was nodding her agreement with Cassandra. "All right. But the moment we engage, you three are below decks, you hear me?"

"Do we *hear* him?" Mariah said facetiously, handing the long glass to Cassandra as Spencer headed aft once more. "Are we all shaking in our shoes, ladies? I know I am. Men! Do they think wearing skirts means we can't fight?"

Lisette laughed, and Cassandra put the long glass to her eye, hoping the full moon provided enough light to be able to see Courtland aboard the

Spectre, as the sloops were running nearly side-by-side. But she couldn't see him. Ah, no, there he was, standing beside Chance, who was barking out orders as he watched the mainsail, checked the direction of the wind—at least that's what she thought he might be doing.

She supposed Chance looked quite dashing as he played the captain, his fair hair wild around his face, his shirtsleeves glowing white as they whipped about in the night breeze. But it was Courtland who drew her eyes; that solid, strong man, his expression formidable in its intensity, his demeanor that of a man deep in thought, considering all angles of a thing before moving, and then moving decisively—correctly.

But then Billy came up to him, handing him two braces of large, ugly pistols, each pair laced together from thick strips of leather Courtland hung about his neck. What good would pistols be, unless they planned to board one of the sloops following them? In case they were boarded themselves and expected hand-to-hand combat?

Assuredly, sand had been spread on the decks of the *Spectre,* as well.

"Oh, God," Cassandra said, lowering the glass. She knew so little about what happened during a sea battle, but perhaps that little was still too much.

Ainsley gave another command. They were in tight quarters, four swift sloops running so very near together, but that's how privateers fought. Slipping, cutting, sailing close to the wind, closer to danger, in pursuit of their prey.

Cassandra grabbed at the railing as the *Respite* turned toward the barely visible shoreline, the sails filling, flapping loudly, so that Cassandra knew she'd have to shout to be heard, not that she could think of a single thing to say save to warn, "Go below! It's starting!"

Lisette, tall, slender, but stronger than she looked, both in mind and body, pulled Mariah to the stairs leading below decks, but Cassandra stayed where she was, keeping a white-knuckled grip on the rails as she strained to see the *Spectre.* It was turning away from them now, and she quickly lost sight of all but the yellow light of a few lanterns in the dark, even as the *Respite* completed its dangerous maneuver near the shoreline—its hull purposely designed to be shallow enough to avoid the rocks—and was now heading in exactly the opposite direction.

Cassandra, desperate to not lose her balance, ran to the starboard side, grabbing on to the rail with one hand while holding tight to the long glass with the other in time to see that one of the pursuing sloops, either reacting too slowly or not reacting at all, was about to be sandwiched between the *Spectre* and the *Respite.*

No more than fifty yards of night-black Channel water divided the *Respite* and their pursurer now, and she could see the tips of the *Spectre*'s mainsail as Chance flanked the trapped sloop. It was being fed into a funnel, had nowhere to turn, but would have to hope its speed could pull it through the narrow tunnel of space left to it, leaving the *Spectre* and *Respite* heading in quite the wrong direction.

They *were* going to attempt to board the sloop. That's all Cassandra could think, as surely they were too close to fire on the other ship—except that they were also too far apart to board it. Their guns had been run out, yes, she'd heard the rumble, and felt it, beneath her feet—but so had the guns on the other ship. If they fired, they'd only succeed in sinking each other, and that was madness.

No, the sloop was going to be past them, free, while their ships moved on in the wrong direction, perhaps to attack the second sloop that already seemed to be turning, running away, as if it wanted no part of the fight. But why let this first one pass them by?

She lifted the glass to her eye yet again, the full moon sliding out from behind a cloud just in time for her to be able to see some of the faces of the crew on Beales's ship as it entered the funnel that was the other two sloops. Some of the crew were running, all were shouting…while one older seaman surprised her by solemnly throwing her a kiss and then simply standing very still and making the Sign of the Cross before bowing his head in prayer.

He had just clasped his hands together in front of him when the deck he stood on exploded.

Cassandra was thrown to the deck as the *Respite* rolled to port before righting itself again. She was forced to crawl across the sandy boards, back to the railing, pulling herself upright. The seaman who had thrown her the kiss was gone. The sloop's gunports were gone. Most of the side of the sloop was gone.

She held on to the rail as the *Respite* moved on past, struggling to recognize that what she was looking at was still a ship.

"Good shooting! Hold tight, boys! We're nearly clear!" she heard Ainsley warn loudly. "Her powder magazine will blow any moment!"

The huge fire on the other sloop lit up the area nearly as clearly as summer sunshine. Cassandra held on, going to her knees and melding herself against the rail, looking up to see the other sloop's shattered mizzenmast disappear past the *Respite.* And then she saw a large, gray-haired man, standing alone at the very rear of the sloop, clasping the railing and first looking down at the fire that raged everywhere on what was left of the deck, then at the dark water below his feet.

"Richard Oakes!" Ainsley shouted, and the man's head whipped around toward the *Respite.* "A true sailor you are, Richard! Never learned how to swim, did you? She's going to blow, Richard! Jump or burn!"

The man shook his fist at Ainsley. "I'll see you in hell, Geoff Baskin!"

Cassandra shot a quick look toward her father,

just in time to see him bow with exquisite elegance as he called out, "You first, Richard!"

Cassandra shut her eyes tight, not wanting to know what would happen next, and nothing did, not for several seconds, as the *Respite* cleared the other ship, the sails caught even more wind and seemed to begin to race gracefully across the water.

Moments. It had all happened within a few moments, but Cassandra knew she would remember those moments for the remainder of her life, especially when she at last caught sight of the *Spectre* just before the crippled sloop exploded with a terrifying amount of force and noise, and then almost immediately disappeared beneath the dark water.

That terrible flash of yellow light had served to outline the *Spectre* in the dark, and the fact that the mizzenmast was now in two pieces, the topmost part lying smashed on the deck. Where she had last seen Courtland and Chance.

"EASY...EASY...JESUS, Kinsey, don't let him *swing* like that! Watch his leg!"

Courtland stood in the longboat, watching as Rian's giant, Jasper, raised his massive arms to grab hold of Chance the moment he and the stout net sling he was lying in dropped low enough.

"Stop being such an old woman, Court!" Chance yelled down to him in between singing snatches of a song having a lot to do with a woman named Kitty and how, for a penny, she would let a man touch her great-grand— Well, Courtland really wasn't listening anyway. He hadn't been listening for the past several hours as Kinsey worked to bring the damaged *Spectre* into the lagoon and Courtland had held down Chance after they'd poured half the rum onboard down his gullet before Jasper set the man's broken leg.

One errant ball. Two close-on broadsides, one errant ball. Remarkable in itself, but did that ball have to split the mizzenmast in two and send it crashing down on Chance's leg?

Courtland had not quite escaped injury himself, but a bump to the brainbox would have to be delivered with more force to have done any real damage, or so Billy had told him as he'd wrapped a bandage around his head.

It was two hours past dawn, after the longest night of Courtland's life, but at last they were home.

Ainsley, after keeping the *Respite* close while the *Spectre* limped along, had been ashore for some minutes, and Courtland swore he could feel Cassandra's eyes boring into his back as he assisted Jasper in lowering Chance against the boards and they were rowed toward the shore.

There was probably going to be hell to pay, or she'd cry all over his neck—God, she wouldn't do that, would she? Not until he'd had a chance to speak to Ainsley, to explain to Ainsley, to promise to Ainsley…

"How is he?" Ainsley called out as the crewmen jumped into the surf and pulled the longboat up onto the shingle beach.

"Drunk as three sailors, sir," Courtland called back to him, hopping over the side into the knee-deep water, "and happy to point out to anyone who will listen that none of *his* broadside went wide. *Sir,*" he ended grinning.

Ainsley's smile was tight. "Very well. You'll carry him, Jasper? Thank you. Spencer, Rian? Let's get him inside before he sobers up and realizes how much pain he's in, gentlemen."

Everyone made their way through the shore fortifications toward the house, the crews of the two ships heading to the village to refresh themselves at The Last Voyage. Cassandra stood her ground and Courtland, knowing he had nowhere else to go, stayed also, busying himself securing the longboat to the cleat hammered into the shingle.

"We will never speak of this, not ever," she said at last, her voice firm, taking on the tone, he thought, of Mariah, or the always composed Eleanor, or perhaps even Chance's own Julia at her most imperious. God, there was a thought. A lucky thing for Ainsley that he'd be well at sea before Julia found out what had happened to her husband.

Unless he wished to tie the rope into knots that would never be untied, Courtland had nothing else to do that would keep him from looking at Cassandra. "Agreed."

"We will never speak of that man, that Lieutenant."

"Also agreed. Although I will say it's probably a good job that we'll be leaving soon, even though I doubt anyone will be able to remember just how the man came to be dead in the middle of that melee."

She wrung her hands in front of her, her only sign of nervousness. "It couldn't be helped. He was in the employ of Edmund Beales. Please don't be upset for him and please don't ask me to pray for his soul."

Courtland nodded, holding out his hand so that Cassandra took it, and they began walking up the beach. "Are you all right?"

He wasn't sure if the sound she made was a short laugh or a suppressed sob. "I have never—*never*—been so frightened in my life as when I saw that huge mast and sail where I'd last seen you. I thought…I thought…oh, God, our lives have just begun, they can't be over. And I was so…so *angry.*"

Now he smiled. "Yes, I'm noticing that. You've always favored anger above tears."

"I am *not* having a tantrum, Court. I'm not a child. I'm angry! But neither serves any purpose, does it? I'm so…so weary of all of this. I'm angry with what's happened, what's happening now. I'm angry that I had to see Papa in a way I've never before seen him—brilliant, yes, but…but *ruthless*—and acting in a way that makes me realize that the past belongs in the past, never out in the sun again. And I'm angry with myself for being so stupidly angry, for not realizing sooner that no matter who we are now, we were once not so…not so *nice.*"

"Callie, it wasn't all like that. Yes, Ainsley was a privateer, but sanctioned and approved by the Crown. And look at how he cared for all of us. If it hadn't been for your father, I—"

"No! Don't say anything! I'm not asking you to defend him. He doesn't need defending. He's a good man. I know that, and I love him very much. Last night didn't change that."

"Then maybe you might want to go tell him that," Courtland said, reaching for her. "Knowing him as I do, he's probably wondering what you thought about actions he had no choice but to take last night."

"No, not yet. I need *you* to understand." She held up her hands, keeping him at a distance. "I…I want it *over,* Court. Poor Papa. He wants so much to be good. And you, Court. I understand now, why you're so careful, why you're happiest when…when everything is quiet, peaceful. I want that, too. I want us to be able to be together without worrying about what Edmund Beales might do next. About whatever was done in the past coming back to destroy who we are today."

He pulled her against him and let her cry.

At last he took hold of her shoulders and gently put some distance between them. "If I promise to go back to being upstanding and dull and boring and… stodgy, will you stop crying?"

"And practical," she added, wiping at her face with the edge of her cloak. "I watched Chance when he was *performing* at the gaol, and as he captained the *Spectre.* And I thought, isn't he magnificent? And I thought, oh, I'm so glad Court isn't like that. It's not that I don't love Chance, that I don't love Papa. I love them with all of my heart. But they're…" she summoned a small smile. "Well, they're *exhausting.*"

Courtland bit back a laugh at the rather astonished look on Cassandra's face, for she seemed to have learned something about herself that she hadn't previously known. "I think, sweetheart, you're attempting to tell me that the reason you're…drawn to me is because I'm boring."

Her bottom lip began to quiver again, but this time she laughed. "Why, Courtland Becket, I think you're right. And I'm not drawn to you. I love you."

Courtland stopped once again, turned her to face him. "You shouldn't have said that."

She looked up at him, blinked.

"I wanted to speak to Ainsley first, ask his permission. I think I have it, but I wanted to ask him, formally, and then propose to you in some romantic way while telling you that I love you with my entire heart and soul."

Cassandra pressed her fingertips to her mouth, smiled. "I…I think this is a very romantic way. Save for that bandage, which makes you look just a little bit silly. Say it again."

He shook his head, wondering what had kept him from saying the words before this moment. Hell's bells, he'd taken her to his bed. Granted, that act didn't equate love, not for a large population of the world, but he wasn't the rest of the world. "When we fired the broadsides, I held my breath until I could see the *Respite* was undamaged. God, I was shooting at the ship that held my world, Callie. I never want to be put in a position like that again. I love you," he ended, lowering his mouth to hers until his lips were only a whisper from hers. "I will love you forever."

He held her close as they shared what somehow seemed to be their first kiss, filled with a sweetness that hurt his heart, which threatened to unman him. She was his. So precious to him…and now his equal, his woman, his love…

"We have to go inside now," he murmured against her hair as she clung to him, the two of them more than a little breathless. "Like you, sweetings, I wish this was over, but we both know it isn't. I want you to go upstairs, get some rest, while I speak to Ainsley."

"I know. Papa told me Edmund Beales will most likely come here, perhaps even today."

"We'll talk about that, yes," Courtland said, lifting her hand to his lips. "But first we'll speak of something much more important. Once we're at sea, I believe your papa may be able to marry us. Would you like that, or do you want to wait until we're in Hampton Roads, and you can gather bride clothes and—"

Cassandra gave a small cry and wrapped her arms around his neck, placed a swift, hard kiss on his mouth. "Does that answer your question?"

"Yes, I suppose it does," Courtland said, believing he might just be grinning like the village idiot. He took her hand again as they mounted the stone steps to the terrace.

His hand on the latch of one of the French doors leading into the drawing room, he kissed her once more, and then asked her to please check on Eleanor and the baby before going to her own chamber to get some rest.

She started into the drawing room as he pulled open the door and stood back, bowing grandly to her as he gestured that she should precede him. She dropped into a small curtsey and then smiled at him over her shoulder as she stepped into the room. "As your wife, it's my understanding that I'm to obey you, but as only your affianced bride, I think I'm first going down to the kitchens to find Bumble and something to fill my— *No!*"

Courtland reached for her but she was snatched away from the opening before he could get his hand on her arm.

In a single beat of his heart, he knew. *Beales.*

Court slammed the door and bolted for the balustrade, vaulting over it, his left ankle collapsing beneath him as he landed hard on the mix of sand and shingle a good fifteen feet below the terrace.

Ignoring the pain, he pushed himself up, scrabbled and staggered toward the secret opening hidden among the stones of the foundation of the house. Pushed on the correct stone, even as he heard boot heels hitting the stone steps, pursuing him.

In a moment, he was inside Becket Hall, in the windowless storeroom adjoining Odette's Voodoo retreat, the doorway closed and once more invisible to anyone who didn't know its location.

Above him was his family; everything and everyone he loved. *Cassandra.*

"Think! Don't wonder how. Just know it's happening," he ordered himself in a fierce whisper as he felt his way through the deep piles of belongings stored there before they would be loaded onto the *Isabella,* the *Respite.* He found the wall and moved along it, searching for the door to Odette's secret altar room.

Disoriented by the complete darkness that didn't become much lighter even as his eyes began to adjust to it, it took him precious minutes to work his way around the large, oddly shaped room and find the hidden door. Precious minutes he wasted searching rather than thinking about how in hell he, probably the only man in Becket Hall without a pistol pointed at him, was going to make a difference.

His hand closed over the recessed ring that was the latch for this side of yet another hidden door, the one

Cassandra had disappeared through, laughing, teasing, that night so many lifetimes ago, to change out of her gown. He pushed it open, moved into another dark room save for the few candles burning on Odette's Voodoo altar.

He had gotten somewhere. He had gotten nowhere.

Cassandra.

"Stop it! Don't react, don't imagine—*think!*"

"Better to arm yourself, and follow me," Jacko said, striking a match against a stone candleholder on the altar and holding it up so that Courtland could see his face. "You and me, boyo, and one old, dyin' woman who refuses to lie down like she should. Unless we can make our way unseen to the cannon floors where our men have no notion of what's goin' on, we're all they've got."

"Jacko—thank God." Now Courtland could see better, enough to see that Odette was sitting in her ancient rocker, twisting her hands in her lap. "How… how did Beales get this far?"

Odette set the chair to rocking. "Loringa…stronger than me now…stronger than me. The bad *loa.* Hid her from me…"

Jacko rolled his eyes, snorted. Jacko had never put much stock in Odette's powers. "Trickery, boyo, plain and simple." He lit another fat candle and handed it to Courtland. "Now let's see what all we can find in that storeroom to arm ourselves."

As they went through the piles and piles of belongings, pulling out knives, swords, a few pistols and some shot, Jacko explained what had happened.

There were only six men stationed on each of the two cannon floors, one group watching the Channel, the other with their eyes on the land approach to Becket Hall. The remaining men had all gone for their women and children, scattered throughout a few of the local villages, in preparation for boarding the *Isabella* and leaving Romney Marsh for good, confident that Ainsley and the rest would return shortly after dawn.

That left Bumble and Edythe in the kitchens, Odette in her bed, Sheila Whiting sitting with Eleanor, a young girl from the village in the nursery with Spencer's children, Onatah tending young Jack, and Jack himself working away in Ainsley's study, doing who knew what in preparation for Ainsley's return.

"And me," Jacko said, strapping a cutlass to his ample waist. "I was over to The Last Voyage, and makin' my way back along the beach when I spied the wagon comin' up the drive just like it belonged here. Odette was sittin' right up there on the seat, wavin' to the windows while whoever was drivin' the thing kept his head down. Stopped me, it did. Odette? What in blazin' hell was she doin', out and about, sick as she is?"

By the time Jacko's rum-dulled brain had realized what was happening, it was too late, the wagon had passed beyond the point where any number of cannonballs could reach them, driving straight up to the front door.

"Probably knocked on the door and then walked right in, her and everyone hidden in the wagon," Jacko said, shaking his head. "Only black face for all the Marsh, probably, and lookin' so much like Odette? Our men just watched, seein' nothin' to bother them. Edythe, I'm thinkin', opened the door and let her in, and the others followed. *Beales.* Nothin' else for me to do but come in here, figure what to do next."

"Loringa destroys, that's all she knows to do," Odette said from the doorway, swaying slightly as she braced her thin frame against the doorjamb. "I leave this room and she'll know I'm here. It's taking the good *loa* and all I have to keep her away this long. Help them. Hurry."

CHAPTER TWENTY

CASSANDRA SAT VERY still on one of the pair of couches pushed back against the wall by their dozen or more captors, Lisette beside her. They held hands as Mariah was escorted out of the drawing room at pistol-point, to be taken upstairs to Eleanor's bedchamber.

Mariah hadn't wanted to go, but then Edmund Beales had asked whose two "darling little children" had been located in the third floor nursery and removed to Eleanor's bedchamber, to be with the invalid and the infant being minded by the fierce-looking old harridan with the braid.

Mariah ran toward the hallway then, pausing only a moment to look back at Spencer, who sat cross-legged on the floor with his hands tied behind him. Rian laid sprawled beside him, cradled in Jasper's strong arms, still unconscious from the blow he'd taken when Beales had casually swung the hilt of his pistol at the head of the man who had dared to burn down his French estate.

Although his leg was strapped between two pieces

of the splintered mizzenmast and he was far from being able to do much more than curse in his frustration, Chance's wrists were also bound as he lay slumped on another couch.

Only Ainsley remained free, standing in front of the fireplace, beneath the portrait of his dead wife.

Jack was nowhere to be seen. Nor were Jacko or Odette. Was that a good thing or a bad thing? Cassandra didn't want to think about that at the moment.

The French doors opened and three heavily-armed men reentered the drawing room, the lead one shaking his head as he looked to Beales. "Ran off into the weeds somewhere. We made a full circuit of the house, but we couldn't find him. Didn't chance looking in the village, seeing how you said you wanted to be in and out of here without a fuss. Didn't figure on so much company, did you, Cap'n?"

Cassandra bit her bottom lip between her teeth to keep from smiling. Courtland had escaped them. The crews from the *Respite* and the *Spectre* were only a quarter mile away in the village. There was still hope.

"Another way of saying you are, as always, a bloody coward, Thibaud. And lazy," Edmund Beales purred as he sat in her papa's favorite chair that he'd had placed in the very center of the room, as if he was a king holding court. "Thank you so much. Geoff? By my reckoning we have no more than, oh, a half hour or so before we could be disturbed. I believe it's time we were finished with this, don't you?"

"As long as you draw breath, Edmund, this won't be finished," Ainsley said in much the same tone he might use to offer a guest a glass of wine.

Beales smiled, and Cassandra had to avert her eyes, for he was the embodiment of evil in any case, but even more so when he smiled. "I had so hoped to watch from a convenient balcony as you were hanged in chains. It angers me that I'll be denied that particular delight. But," he added, shrugging, "as long as you're dead, I imagine I can deal with my disappointment. Now, the Empress. Where is she?"

"Nowhere you'll find her," Ainsley told him.

"Oh, I don't have to find her—you're going to be happy to tell me where she is. I most certainly didn't believe you were going to have that cripple over there bring her to the gaol, all nice and tidy. But you told him where she is, didn't you? Your fine and lovely family—they all know. Which one, do you suppose, will be the first to tell me?"

"No one else knows, Edmund. The Empress is not a possession I'm particularly proud to own."

"You *don't* own her—I do!" Beales had half risen from the chair but then sat back, crossed one leg over the other. "Excuse me. I don't mean to lose my temper. So wasteful an emotion, don't you think—anger? Especially when I have at my disposal so many possibilities for persuasion. Thibaud—the girl. Bring her to me, please."

Ainsley stepped forward quickly, to be stopped by

the barrel of a pistol shoved into his side as Thibaud approached the couch and grinned down at Cassandra.

"You don't frighten me," Cassandra heard herself say, her own voice seemingly coming to her ears from a distance.

"Ah, sweetings, I can change your little mind about that fast enough," Thibaud said, pulling her to her feet and dragging her in front of Beales, twisting her arm so that she was forced to bend her knees until she was at eye level with the seated man. "See if you can hold on to this one, Cap'n, huh?"

Beales inhaled sharply. "There remain moments, Thibaud, that our long friendship is all that keeps you alive. Now take your hands off her," he said coldly as he took hold of Cassandra's other wrist, smiled at her. "Don't worry, my dear, I won't let him hurt you. Not when I've already promised him my own darling Lisette. He's coveted her for a long time. Haven't you, Thibaud? Or have you changed your mind now that you've seen the redhead, hmm?"

"Bastard!" Spencer shouted, trying to rise, only to be knocked back down courtesy of a rifle butt to the stomach.

"Some one of you idiots tie his feet, for God's sake," Beales said in disgust. "And gag him. Gag them all. Damn you, Geoff, you always kept a menagerie about, didn't you? Tell you what—you there, Dominic, is it? Yes, of course, Dominic. Lovely name. Can you spell it if I were to ask you to, do you think? Never mind. Dominic? The very next man says a word, shoot him, or I'll have you shot." He leaned past Cassandra, to smile down at Spencer. "Do *you* understand, wharf rat, *hmm?* Tut-tut—careful now, don't speak! Just nod."

"No more of your tedious theatrics, Edmund. You've made your point. Let my daughter go," Ainsley commanded.

And the visibly shaken Dominic promptly shot him.

"Papa!" Cassandra wrenched her wrist free from Beales's grip and ran to her father, going down on her knees as he lay there, holding one hand to his shoulder as blood seeped out from between his spread fingers.

"Not *him,* you fool! Incompetents," Beales said, getting to his feet, a pistol in his own hand. "It's my curse to be surrounded by incompetents. Oh, and Dominic? This is for you—your name is spelled *D-E-A-D.*" He raised the pistol and fired, a small black-edged hole appearing in the center of the man Dominic's forehead before he crumpled where he'd stood.

AT LEAST THEY HAD A PLAN, one born more of desperation than genius, but it would have to do.

If only Odette hadn't insisted on coming with them, damn it, but she'd been adamant that she was the only one who could possibly defeat her twin, make their work easier by ridding them of her Voodoo protection of Beales.

Courtland led the way up the twisting staircase from Odette's altar room to the door that led into the kitchens. He and Jacko had discarded their boots to keep their footsteps undetected, and he'd dispensed with his jacket and neck cloth. At his quick count, he believed he was carrying a total of nine knives—two in each boot, one in the harness that held the stiletto he'd already killed with once in the past four and twenty hours, one in each hand, one in his waistband. And one, God help him, held tight between his teeth.

He had a moment of insane silliness as he thought that Cassandra probably wouldn't have liked to see him this way. Or perhaps, at the moment, she would.

On the island, Courtland had always remained on shore, close to Isabella, close-mouthed and private, the odd child out. Just as, grown, he'd considered himself the odd man out, different from the hey-go-mad brothers and even sisters who ran toward adventure rather than away from it.

He'd sought order, never chaos. He'd never been a privateer or a pirate. He may have ridden out as the Black Ghost when he'd seen no other choice left open to him, had his share of fevered pursuits and partaken in one or two skirmishes, but those actions he'd considered to be practical, measured, a job of work, and necessary—but not an adventure.

He'd never gone to war, never been in a real battle, had never deliberately looked for trouble.

But he was more than willing to fight now, more

than ready to kill. He had to tamp down his immense anger and remember that he worked best, accomplished most, with his mind.

He went into a low crouch as he slowly depressed the latch, eased open the door, held his breath as he waited for the sound of a shout, the impact of a bullet or knife. But the hallway was clear, and he motioned for Jacko to follow him, the older man holding on to Odette's elbow to help her climb the last few steps.

They turned to the left, to enter the main kitchen, make sure it was clear of intruders before heading for the hidden staircase, and Courtland nearly tripped over Bumble's peg leg. The man who had been with Ainsley from the beginning, as sailor and cook, had so looked forward to traveling with him to Hampton Roads, lay sprawled on his back in a pool of his own blood, his throat cut from ear to ear.

Her head on his chest, Edythe's body lay beside him, the hilt of a kitchen knife protruding from her back. Edythe, who'd survived the island, only to die in a kitchen.

Courtland took the knife blade from between his teeth and slid it into his waistband. "There was no reason for this."

"Beales never needs a reason. Bastard," Jacko breathed, shaking his head. "Come on, no time to waste."

With one last look at the bodies on the floor,

bodies that gave mute testimony to Beales's penchant for senseless violence, Courtland tucked the knives into his waistband and worked the lever that moved the large cupboard, exposing the staircase to the cannon floors. He held out his hand to Odette, who looked past him, at yet another steep flight of stairs, and shook her head.

"I go to where Loringa waits for me, calls to me. Good and evil, with one dies the other, and the world is balanced again. When she is found, throw her body on the shifting sands, the doorway to Hell. Let the devil have her back."

"Odette, please," Courtland whispered hoarsely. "You're in no fit condition to—" He turned his head in the direction of the sound of a pistol shot. Then, moments later, a second shot. "Odette—now."

She backed away from him as Jacko gave him a push toward the staircase. Courtland leaned toward the opening as the cabinet swung back into place, his last glimpse of Odette telling him that she was most probably on her way to Jacko's conservatory.

"Jacko, we can't leave her here to—"

"It's like the Cap'n says—we make our own choices. Her sister. Her fight and her right. Now move!"

They climbed the staircase as quickly and quietly as possible, Jacko turning off at the first landing, Courtland continuing on up past that floor, past the second floor of Becket Hall—which had all the bedchambers—and up to the other cannon floor. Decks, some of those who knew about them called these hidden floors, for the cannon and munitions stored there were much like the gun decks on the *Respite*.

It was his and Jacko's plan to send two of the men to circle through the marsh grasses to the village as quickly as possible and have the rest of them arm themselves, reconnoiter first the attics and nursery, then the bedchambers, and then finally split their small force between the interior of the house and the terrace, attacking from both positions at once.

They would eliminate their enemy from the top down, leaving Beales with as few of his men as possible before attempting to broach the drawing room, hopefully with the crews from the *Respite* and the *Spectre* joining in on the assault.

It wasn't a perfect plan. Those they loved could very well be caught in the crossfire, just as the sloop had been caught between the *Respite* and the *Spectre*. But it was all they had.

He ran into the low, cavernous space, no more than seven feet from floor to ceiling but as wide and long as Becket Hall itself, and a half dozen men turned to look at him owlishly as he began pulling the knives from his boots and waistband and tossing one to each of them. If they had to kill, they would kill without sound. "Quietly, men, to me. It's Beales. He's got the Cap'n. He's got them all…"

"PAPA, LET ME TELL him where it is," Cassandra pleaded quietly as she bent low over Ainsley, holding a folded pad of cloth against his wound while Lisette wrapped his shoulder in several strips she'd ripped from her petticoat. "Please. If I tell him, maybe he'll just go."

"No. He plans to kill all of us no matter if we tell him or not," Ainsley told her, wincing as Lisette tied a knot in the ends of the last strips. "We simply need time for Courtland to make his way to the village, bring the crew. It's a hell of a thing, pardon me, ladies. We can keep most anyone out, but once they're inside, we're no safer than any other household. Edmund knows he doesn't have much more time—so we have to outlast him. Just stay alive, Cassandra. For me. For your mother. For Courtland."

"I should have found a longer scissors that day," Lisette whispered fiercely, "and he'd be dead now. I am so sorry to say he is my father, Mr. Becket."

Ainsley reached up his hand and patted Lisette's cheek. "We are privileged to choose only our friends. It was my mistake all those years ago, my dear, never yours. Now, please, if you ladies don't mind, I'm not going to remain here on the floor."

"Papa, you should stay where you are," Cassandra said, but the look on her father's face told her she was wasting her breath on a fruitless argument. Between them, she and Lisette helped him to his feet, at which time Beales ordered them both to return to the couch.

"My most sincere apologies. And how are you

feeling, old friend? A flesh wound only, I'm assured, as that fool, luckily, was a very bad shot. But do you know what, Geoff? I think I'm bored. Truly. As well as most unfortunately pressed for time. Not that you don't have a lovely home, and you're most certainly a gracious host, but it will soon be time for luncheon and, alas, our old friend Bumble refused to feed me. You know what's going to happen here, Geoff, we both know that. So, as you said, no more theatrics."

"Theatrics are all you know, Edmund," Ainsley said steadying himself by placing one hand on the mantel. "You always hope to play a role, but you lack talent. Ambition, you understand, is *not* talent."

Cassandra looked around the room as her father spoke, obviously attempting to engage all of Beales's attention and anger, keep him occupied, thus buying them precious time for Courtland to summon the crew.

He'd been right. All his inventiveness, all of his plans, had been meant to deal from strength, Becket Hall a fortress meant to keep evil out, to never have what happened on the island happen again. But now evil was inside, and even though she knew there were men stationed on both of the cannon floors, those men had no idea what was happening here in the drawing room. The drawing room had become another island.

Chance was sitting up now, propped against some pillows, obviously in pain, both because of his leg and because that leg rendered him powerless to do anything but glare at Edmund Beales.

Rian had regained consciousness, thankfully, but like Spencer and Jasper, he was now bound—his arm tied to a leg of a heavy table—and the three of them were gagged, horrible rags stuck into their mouths.

The only good thing Cassandra could think of was that Spencer and Jasper had managed, while Rian was being tied up, to have themselves moved so that their backs were against the wall backed by the terrace. Like her and Lisette, still ordered to remain on the couch already against that same wall.

Bunched together so that their captors could watch them more easily. But also out of the line of fire when Courtland and the others came to rescue them. Hopefully.

Only Chance, on the couch in the middle of the room, and Ainsley, once more at the fireplace, were any distance from them.

But what was happening upstairs, with Mariah and Eleanor? Please God that Eleanor was all right, and that Mariah didn't take it into her head to be brave….

"Thibaud, bring our other friend in here," Beales ordered the increasingly sullen-looking man who was the only other one in the room that seemed to be of the same age as Beales and her papa.

"What for?" Thibaud asked, getting to his feet while he wordlessly signaled for the remaining armed men in the room to direct their pistols at their captives. “Let him die where he is, I say. No sense linin’ them up like cordwood, unless you’re thinkin’ of having me paint the scene for you to look at in your dotage. We were through with this, Cap’n. You told me so. But you’re never through, are you? You never fill up on the taste of it.”

“Nor do you, Thibaud, for all you complain,” Beales said to Thibaud’s back as the man left the room. “My old friend waxes poetic,” he said, retaking his seat, his freshly reloaded pistol trained on Ainsley’s chest. “I should buy him a petticoat, and perhaps a Bible. Oh, don’t frown so, Geoff. It’s not that Thibaud is right, our old friend Liam, no matter that he has played at being French these last many years. But enough! Your family dies easily or it dies hard, Geoff, it’s up to you. I’d have this over with by now, as humanely as possible, truly, if you’d just tell me where I might find the Empress. Come, come, what are a few more breaths when eternity beckons? Isabella must be anxious to see you.”

Cassandra clapped her hands to her mouth to stifle a gasp as Thibaud and another man reentered the room, dragging a badly beaten Jack Eastwood between them and then dropping him on the floor in front of her father. Jack rolled onto his back, his arms flung wide, clearly unconscious, his face bloody, one side of his face cut and horribly swollen.

“Surprised, Geoff?” Beales asked, getting to his feet. “Perhaps you thought he was dead, *hmm?* He should be, lying to me that he knew nothing of the Empress, but one never knows when one might need a bargaining chip. Now, are you ready to bargain, Geoff, or must I be put to the tedious business of picking who dies after this one." He put his heeled boot on the center of Jack's chest, and leaned forward, putting most of his weight on that foot. "Dear, dear, I think a few of these ribs might be broken. Not that he seems to feel the pain."

Jack moaned, but didn't stir.

"Thibaud? Once again I call on you for your assistance. In the interests of brevity, please take two of the men with you and bring down the ladies. They must be fretting, locked away up there. Oh, and the charming little kiddies, as well. A hard and fast rule of mine, Geoff," he said as Thibaud and two others headed for the foyer, "never leave a whelp alive. They have this lamentable tendency to grow up, wishing to seek revenge."

Ainsley Becket looked levelly at his old enemy, saying nothing.

Cassandra's brothers struggled against the ropes binding them.

Beside Cassandra, Lisette quietly began to pray.

Strange. Cassandra didn't feel at all like praying or even crying. She wasn't frightened, afraid to die. She was, once again, angry. Very, very *angry.*

She wanted Edmund Beales dead, and she wanted to watch as he died.

For all her protestations, all her supposed beliefs, it would seem that she was indeed her father's daughter….

BECKET HALL HAD NEVER before seemed so immense, so full of places a man could hide, ready to jump out at them. Still, Courtland bypassed the servants' rooms and headed straight for the nursery. The three adjoining rooms were empty. Spencer's William wasn't at play with any of the toys littering the carpet. The infant, Elizabeth, was not in her cot.

Courtland was still staring at the overturned rocking chair when Jeremy Wilkins skidded into the room. "Nobody nowheres else, Court. Now what do we do?"

"Now we go downstairs, to the bedchambers, careful not to take aim at one of our own, because Jacko has the others down there, already doing what we were doing up here. Pass the word, Jeremy, knives only unless forced to fire. I told you—off with those boots, man, we need to be quiet. Remember, nobody knows we're in here."

They joined up and made their way back to the servant staircases at either end of the house, Jeremy leading three men, Courtland the other two: Cholly, a seaman from the long ago *Black Ghost*—and Demetrious, once the ship's chandler. They descended quietly, swiftly, coming out into the hallway and quickly moving into the first bedchamber on the left, Fanny's old room.

Courtland hadn't expected anyone to be in the chamber, unless it was to look for valuables, and he pointed Cholly at a second door, Demetrious at a third, as they made their way down the hallway and then turned into the main hallway and the largest, center chambers.

He had just stepped out of Ainsley's bedchamber when he heard a child's cry and motioned for everyone to flatten themselves against the wall.

Eleanor and Jack's chamber, of course. With Eleanor still confined to her bed, it would only make sense to bring the other women to her.

Cassandra.

He put a finger to his lips, then lifted the knife he held, wordlessly ordering them to have their own knives at the ready.

At the other end of the hallway, Jacko was already on the move—as if he'd only been waiting for Courtland to show his face—his footsteps light, quiet, almost graceful, as only a large man could manage.

Jacko stopped in front of the door that led directly into Eleanor's dressing room, nodded to Courtland, and then he and his men slipped inside.

Courtland pointed to himself and then to the heavy double doors to the bedchamber, and then pointed to Cholly and Demetrious, put his fists together and then pulled them apart, hoping they'd understand that he wanted them to take the doors, pull them both open at once.

Cholly nodded, and then whispered in Demetrious's ear. The old man who had not fired a pistol or swung a sword in nearly two decades looked at Courtland, and grinned.

Courtland, now with a knife in each hand, put his back against the far wall and waited for Cholly and Demetrious to get into position, their hands on the door latches. He took a deep breath, and then nodded his head once.

The doors were pulled open, Cholly and Demetrious stepping out of the way, and Courtland launched himself into the bedchamber, through the small vestibule, past the drawn-back, emerald-green velvet curtains, and then went down, rolling to his left, coming up just as quickly, and praying Jacko had already made his own entrance.

He had. Jesus, God, he had.

The scene in front of Courtland was like some horrible tableau, everyone posed in place, nobody moving.

The women were all massed on the large bed.

Eleanor, looking deathly pale but yet also managing to appear indignant, holding her newborn son close against her chest as she glared up at the large, older man who held his hand out to her, as if asking her to leave the bed, come with him.

Mariah, sitting close beside her, her children held tight in her arms.

Sheila Whiting, Onatah and the young girl from the

village—Betty? Mary?—perched on the edge of the bed, strung together at their waists like beads on a chain with the thick, silken cords from the draperies.

There were four men in the room. Beales's men. Three of them with their pistols trained on Jacko and the six men standing behind him. These men moved first, shifting their collective gaze toward Courtland and the men with him, now all six from the second cannon floor, and immediately dropped their own weapons.

The fourth man turned his pistol, pressed it against Eleanor's head. Courtland noticed that he had a second weapon, tucked into the sash at his waist. Except, within a heartbeat, that pistol, too, was in his hand, and leveled at Jacko not six feet away.

"Jacko, back from the dead, are you?" the man said, grinning. "Geoff told us you were dead. Gone to fat, haven't you? Shameful."

"It's over—you can count, can't you? Your cowardly hirelings can. Hand over the pistols, Liam," Jacko said quietly, smiling that extraordinarily friendly smile that made his eyes dance, yet held all the menace in the world. "You're a dead man and you know it. It's up to you how long you want me to keep you alive before I send you to Hell. Hurt her, and you may die from now till Christmas. Maybe halfways to Easter. An inch a day. You know I know how to do it."

"Where's…where's Jack?" Eleanor asked, attempting to turn her head away from the pistol that pushed into her temple. "Jacko, please. Where is my husband?"

"Waitin' on you downstairs, my angel," Jacko said in a voice suddenly so gentle, so alien to the man Courtland had known for most of his life that he had to take his eyes off the man called Liam and look at him. "It didn't end then, and it won't end now. Not for you. I promise."

Courtland stealthily slipped the heavy knife in his right hand into his waistband and pressed his upper arm once, twice, against the side of his body. The stiletto slipped into his palm. He could do this, he knew he could do this; he'd practiced for years, fashioning his weapons for everyone else. He knew the weight of the stiletto, its balance. The distance wasn't that great, no more than twenty feet. He narrowed his eyes, refusing to see Eleanor or Jacko or any of the women. He saw only the man holding the pistol on his sister. He took one deep breath, a second, and held it. He could do this. *Please God, let me do this.*

"Why, Jacko, I think I'm going to cry, really," Liam said, laughing. "This one's special to you? Didn't think anyone was *special* to you. Hard as nails, that's the man I knew, and twice as bad as any of the rest of us. An old woman now? Makes a man feel sort of sick to see you brought so low. I'm tired, too, Jacko. So tired of all of this. Too many years, you know? So I'm dead, that's what you say? Fair enough. But I think I'll take her with me."

Courtland flipped the stiletto in his hand, gripped the tip, pulled back his arm.

Liam cocked the pistol aimed at Eleanor's head.

Jacko's shouted *No-o-o!* came at the same time, as he launched his bulk across the carpet, colliding with Liam a split second after the stiletto slammed home an inch below the man's Adam's Apple.

The sharp bark of two discharged pistols set Mariah's children to crying and Sheila Whiting to screaming at the top of her lungs.

Courtland didn't realize he was moving until he caught Jacko's bulk and somehow turned him so that he fell half on the bed on his back as Liam's body slid to the floor.

"Jacko, no!"

"Move away, Elly," Courtland commanded, ripping at Jacko's shirt that was already soaked with blood. "Sheila, shut up!"

"But I'm shot! He shot me!" the young woman cried, holding a hand to her head. "The bloody bastard shot off my ear!"

"I've got her," Mariah told Courtland tersely. "Court, how bad is he?"

Courtland looked at the wound, looked at Jacko. The man had never lied to him. He shook his head and said, "I'm sorry."

"All right, boyo…all right. Only…never thought I'd die in bed…"

"Oh, Jacko," Eleanor said as she stroked his face,

with the baby still in her arms. "You saved me again. Life shouldn't ask so much of one man."

Jacko looked up at her. "You…you know?"

"Shh, it's all right," Eleanor told him. "I've always known. It's all right. I understand. I love you, Jacko."

"I…" Jacko slid his gaze to Courtland. "Shots… they heard them…go. Go!" He struggled to rise. "Up to you now. Finish it, boyo. Finish it…"

"No, Jacko, don't go…" Eleanor whispered as the big man closed his eyes and died.

Courtland eased the body to the floor and got to his feet. "Cassandra?" he asked tersely. "Why isn't she with you? Where is she?"

Mariah was holding her daughter's blanket to Sheila Whiting's bleeding ear. "Downstairs, in the drawing room. Lisette, too. Everyone's in there. A dozen, no, now less men, and Beales. Ainsley has something he wants. I don't know what. Hurry, Court."

"The Empress," Courtland said, making the word a curse. But, at the same time, the stone gave him an idea. "Three of you, stay here—Demetrious, Cholly, Wilkins. The rest of you come with me, down the servant stairs to Ainsley's study. They know we're coming now. Let's do what Jacko said. Let's end this."

THE SHOTS COMING FROM the second floor probably saved Jack Eastwood's life.

Edmund Beales took his booted foot off the man's

chest and turned toward the foyer. "Thibaud! Thibaud! Answer me!"

But there was nothing…no more sounds came from the second floor.

"I remember something you told me, Edmund, a long time ago," Ainsley said, looking at Cassandra and—dear God, the man *winked* at her. "If a man believes himself invulnerable he, in reality, only makes himself vulnerable. When attacked, he can't believe the attack is happening, and will not react quickly enough. Because he has only his own supposedly perfect plan, seeing no need to consider alternatives. You're brilliant, Edmund, and always were. But you were never invulnerable."

Beales was still standing in the doorway, his pistol pointed at the empty staircase. "Shut up, Geoff."

Cassandra silently agreed with the man; silence seemed like a practical option. But her father spoke again.

"I was to hang, be neatly locked up in Dymchurch gaol while you attacked my home. You even staged that near riot at the gaol, just to watch to see how many of my men had come to Dymchurch. You must have been quite pleased, believing you'd so brilliantly scattered our forces, muddled our minds. You would face only a few women, perhaps some old men—just like before, on the island. The same sorry, sick plan as before, Edmund, a variation on a theme of yours—puffing yourself up as strong by attacking the weak. My family was going to tell you where the Empress is hidden in order to save their lives, even though you've never been known to keep a bargain. And you were to escape very neatly, before anyone even realized you'd been here, patting yourself on the back all the way to your grand and powerful new life in London. Yes?"

Beales looked wild now, panicked, as he ran back into the room, charging at Ainsley, waving the pistol near his face. "I said, shut your mouth!"

"But it didn't work out that way, did it? I'm here. My crew is here instead of in Dymchurch, and obviously now summoned from the village by one of my pesky family—one of the *menagerie* you so despise, always despised. A man is loyal to himself and no one else. Isn't that your credo, Edmund? I was too soft, too shortsighted, wanting only to return to England with my family, live a quiet life. I had no *ambition* beyond providing well for my family. But that was all right. You had enough ambition for both of us. You helped to make me a very rich man. You'd just never intended that I'd keep any of it, that I'd leave you."

"Papa...please..." Cassandra whispered as Beales turned his pistol on Ainsley. "Just let him leave. Let him go."

"Yes, why don't we do that. Splendid idea, Callie. We'll let him go."

"Court!" Cassandra half got to her feet, but

Lisette pulled her back down as Courtland stepped into the doorway.

He was alone.

Courtland held up the small leather bag, tossed it into the air, caught it again. "Well, now—look what I found."

Beales kept his right arm outstretched, pointing the pistol at Ainsley's head. He smiled, and Cassandra flinched. "Another of your misbegotten whelps, Geoff? Seems he at least knows who is in charge here."

Courtland walked fully into the room. "Yes, I do know who's in charge here, actually. *I am.*" He tossed the bag in the air once more, caught it this time in both hands, as if he'd almost dropped it. "Deceptively heavy," he said, smiling. "And yet, so I'm told, fragile. But you know, I am feeling this almost overpowering urge to throw it at the wall behind me. As a matter of fact—I think I will."

"No!"

Becket men crashed in through the three sets of French doors. Others ran in behind Courtland, aiming their pistols at Beales's men, who dropped their own pistols and raised their hands so quickly that Cassandra actually believed she could see some terrible amusement in their quick capitulation.

Which left Edmund Beales, his loaded pistol, and Ainsley Becket standing beneath the portrait of Isabella.

"Put down the weapon, Beales," Courtland commanded. "You're beaten."

"No! I'm *not* beaten. I'll never be beaten! Tell your men to put down their weapons, or he dies. I'm leaving, and Geoff, you're coming with me. He comes with me, as far as I decide to take him. Saddle two horses and have them brought around to the front of the house. Disobey, and he dies now. *Do you hear me!*"

"Well, now, what *do* have we here?"

All heads turned toward the hallway as Ethan Tanner, Earl of Aylesford, accompanied by an equally travel-dusty Valentine Clement, Earl of Brede, looked in from the doorway.

"I really couldn't say for certain," Valentine said, pushing his windblown hair away from his face, "but we may have interrupted a small party? Our ladies will be considerably vexed to have missed it, following along in the coach the way they are. Shame, that."

Ethan, the epitome of the London peer, resplendent in his London clothes, dusty as they were, smiled at Valentine. "Still, how can we ask this man to stay until they arrive? He really does seem in a hurry to be away, doesn't he?" He turned back to Beales, bowed. "I believe you asked for a horse, sir. I am delighted to oblige. My very own Alejandro is just outside, saddled, still fairly fresh, and at your service. You'll know him at once—magnificent beast if I do say so myself. White as a cloud, swift as the wind. Valentine, Courtland? Let's all stand back, shall we, give our departing guest a clear path to the door?"

"Take my mount, Ainsley," Valentine said, "with my compliments."

"I'll return shortly," Ainsley said as he walked ahead of Beales, the pistol pointed at his back.

Beales actually laughed. "Of course he will. You! The Empress—now!"

Courtland tossed the pouch at him and Beales snatched it from the air.

Once they were clear of the foyer, Cassandra and Lisette ran to the front windows to watch the fun.

Because Alejandro was a very singular horse, a magnificent Andalusian given to Ethan and trained to do the most marvelous tricks. Cassandra had seen him bow on command, paw the ground as he counted to ten…and one most fascinating defiance of gravity wherein he actually leapt a good five feet straight up into the air from a standing start, all four hooves leaving the ground.

Her papa was slowly backing down the outside stairs now, Beales behind him, using him as a human shield, the pistol pushed into Ainsley's back.

Ethan, hands raised and empty, followed, speaking, most probably helpfully offering to untie the two horses from the wrought-iron posts at the edge of the drive. Everyone else remained inside Becket Hall, watching from the door, the windows.

Beales smiled as he settled himself in the Andalusian's saddle, still with his pistol trained on Ainsley. He said something, and her papa shrugged, then mounted Valentine's horse, as if he was indifferent to being forced to accompany Beales in his escape.

Becket Hall men had quickly cut the ropes holding Rian, Spencer and Jasper. Courtland joined Cassandra at one of the windows, his hands on her shoulders.

No one had resisted. No one said a word now.

Beales had to think that he'd won, yet again. *It is when you believe yourself invulnerable that you are most vulnerable.*

The horses turned, started off down the drive, and Lisette squeezed Cassandra's hand a moment before Ethan's raised voice carried across the wind coming in off the Channel: "Alejandro—*courbette!*"

"Oh my, I forgot that one!" Cassandra said, watching avidly.

Alejandro immediately stopped, reared upright, pawing at the air, then proceeded to actually *jump* in place four times on his hind legs before gently, gracefully, lowering his front hooves to the ground once more.

Edmund Beales, however, was no longer on the stallion's back….

CHAPTER TWENTY-ONE

EDMUND BEALES, KNOWN TO his gaolers and the court as Geoffrey Baskin, the infamous Black Ghost who had been the scourge of the Waterguard for too many years, was hanged in chains at Dover Castle the day before Christmas. Only Billy, still wearing a black armband in memory of his friend Jacko, attended the execution. He wanted to be sure the man was dead.

Because Ethan and Valentine had ridden back to Becket Hall as quickly as possible after receiving a pardon for Geoffrey Baskin, pirate, but they hadn't procured one for Geoffrey Baskin, smuggler.

The trial had been quick, for the Black Ghost was a wily fellow, and had already escaped Dymchurch Gaol in an attack that had left the good Lieutenant Tapner dead. There had been no pardon for that murder, either.

Ethan and Valentine had been sad to have to turn in the man they'd fought so hard for in London, but they, as good citizens, could not condone the murder of the Lieutenant. They'd driven "Geoffrey Baskin" directly to Dover and presented him to the Honorable Frances Roberts, who had quickly seen the advantage to himself in accepting the prisoner without doubting his identity.

Both Mr. Roberts and Sir Horatio Lewis both had attended the execution. The Reverend Thomas Carstairs had said a prayer for the condemned's immortal soul as the trapdoor was dropped.

Sadly, all three men, in oddly coincidental separate coach accidents on their way back to their homes, perished. But, then, traveling Romney Marsh could be treacherous in the wintertime.

Beales had remained mute throughout his brief incarceration and trial, his silken tongue silent.

Billy still kept it, pickled, in a jar beneath his bed.

THEY'D FOUND ODETTE and Loringa in the conservatory that had been Jacko's pride for so many years, his long hours devoted to the nurturing and growing of beauty the aberration that had made the ferocious Jacko human.

There was no outward sign of the intense struggle that had taken place there. Not a flower or plant had been disturbed. The orchids that had arrived only that fall from South America were still lined up smartly in their pots. Three small lemon trees were blooming, and the air was warm and heady with the smell of dozens of varieties of roses. Pots of tulip bulbs were being forced on a table in one corner. A palm tree, like those on the island, pushed up toward the thirty-foot high glass ceiling.

A place of beauty, a haven of peace. Living, growing, unquestioning friends, companions to a man who could then possibly forget, for a moment, who he was, who he'd been, what he'd done…

The women sat in facing chairs, Odette's thin, wasted body clad in her funereal black, the woman who had once been her mirror image dressed much more colorfully, her features looking younger, if not as peaceful.

Their hands were still clasped on the arms of the chairs. Their posture was alike, and remarkably straight. Neither woman had a mark or cut on her body. They simply sat there, their eyes open, staring.

They were both dead.

And the world was balanced again….

"CHANCE, SIT DOWN! I don't trust those things," Julia Becket ordered as she entered the drawing room, carrying a plate of cookies plump with raisins. She was quickly surrounded by children all clamoring for one of their own as she reminded them that it was time they were all up in the nursery.

"Court made them for me," Chance said, already sitting down once more and placing the crutches on the floor beside him. "You can't believe he would endanger his own brother by handing him inferior worksmanship."

"Well, you never know," Courtland said, winking at Cassandra, who sat close beside him. She'd been close beside him for the past several weeks, not that he was about to complain about that fact. "And it isn't as if I've been keeping score, you understand, but I think I still owe you at least one good thumping. It's just like you to break your leg to avoid that thumping."

"Don't," Chance warned him. "You remember what happened the last time we fought. It's too damn cold tonight to have Julia dumping a bucket of water over our heads."

"I heard that," Julia said, retying Alice's bow.

"I didn't," Lisette said from her own seat next to Rian. "They had an actual fistfight? And you threw water on them—like they were cats?"

Rian lifted his wife's hand to his lips before helping her to her feet. "Come upstairs with me, sweetheart, and I'll tell you all about it. Our Chance and Court have a long history of tugging at each other. Chance is still probably attempting to figure out some way to save Court's skin, so they'll be even again."

Cassandra squeezed Courtland's hand, as mention of what had happened—had nearly happened—in this room only a few short weeks ago still had the power to give her nightmares. He'd held her close every night, ready to wake her, soothe her, if she began to stir or cry out in her sleep.

Even the Yule log burning merrily in the fireplace, the holly branches Morgan had tucked into every conceivable corner, couldn't as yet quite rid the drawing room of the memory of that horrible day. It was, he thought, good that neither Elly nor Jack had seen what had occurred in this room, keeping their memories free to enjoy their home. As it was, they'd already moved into Ainsley's bedchamber, Eleanor's bedchamber remaining vacant since the day Jacko had died there.

Courtland had nightmares of his own, all of them centered around that moment on the terrace, when Cassandra had looked at him in sudden horror, and then been snatched away. If he had broken his ankle in the leap from the terrace, if he hadn't been able to reach the secret portal before Beales's men caught up with him, if Jacko hadn't been there to tell him what had happened, if he'd taken too long to execute his plan, if Cassandra hadn't still been alive when he'd figuratively rolled the dice and carried the Empress into the drawing room…

Spencer picked up young William, still munching on his cookie, and lifted him up and over his head, settling the giggling child on his shoulders. "Good night, all, and Happy Christmas yet again. It's difficult to believe that we'll be leaving in the morning. I probably should help Mariah finish packing up whatever's left in our rooms that's not too large to fit in any of our cases."

"Sail off before Fanny gets here," Cassandra warned him, "and she'll just swim out after us. Valentine promised they'd be here as soon as he could tear them away from his sister's house party. Knowing Fanny, they'll drive all the night through, if necessary."

"Callie, sweetheart, are you sure you've packed up everything you want to take with us?" Courtland asked her as Spencer's words seemed to have everyone getting to their feet, bustling off to do whatever they felt still needed to be done.

"Yes, I'm fine," she said, laughing as Morgan and Ethan, each of them chasing one of their rambunctious young twins, somehow managed to herd them toward the foyer. "Jasper carried down most of my cases this afternoon."

"Then come help me," Courtland said, because the object he had in mind wasn't really packing up their belongings, but getting Cassandra to himself for a while on this, their last night in England.

"All right," she said, getting to her feet. "But first I want to stop in and see Elly and the baby, make sure they're all right. Not that they aren't, but Elly's had her hands full, keeping Jack in bed until he's healed."

"She's not the only one having trouble keeping someone in bed," Courtland muttered under his breath, and then smiled at his poor joke. But he couldn't get enough of Cassandra, not now that he knew that the love he'd thought he felt for her was as nothing compared to how much he loved her now, having almost lost her.

He said his good-nights to Chance and Julia and headed down the hallway to Ainsley's study. Knocked, and was bade to enter.

"Court," Ainsley said, sheaves of paper in his hand, others tucked into the black silk sling he still wore on his left arm, "you're just in time. Help me with these, will you, please?"

"Certainly, sir," Courtland said, taking the papers and piling them neatly on the desktop, noticing that the top sheet was a letter signed by Marianna Warren. He looked around the large room, at the bookshelves missing quite a few volumes, at the map table that he'd never before seen not littered three inches deep in maps and charts. All those years, the Empress had been stored inside that table. "I would have thought you'd be the first one packed and ready to go. It's fortunate that we had time to linger this long, isn't it?"

Ainsley nodded, seating himself behind his desk. "I wouldn't have left so soon in any case. Not until I knew everyone was all right. Poor Jack, he got the worst of it." He looked to the empty couch directly across from the desk, at the permanent indentation in one of the cushions. "And Jacko…"

"He died as he wanted to, sir. Protecting Elly."

"Circles, Court. The world moves in circles sometimes, each one tightening in on the last one. It takes all the energy we have to break the circle, move forward to a new future without dragging the worst of the past with us." He opened the middle drawer of the desk and pulled out the pouch holding the Empress, laid it on the desktop. "What do we do with this?"

"I'd like to see it at the bottom of the ocean," Courtland told him honestly.

Ainsley smiled. "What? The most practical of my sons, willing to toss a fortune into the sea? People have died for this stone, Court, my own wife among them. But a stone didn't kill them. Greed killed them. Greed, ambition, superstition."

"I can speak only for myself, but I doubt that any of us wants the thing in any case, sir."

"Yet it's ours, isn't it, paid for in blood." Ainsley picked up the pouch, held it in his hand for a moment before replacing it in the drawer. "Very well, I'll deal with it. One way or another, the Empress should stay with the Becket family. As I told Cassandra, bad luck wears off."

"Bad luck? But you said the stone was blameless," Courtland pointed out.

Ainsley tipped his head to one side, shrugged. "True. But I also never said I wasn't superstitious. We'll leave it to another generation to decide what's to be done with the Empress. It's enough that my family is being scattered to the four winds."

"Spence and Callie and I will still be with you, in Hampton Roads or nearby," Courtland pointed out, carefully not mentioning Rian, Ainsley's "beautiful boy," once believed lost to them, who would be taking his Lisette to her family home in New Orleans, or Morgan, Chance and Fanny, who would all remain in England. "We…we could stay here, you know. Now that Beales is gone, the Black Ghost is gone."

"No," Ainsley said quietly. "Becket Hall belongs to Eleanor and Jack now. Eleanor would never be truly happy anywhere else. And God knows I've hidden here long enough. I wouldn't have believed it possible seventeen years ago, Courtland, but there's an ending to everything, even penance. I only wish the others could be leaving with us. Jacko, Odette, Bumble, Pike, Edythe and all of the others. They deserved better than they got."

"Yes, sir," Courtland said, pouring his adoptive father a glass of wine and placing it in front of him. "This will be a long night for all of us, saying good-bye to old friends. But new friends await us."

Ainsley lifted the wineglass in a toast. "Then I'll drink tonight to old friends. Good night, Courtland."

CASSANDRA YELPED satisfyingly when Courtland's hands squeezed her waist as she was bent over a large seaman's chest, trying to make some sense out of the jumble of shirts and smallclothes he'd thrown into it willy-nilly.

"You shouldn't sneak up on me like that," she scolded as she straightened, putting a hand to the small of her back, easing her spine back into line, he supposed, as she'd been bending and stretching for what seemed like weeks, choosing and folding and packing…and then choosing again, folding again, unpacking and packing again. He'd decided that all the fuss had kept her mind away from unpleasant thoughts. "You know, if you continue to refuse to be serious about this, you're going to leave without everything you need."

He slipped his arms around her waist, drew her close to kiss her hair. "If all I take is you, I'll have everything I need."

"Oh, Court, that's so sweet—now let me go, I want to finish this."

He stepped back, and she picked up another stack of shirts from the piles on his bed. He watched her, being so very domestic, and remembered a time when she would sit on a blanket on the beach, playing with her favorite doll. Until she spied him, of course, and forgot the doll in order to get up, follow him, pester him with endless questions while he was attempting to be so grown-up, so very serious.

She'd always been able to infuriate him. And make him laugh.

She'd lost her mother, but Ainsley had made sure that she'd had a childhood…something Courtland had never experienced. When Courtland had watched Cassandra at play he would feel very young…and then, sometimes, very, very old.

But time passes, and has a way of evening things out. Now they were equals. Friends. Lovers.

"I sat with your father for a while after you went upstairs," he told her as she picked up his brushes from the dresser top and then put them down again, probably realizing that he might want to brush his hair in the morning. "He's feeling rather…maudlin."

She stopped what she was doing and turned to face him. "Should I go down to him?"

"No, I don't think so. Let him say his goodbyes in his own way. Now, stop this, all right?"

"But you've made such a mess—don't do that! I took everything out of the chest to fold it, put it back in correctly, and now you're—Courtland!"

But Courtland had already scooped up all of the clothing on his bed and dumped it back into the chest. "There, all done. I like my way better."

"Well, I don't. We're going to be in close quarters for several weeks on the *Isabella,* and every time you want to find a clean shirt, you'll be dumping everything on the deck and—"

He grabbed her, picked her up, and tossed her onto the bed. "There. That's how I like to see my bed. With you in it."

Cassandra rolled her eyes and then scooted to the head of the bed, pushing up the pillows so that she could sit propped against them. "Well, you could have simply *said so,* you know."

"I thought about it," he told her, unbuttoning his shirt as he put a knee up on the bed, "but that was more fun."

She pulled the ribbon from her hair and her curls tumbled free. "Fun? I love you, Courtland. I don't know why anyone would call you stodgy."

"I love you, too," he told her, reaching for her, grinning. "Do you realize, Callie, that by this time tomorrow night your father will have married us at sea? This is your very last chance to be a wild, wanton woman. Not that you haven't had considerable practice these last weeks."

She leaned over, finished opening his last few buttons for him, opening the buttons on his buckskins, teasing him with the lightness of her touch, the surety that she could rouse him with only that slight touch. "My last night as a wanton? Not according to Morgan, it isn't. There, all done." She turned her back to him, lifting her hair from her neck. "Now help me with my buttons, the way you did the first time I wore this gown."

"Not yet a wife, and already giving orders," he said as he knelt on the mattress and began opening the small satin-covered buttons that began at her nape and seemed to go on forever, especially as she was wriggling about now, one hand beneath her skirts, rolling down her silken hose. "No, leave them." He bent to kiss her nape, nuzzle against her soft, perfumed skin. "Please."

She eased back against him and he gently pushed down the top of the gown Morgan had ordered altered for her, the one that seemed to demand a complete lack of underpinnings, and learned that this was still true. He'd hoped that was the case, all the evening long.

He cupped her bare breasts as she arched her back, tilted her head, giving him total access to her long, slender throat. He kneaded, gently pinched, lightly stroked, feeling her nipples tauten, watching as her chest rose and fell rapidly, the effect of his touch on her fueling his own passion.

They'd made love nearly every night for the past few weeks. Sometimes gently, slowly, building their passion, prolonging their combined release. Sometimes quickly, fiercely, as if to chase the world away, put the past behind them, live only in the moment. Tonight, their very last at Becket Hall, it would seem, would be one of those nights.

"Yes…so good, Court. So good…damn this stupid gown!"

She lifted herself slightly, began working to hike up her skirts, her tugging becoming more frantic as he rubbed her nipples between his fingers and thumbs, her breath coming faster, her soft moans of pleasure urging him on.

Some small disinterested part of him heard the thin fabric rip.

With a frustrated cry, she pulled away from him before turning about, all but attacking him, and he pulled her close, between his thighs, as she wrapped her silken-clad legs around his back. He held her balanced just above him as she reached down between their bodies. Finding him. Guiding him…

She ground herself against him as he moved deep inside of her, their movements mirroring each other, holding on, flying high. Falling, falling…falling through time and space and future and past, only to find each other…and hold on…hold on…

COURTLAND TIED the strings at the top of Cassandra's cloak and kissed her before pulling the hood up and over her curls. It was cold on the terrace as the sun had yet to make its way above the horizon far out in the Channel, so that they were caught there in a thick, otherworldly, predawn Romney Marsh mist.

"Do you think I'm being silly?" she asked him, raising her hand to his cheek, biting her lip to keep from crying as he turned his face into her palm, then kissed her fingertips.

"No. Everybody says goodbye in their own way. This is yours. I like it."

Holding hands, they walked down the stone steps, the wind that would soon fill the sails of the two ships whipping their cloaks around their legs. They crossed the wide sand-and-shingle beach, bits of watery ice from last night's rain crunching between the pebbles as they stepped carefully toward the tide that was coming in to meet them, that would soon carry them away to a new life.

She could already see men climbing into the

riggings of the *Isabella* and the *Respite,* doing whatever sailors do to prepare for a voyage, and she squeezed Courtland's hand. "It's happening. It's really happening. We're really leaving."

Courtland turned her around, his hands on her shoulders as he stood behind her, to watch together as the winter sun at last made a rare appearance and the many windows of Becket Hall began to blaze as if the entire building was on fire. She felt some of that reflected warmth melting something in her breast as she committed the sight to memory, hoping she would be able to see Becket Hall this way again someday, but not knowing if she ever would.

She raised her hands to cover his, sighed. "Our last morning…" she said quietly.

"No, sweetings," he told her. "Our very first…"

EPILOGUE

Hampton Roads
January, 1816

HE LEANED DOWN, lifted the latch that held the gate shut on the white picket fence, and stepped inside the winter-brown garden that still seemed to radiate a sense of order, of belonging…and the promise of another spring to come.

A tall man, no longer young, not yet old, the years and the silver in his dark hair rendering him even more handsome than the youth he'd been several lifetimes and heartbreaks ago, he walked with a grace that was innate to him, even as his heart threatened to break free of his chest.

He saw her a moment later. She had her back partially to him as she snapped off the hard, round heads of last summer's roses.

He'd seen her only once before, nearly four years earlier, but her face remained clear in his mind. Her body, lithe and tall, her smile open and honest, her light brown hair cut unfashionably short, suiting her intelligent gamin face, highlighting her wide green eyes with the small laugh lines around their edges.

She was dressed now as she had been then; a long, fairly full brown woolen skirt, and one of her late husband's too-large white shirts hanging over that skirt and belted at her slim waist; open at the collar, that collar turned up, perhaps to keep the late winter sun from her neck, although the large, battered straw hat she'd brought into the garden with her was hanging from a nearby tree branch. She wore a sleeveless sweater, also too large for her slender frame, and its pockets bulged with whatever she'd carried with her into the garden.

She was, then and now, the most unique woman in the world.

He approached slowly, wondering if he was mad, if he'd misunderstood her letters, if he was meant to ever be happy again.

"Marianna?"

She stopped what she was doing, remained still for a few moments, and then stood up very straight, turned to face him.

Slowly, as he held his breath, feeling less a man of the world than he did a raw youth, she began walking toward him along the brick path, stripping off her gloves. She stopped not two feet in front of him. Smiled.

"Well, Ainsley," she whispered, tears dancing in

those beautiful eyes as she raised her face to him, as he bent to capture her mouth, "it certainly took you long enough…"

MILLS & BOON®
Super
Historical